David Dale was born in the city of York in 1949 and educated to post graduate level with a Post Graduate Certificate in Education and a degree in East Asian Studies studying Japanese, Mandarin, Mongolian, Cantonese and classical Chinese. He speaks Mandarin and some Japanese, and has a Japanese wife and six children.

He has worked for Hebei television and various other creative jobs in China. He has a passion for illustrating and cartooning and has illustrated for BBC York. He is also a member of 'York Writers'. He has worked and lived in Germany (RAF Wildenrath BFPO 42), China (Shijiazhuang and Beijing), Japan (Kyoto and Wakayama), the Caribbean (St Kitts and St Thomas USVI), USA (Houston TX and Cut-off Louisiana) and Sardinia (with RAF Harrier Squadrons 3, 4 and 20). He also worked as a merchant seaman in the Gulf of Mexico. All his novels stem from personal experience and as such possess an element of truth. He currently works at the University of York in a non-academic role.

Dedicated to Jeany (Ms Nie Jin Mei)
Forever missed.

DAVID DALE

NIGHT WITCH

AUSTIN MACAULEY
PUBLISHERS LTD.

A CIP catalogue record for this title is available from the British Library.

ISBN 9781786128942 (Paperback)
ISBN 9781786128959 (Hardback)
ISBN 9781786128966 (E-Book)
www.austinmacauley.com

First Published (2016)
Austin Macauley Publishers Ltd.
25 Canada Square
Canary Wharf
London
E14 5LQ

Acknowledgments

I owe my sincere gratitude to my friend Phillip Elcock for his patience and encouragement throughout the writing of this novel.

This is a murder mystery novel set 1989 in Shijiazhuang, north China, the year of the June 4th incident in Tian-a-Men Square and centres on the miserable life of *Jin-Mei* the divorced wife of the local police chief *Bo-Cheng*. Her life changes when she meets *Jason Lamont* a Head Teacher from her local language school with whom she envisages a better life. As a student she comes across *Pepper* who she instinctively distrusts and feels threatened by.

Her life is turned upside down when she is raped by four of her ex-husbands' police department colleagues on *Bo-Cheng's* orders. The consequences of the rape are far reaching as *Jason* goes on the run for assaulting *Bo-Cheng*. *Jin-Mei* is then taken in by a *Dr Jenna* a lesbian colleague at the hospital where both she and *Jin-Mei* work.

One of the rapists, *Fei-Liao* is brutally murdered and a suicide ensues. *Bo-Cheng* is then mutilated in his hospital bed and his guard *Pang* is murdered as he slept. The police search for *Jason* who evades capture with help from *Douglas* an old colleague and so the finger of suspicion then moves to others in the complex puzzle. *Jason* is then torn between the love he has for *Jin-Mei* and his fascination for *Douglas's* operative, a playgirl named '*Bunny*'.

Jenna and *Jin-Mei* fall out over *Jenna's* relationship with *Pepper* and *Jin-Mei* returns to her own apartment. The daughter of *Jin-Mei's* neighbour returns home from Beijing and declares her undying love for (Pang Xi) *Jin-Mei's* son, a casualty of the Tian-a-Men Square incident and presumed dead.

The story ends with *Jin-Mei's* paralysed husband being looked after by *Jin-Mei's* neighbour *Miss Sha* who makes sure he ends his days at her mercy. *Jin-Mei's* son turns up in Beijing along with her neighbour's daughter and declares his intention to marry her. *Jenna* and *Pepper* are arrested for the murders. *Jason* flees China, only to find *Bunny* next to him on the plane. *Jin-Mei* and the Inspector on her case (Inspector Fang) realise they share a fondness for each other as they return to Shijiazhuang.

A letter is sent from *Jason* to *Inspector Fang* confessing to the murders in order to help procure the release of *Jenna* and *Pepper* while the true murderer remains undetected, caring for her victim in the comfort of her secluded apartment.

JEANY MEETS JASON

A vortex of yellow sand swirled across the pavement and then dispersed amidst the rush hour throng. Yu Hua Road was now besieged by a noisy procession of car headlights bumper to bumper as they snaked their way back through the smog from nowhere. On each side of the thoroughfare, an army of faceless figures marched in both directions without discourse, back to their high rise homes. Dark winter clouds hung low over the city as an eerie depression stormed through the busy streets whipping up dust and debris into the bleak night air, a sure sign that a severe chill was fast setting in.

Nie Jin-Mei pulled her raincoat across her front, as the gale lashed at her long black hair, blowing it in all directions. With her face shielded, she leant into the bitter wind that nipped at her skin. The sand laden cyclonic gusts sweeping down from the Mongolian Steppes were sharp, cold and penetrating. There was a feeling in the air of impending tragedy, although she couldn't quite explain it.

As she made her way towards her apartment complex, the howling wind, like a possessed demon, drowned out the real and restless world around her. Humanoid shapes passed her on all sides like an army of automatons, impervious to each other's feelings. Alone with her thoughts and sorrows she struggled onwards, her head bowed into the oncoming wind.

Startled, she stopped as a gigantic juggernaut with its huge double trailer thundered past. She froze, her body trembling. She could feel frigid perspiration running down her pallid face and her heart pounding deep inside her chest. Her shallow breathing raced. The shock that should have brought her out of her daydreams didn't, instead it sent her into a surreal state of mind. For what she heard wasn't the juggernaut, but an army of tanks thundering across Tian-a-Men Square, crushing the young students in their path; in her mind, she could see images of her son Pang-Xi being mown down by Li-Peng's tanks of hate.

For a few moments she stood there, traumatised by the recurrent imagery that had haunted her since June 4th, the day The Central Kingdom murdered its children. She stood there, shaking, with her eyes closed, motionless, as the crowds, the traffic and the driving wind swirled around her. Tears for her son ran down her cheeks and evaporated into nowhere.

Stark reality drifted back and she began to move. With her teeth clenched, she stared into a blurred uncertain future as anguish born tears trickled down her face. For the mighty juggernaut had summoned up devilish ghosts that she was ill-equipped to deal with. The sky overhead was getting dark, she glanced at her watch and increased her pace; she needed to get home.

On her arrival back at her apartment complex she stopped for a moment at the black iron gates, and looked up at the three rectangular grey concrete blocks and their high perimeter fence, that was now her home. She stared up at her window on the top floor and sighed. Now weary, she entered her block with the wind at her back. Unsure of why she had rushed to get back, she climbed the stairs to her apartment, pulling herself along on the crude wooden bannister, her footsteps echoing in the vacuous stairwell. The sound of the ferocious wind outside was all but stifled by the building's sheer concrete walls.

The metal door creaked as she entered the dark confines of her empty living room. The threadbare curtains cast an eerie shadow over the once warm family room that had now become unwelcoming and desolate. On the far side of the living room was a leather sofa. Many years ago her son had played and slid on its shiny soft fabric, but now the lack of love had hardened its skin and roughened its once smooth exterior. Its cushions were strewn across the floor; only a slip of paper lay across one of its arms. She snatched the note from where it sat, screwed it up and threw it into a far corner of the room. She had been here before; she didn't need to read it.

Having closed the door and bolted it securely she stood at the window and gazed across the mighty city of Shijiazhuang that spread out before her. Tall modern buildings stood proud above the haze and the city smog as if they alone had found a way of rising above the depths below.

She turned, glanced around the dimly lit room and then slumped down into the easy chair. She rubbed her moist eyes and then reached for the phone.

"Nan, He's done it again."

"Jin-Mei! Who's done what again?"

"That ex-husband of mine, he keeps turning up without a word and then without a thank you, he leaves."

"So he gone, that's good isn't it?"

"Yes but he keeps coming back."

"So you think you'd be better off without him?"

"Yes of course; I mean we've been divorced ages."

"So why let him back into your apartment?"

"Nan, he's got a key, I think he believes he has the right to come and go as he pleases, I'm sure he thinks it's a free hotel."

"Change the locks."

"He'd just kick the door in."

"He's not that bad, is he?"

"Yes he is. He shouldn't be here in the first place. He's suffocating me."

"Jin-Mei I don't know what I can say, just be happy he's not there now."

"Nan, I'm just tired and fed up of being taken for granted."

"You're a woman, get used to it."

"I can't, I mean how many more times is he going to turn up as if he owns both me and my apartment?" For a moment Nan remained silent as if she had been distracted by someone, then she returned to the phone. Jin-Mei continued.

"Do you remember last April when Pang-Xi and the others headed off to Beijing?"

"I remember of course, very sad."

"My so called husband never discussed our son's disappearance, not once."

"Maybe he was in shock or full of remorse," she suggested.

"Yes maybe, but during the June 4th Incident, he came, stopped overnight and then left."

"Even though he didn't say much, he must have cared for his son, surely," argued Nan.

"He didn't care that my world and my sole reason for living had dissolved into nothing. Nan, he knew that our son was never coming back and yet he left me to mourn alone."

"What do you expect me to do?" she asked with a tone of resignation in her voice.

"I know its short notice but can I come over and see you?" Jin-Mei begged.

"No, not tonight, I have guests. I'll be seeing you at work during the week. We'll talk then."

"I'm on Ward Three tomorrow night; I'll catch up with you then. Sorry to have bothered you," she said as she put the phone down. With her problem unresolved by its sharing she sighed, and without a sound she crept into her double bed.

The sky over the great city became overcast and then rain began to beat against the window's grimy panes. It was as if the torrent outside and the wind rattling against the sash windows frames, were compressing the room making feel smaller and smaller, forcing its walls to close in on her.

As thunder and lightning cracked outside lighting up the heavens, inside wallowing in her morbid feelings of insignificance, she lay there in the darkness. Again and again she asked herself, 'Is this the kind of life God had planned for me, or is it that I'm in some way to blame for my own misfortunes?' Lights from the bustling streets below, one after another, tracked across her ceiling and down the far wall, only to disappear into oblivion. Her moist eyes stared up at the restless procession of flickering reflections as she lamented over another day's meaningless existence. She told herself she needed to do something and do it soon.

A Fresh Start

The next morning Jin-Mei was awoken by the noise of traffic and voices emanating from the busy street below. She rolled out of bed, swept open the tattered curtains and gazed down from her top floor apartment window now spotless and clean. The morning had just broken and below, the sprawling city of Shijiazhuang was already bustling with commuters, weekend shoppers and pedestrians.

The officially denied events of the summer's troubles had cast a grim shadow over the whole country. China's hero Hu Yao-Bang was no longer and far worse than that, so was her only son. She realised that now there would be no new cultural revolution and no sweeping changes to their mundane existence. Despite this feeling of despondency that permeated throughout the population, she had woken up with a positive resolve. She was determined to turn her life around, once and for all.

She turned away from the window and picked up one of her son's English books from the floor. She smiled to herself as she gripped the dog-eared book with both hands. 'Yes' she thought as she placed the book down without even opening it. She'd known colleagues at her hospital who'd studied English, and she'd seen them go on to emigrate and live abroad. Some settled in the West, while others came back full of praise for the way of life outside the Central Kingdom. She was now determined to begin this new adventure in her life by studying English. What she knew of the language wasn't bad, but she had never had the opportunity to practice with an actual native speaker.

Now full of zest she threw open her wardrobe, pulling out her best clothes that she kept aside for special occasions. Her final choice consisted of a black strapless dress with red high heels. She brushed her long black hair back until it shone and then applied a rich crimson lipstick. She glanced in the mirror; her face glowed with excitement and vigour. She turned to one side and noticed her complexion; it was flushed and radiant. It was as if the stress of these last few months had been lifted from her shoulders. She spun around admiring her favourite black dress in the mirror, she felt rejuvenated and empowered. She smiled to herself as her youthful vitality flooded back. Her raven black hair and dark eyes were in sharp contrast to her fiery red lips; today she felt beautiful. She was now ready to go out into the world with a fresh sense of purpose and one she believed would change her direction in life once and for all.

She trotted down the concrete stair and exited her apartment block and without looking back, headed down Yu-Hua Road towards the hospital. This was the same route that she walked every day, although she'd noticed a large foreign language school in passing, she'd never thought of going inside to take a look. Today she would. Her stomach churned at the thought of embarking on a course of study. Although she had studied English for years, going back to school was going to be a challenging road but one she felt compelled to follow.

With her heart full of trepidation, she entered the foyer of the language school and wandered around the reception area as she tried to get a feel for the place. To her left, she noticed a group of young women and a few children gathered around someone. At the centre of the gathering was a tall Western gentleman. By his manner, he appeared to have authority and was clearly the centre of attention. What kind of man was her ideal? She'd never considered a foreigner, but this tall stranger from wherever he originated, came very close.

At once she felt she would love to learn more about him. He was attractive in a way that she found hard to define; his most riveting features were his mouth and his long narrow nose that gave the impression of being business-like and his lips exuded passion. As she looked on, she felt a sudden impulse. His blond, greying hair brushed back from his face, exposed a high intelligent brow and distinctive deep-set blue eyes. There was something about him – a kind of self-assuredness – call it vanity – he seemed aware of his appeal to the opposite sex. She listened intently and was surprised to hear him converse with the group in Mandarin.

For some reason the man stopped talking to them and looked around. As soon as he saw Jin-Mei, whatever he had been saying or thinking about was gone. He froze motionless, as if hit by a sudden jolt of attraction. His bright blue eyes met hers and at that moment it was as if there was an invisible magnetism between them, compelling them to gravitate towards each other. She had a kind of vulnerability and beauty that begged to be embraced, but the thing that captured his heart, was her warm tender smile. He felt an immediate rapport with her. She stood there unable to take her eyes off him.

Despite a certain embarrassment, at the intensity of her obvious scrutiny, he had gained a first overall impression of a woman he would dearly like to know better, if only to satisfy his curiosity. As if mesmerised, he excused himself and walked over to her, reaching out his hand to shake hers. He drew close to her and kissed her gently on the cheek. It was a fraction longer and more intense than a mere peck. Her heart raced as their two spirits, for a brief moment, embraced. It had been a long time since such eroticism had welled up inside her, and she liked it.

He stepped back a pace. She was still smiling at him and that made him feel exonerated, although he had surprised himself at his own impulsive behaviour. Yes, she was strangely beautiful; her lips were moist and enticing, but he'd never been a pushover for a pretty face, so on this occasion he couldn't understand what had come over him. She was slim with long black hair and there was an intensity in her manner, a bold challenging look, which was so appealing. Her dark penetrating eyes and her sensuous mouth caught his attention.

Once more aware of his immediate environment, Jason composed himself, smiled and shook her hand as if they had known each other for years.

"Welcome to our school. Please stay and look around; I hope you'll become one of my students," he said as he retreated, his eyes still fixed on her as he re-joined the group from which he had been so seductively drawn. Their attention was soon directed back at him, oblivious to Jin-Mei's presence. She stood once again on her own, although now her body chemistry had kicked into action, leaving her with indelible thoughts and a warm inner glow.

Shocked by his own inappropriate behaviour, Jason wondered if he would ever see her again, and if he did, would she even remember that he had kissed her, albeit on the cheek. In China such an action would be sorely frowned upon. This time Jason had got away with it, but he'd have to keep his impulses to himself in future and whatever feelings he had for this woman, he'd have to keep them concealed. Try as he might, the image of her face remained with him for the rest of the day and into the night.

She headed home and as she did, there was a spring in her step that hadn't been there since her teenage years. She felt light as she walked home, from time to time skipping with exhilaration. She went to her empty apartment, but this time there were no tears. She'd been taken aback by this foreigner's audacity. She didn't know if she would ever dare return to the school, or if she did, if she could ever stay away. She closed her eyes and relived that first unforgettable encounter. She'd become an expert in fantasy, for in her years of gloom and misery, it had been her sanctuary and life saver. But the warmth and tenderness she had felt today from this foreigner was no fantasy; he was flesh and blood. Tonight's dream would be about something that was tangible, touchable and accessible.

The Interview

She was now, more than ever before, determined to study English at that school. Although she was in her early forties she felt school-girlish again, and excited at the prospect of being able to see him and often, although to expect anything beyond that would have been wishful thinking. She knew they would surely meet again, but would that initial magic have dissipated by then? Maybe he greeted all female visitors that way. Maybe he was one of those European playboys or a womaniser, who could tell? All she knew was that she needed to be desired and he had given her an unequivocal signal, that she was desirable, and that was enough to lift her out of the doldrums.

The following day, she re-entered the school on Yu-Hua Road and approached the reception desk. She glanced around but there was no sign of the foreigner. One of the young Chinese receptionists asked her to fill out a form and invited her to sit down.

"If you have time, we can have you interviewed by our academic co-ordinator, he'll decide what level you are and allocate a class for you, that's if you are ready to sign up." she said.

"Yes, I have plenty of time," she replied, clutching her handbag, as if someone was about to steal it. She pulled out her glasses and filled in the form, although she remained disappointed not to have seen the foreigner. She turned to the receptionist.

"That foreigner, the one who was in here yesterday, what was his name?" she asked, hoping he wasn't from another school altogether.

"That's Jason. He runs the teaching side of the school," she replied, with one of those all-knowing smiles.

"Really," replied Jin-Mei, trying not to sound too inquisitive. As she waited there, her whole body chemistry started to play tricks with her, turning the just moments before confident and assertive Jin-Mei into a crumbling pillar of nervous vulnerability. The silence was then broken by a foreigner's voice, as it bellowed out from one of the side offices.

"Jin-Mei." Her heart at once began to race. She was barely able to get to her feet; she could feel the strength draining from her knees. She managed to shuffle into the office. "Ah, Jin-Mei, please sit down. Would you like tea or coffee?" She stood in the doorway and stared across the desk at him, unable to utter a word. "Jin-Mei, jin lai" he said, which was an invitation for her to enter his office. She entered as if she were stepping onto a stage watched by hundreds of people, but it was only Jason as he sat there smiling, the epitome of patience. She fidgeted with her ring, which she'd almost forgotten she was wearing. It had become part of her. Though meaningless, it was now a source of embarrassment, as she sat down opposite him.

He was now able to look at her. Hers was a truly original face; sleek oriental eyes with an intelligent brow, smooth rounded cheeks and a slight olive complexion. Despite her slightly protruding incisors, her mouth was her most endearing feature, full and sensuous. He found himself wanting her to smile over and over again, to see that mirth light up his spirit. As he

24

sat there recalling the effect that her smile had had on him, try as he might, he couldn't suppress a shiver of pure sensuousness that ran up and down his spine. He cleared his throat and smiled.

"My name's Jason," he said, looking directly into her dark eyes.

"Yes I remember, we met yesterday in the school foyer," she replied, her eyes dropped towards her handbag held fast across her lap.

"Yes we did. How could I forget? I hope you'll continue to study English with us. We don't bite," he said, his voice deep and resonating. "I'm going to ask you a few questions to assess your English level and then suggest a study plan for you. Are you okay with that?" His eyes were still fixed on hers. She looked up and gave him that smile which had bowled him over the day before.

"Yes, ask whatever you want," she replied, as she adjusted her position on the chair, pulling her black dress over her knees as she did.

"Why do want to study English?" he asked, as he leant towards her, his eyes fixed on her face. Jin-Mei's eyes lowered as she replied.

"It's a long story and I'd rather not go in to the whys and wherefores now. What I really want to do is change my life." He leant back in his chair and smiled.

"I know what you mean, I came to China for the very same reason and I've never regretted it, not for one moment. I think English is a key that can open many doors, which in turn can lead to numerous opportunities, either here or abroad." She sat back surprised at how comfortable she felt with this foreigner; so much so that she was convinced that her decision to study here had been vindicated.

"I've decided to place you in the top class, that's my class, at Level eight," he said with a smile. She couldn't hide the pleasure she felt at being in his class. She grabbed hold of his hand and gave him a broad smile that needed no interpretation. A warm, beautiful sensation swept through her entire body, as the realisation sank in that he had for the second time, singled her out, leaving her gratified and fulfilled.

He gave her a whirlwind tour of the school which ended in the small student cafeteria.

"I take it you like Oolong tea?" he asked, aware that most of the students, both adults and the younger ones, drank it constantly.

"Yes that'd be fine, thank you. Do you ever teach English out of school hours?" she asked, curious as to whether he would be prepared to give her a little private tuition.

"I do, but rarely. One has to be careful. I'd hate to lose my job on account of being accused of having an inappropriate relationship," he said, aware of his own feelings towards her. Her heart sank. Was he telling her that she would never be anything more than a student number? Was he letting her down gently? Her face took on a sad and sullen appearance, which spoke volumes about her disappointment and her expectations. At once he realised the depth of feeling she had been harbouring towards him since their first encounter. It wasn't unusual for female student to have a crush on their male teachers, but for Jason, this reciprocal feeling he had for her, had taken him aback. He placed his hands on hers.

"We can be good friends and of course I can help you, but let's get you up to speed in class first. We can have a coffee together some time and, well I'd like to hear your story, I think that would be nice." Her heart once again became invigorated, as did her radiant smile that he loved so much.

His first instinct was to lean across the table and kiss her passionately, but his rational side prevented him from doing so. Despite this, his body language sent a clear message to her of his stifled desire to embrace her. Their eyes were locked, and as they spoke, both seemed to gravitate towards each other, as if some force were drawing them in. He backed away from her just as a student entered the cafe. Eager to break free from her spell, he changed the topic of conversation.

"Jin-Mei would you like an English name?"

"That would be great, if you give me a name, I'll cherish it forever," she said, for a name in Chinese culture had far more significance than a mere label.

"From today on," he continued "I will call you Jeany. It's similar to Jin-Mei isn't it?" he said as he got to his feet. "I really have to go now. Your class is on both Tuesday and Thursday nights. Both start at 7 o'clock. I'll see you then," he said as he made his way to the door.

"I sometimes work nights at the hospital, so I may miss some of your lessons," she explained.

"I'm sure we'll find a way to catch up," he said with a glimmer in his eye. On leaving the room, he glanced back just once more to catch one last mental image of her sitting there clutching her teacup. "Bye Jeany," he said with a smile. She then gave him a wave as he left the room.

She sat alone, one moment ruminating over her past misfortunes and the next overlaying these dark thoughts with fantasies relating to the many possible futures, waiting to unfold ahead of her. Would she or wouldn't she, would he or wouldn't he? Was this man to play a role in her future or, would someone as yet unknown to her come along and sweep her off her feet? The small coffee shop suddenly filled with students having finished their classes. The sudden influx of young vibrant students made her feel uncomfortable and this realisation brought her back down to earth.

As she glanced around, she noticed that the majority of students were in their twenties, half her age, attractive and full of life and vitality. They laughed and joked with each other. Was their laughter aimed at her? She wasn't sure. No one was looking at her. They were unaware of her presence. All of a sudden, she felt her age. Why would a popular man like Jason fall for her, with so many beautiful young women around? They wouldn't care that Jason was almost fifty, so why should someone like her dare to believe she had any chance of captivating his heart with so many young competitors around?

Once again she became despondent. She glanced down at her favourite black dress that she had cherished for years. It was as if it had suddenly become outdated and open to ridicule, not that anyone noticed. She felt clumsy and out of step with those around her. She stood up and smiled just in case anyone was watching and then left the room, through the foyer and once more into the street. She had some serious adjustments to make and she wasn't going to shy away from making them.

A Week Later

The following Tuesday, Jeany turned up for her class in her new image of stretch denim jeans, a white blouse and a denim waist coat. The shoes had been downgraded to a black pair and she wore her hair up, which emphasised her long elegant neck line. Her lips, that Jason was so drawn to, were a dark red, which matched her painted nails and earrings. Today she felt younger and sexier; her past seemed an eternity away, as she stepped out with renewed confidence into a new but uncertain future.

The class was, as expected, inundated with young and fluent speakers of the English language. She felt uncomfortable and intimidated by their superior skills, but then it dawned on her that Jason had expectations of her being able to cope at that level. She also felt that he had put her there to be taught by him and no one else, and for this reason she would not let him down. Many of the female students were openly flirtatious with Jason in class which irritated her, but his clear blue eyes never left her for long.

There was a kind of rapport that enabled both of them to communicate, without anything being said. Their faces and gestures said it all, and though their friendship as it was, could hardly be described as inappropriate, they were bordering on the brink of an involvement that if it went ahead, could divert their respective fates down irreconcilable pathways.

After class Jason suggested they went for a stroll and a bite to eat. Behind Yu-Hua Road was the Shijiazhuang Museum, and opposite that was a very popular American fried chicken restaurant. It was here that they began to open up as they talked about each other's hopes and dreams. The after class watering hole became a regular habit as each dug deeper into the other's past.

One such evening, she felt it was a good time for her to tell him her story. As they sat over a lukewarm coffee, she grabbed hold of Jason's hands across the table.

"Jason, I can't marry you."

"I haven't asked you to," he replied, eyebrows raised.

"No – what I mean is – if we wanted to get married, we couldn't," she said gripping Jason's hand tightly.

"And why not?" he asked with a smile.

"It's not a laughing matter! What future do we have, if we are never to get married? Jason, it's as if I'm still his wife."

"You say you are still someone's wife?"

Jason's brow furrowed as he stared at her across the table. "Maybe you should tell me what you are talking about, you had better tell me the rest," said Jason his face awash with puzzlement.

"This is China. It's like nowhere else on earth. We all have to tow the party line and no one is allowed to cross it. Not you and certainly not me."

"So what's that got to do with marriage and did you say that you were still married?"

"I'm not married; we just need to be careful."

"So you're telling me now that we need to be careful and behave like good old friends?"

"Yes Jason, certainly in public."

"I'm sure we can do that. I know there's a lot you aren't telling me about your past, why be so secretive?"

Jeany pondered for a moment, with her eyes closed as she stifled the hurt of some long buried, painful memory.

"When I was six, Baba was a teacher and Mama worked in the local hospital. We lived in a nice house with a yard and some chickens. Then in 1966, the Cultural Revolution swept through China. Our family and other non-peasant families were persecuted and publicly humiliated for being one of the 'Black Classes.' Baba and my Mama were thoroughly criticised and sent to the countryside to be reformed. We lost our nice house, and were sent to live in a village dwelling. It was dirty and we had to share the one cold water tap with the whole village. Pigs used to run straight through our home as they wished. I had to watch as my parents were forced to till the land by hand. I've never forgiven the 'Red Guards' for what they did to us. They stole my childhood and reduced our country to chaos. I never got the fine education I would have had, but then later in life, I did manage to educate myself and become a nurse.

"So you take after your Mother then?

"I'd like to think so."

"So everything ended well then?"

"Not really. Despite hating the 'Red Guards' I ended up marrying one. He was introduced to me when I was a student nurse. He had a good job as a police officer and a regular salary, good prospects and connections in high places, what could go wrong?"

"Were you happy?"

"Life isn't just about being happy. Few Chinese women are. I had my one male child, which was the official limit and I was then duly sterilised and sent on my way."

"What did you call your son?"

31

"His given name was 'Pang-Xi' He was a lovely boy but he was hurt when our marriage began falling apart. My husband would find some stupid woman and leave, often returning until the next fling. Then at 16, Pang-Xi left home for Beijing to be with his fellow pro-democracy friends. Trouble erupted with the authorities and you can guess the rest."

"He never came back?"

"Pang-Xi never did. My ex-husband does, but then only when he wants to, but he rarely stays long. I never know when I return home if he'll be in my apartment or not, preferably not, I have to say."

"Why didn't you divorce him?"

"You make it sound so easy. We did divorce, that entailed a meeting of both our families to discourage it. I was so relieved when it eventually became final, although my husband never really had any intention of truly being out of my life."

"So you're a single woman, you are legally free to do what you like, yes?"

"No, you haven't been listening. He won't let me go, and certainly not with a foreigner. He'd kill me first. Divorced or not, I'm still under his control."

"Why didn't you leave?"

"And go where?"

"What he's doing isn't legal."

"Who shall I complain to? Remember he's a policeman and a high ranking one too. So you see, we can be friends for the whole world to see, but we can only be true to ourselves behind closed doors. You do understand don't you?"

"I do and for now we'll keep our business to ourselves, okay?"

"Thank you Jason, I think we'll be alright so long as we're careful."

"You need to study hard and then one day you can leave all this behind."

"This is why I went to your school, to change my life and build a future."

"The past is the past, forget it. Today is ours, and the future I'm sure will unfold as it should. You should be able to start again. Don't allow the demons of the past to trouble you; they can't pose a threat to our relationship, can they?" Jason then smiled.

"What's so funny?" Jeany growled, her sombre mood still insufficiently lifted or reassured by Jason's kind words. He took a sip of his now cold coffee and stared into the half-empty cup as he churned the contents round in a circular motion. She stared, studying every slight facial gesture for any subtle clue as to what might be going through his mind. She grabbed his hands across the table and with eyes that seemed to burn with passion, demanded his attention.

"Talk to me, what am I to do?"

"What is it that you want?" he replied screwing up his face as he did.

"When people see me with you, they look down on me. You're a foreigner and rich. What do you think they take me for? When you go back to your cosy life in England, what will become of me? Have you thought about my position for one moment? I think not. No man will look at me twice after you've gone. I'm sacrificing my good name and all for you, but I feel you're just playing with me. Jason, wo-shi-ge-ren (I'm a person), look at me and tell me you love me."

"Jeany, I do love you," he replied looking irritated that he'd been pushed into saying so.

"Then prove it, let me go back to England with you. Let's run away together, please?" she pleaded, the deep-seated insecurity welling up, all the while nibbling away at her confidence from within. Something inside was telling her that her hold on Jason was getting a little weaker as each day slipped by.

"Don't pressure me. You're moving things on far too fast," he protested. He'd never needed to be committed to anyone. He'd always lived his life as he wished, giving nothing in return. Her sudden proposal had taken him aback and nudged him rudely out of his comfort zone.

"Jason, I'm talking about a new life of freedom and escape from bigotry and prejudice. I want to go where I won't be scorned at for loving a foreigner." He looked at her once more and gave her a warm smile that masked his suppressed instinct to get up and run away.

"Look – I never wanted to get all entangled with anyone, let alone someone with heaps of emotional baggage and endless needs. This is something that I hadn't reckoned on," he said, half wanting to push her away, while at the same time wanting to embrace her and evoke that mirth that had opened the door to his heart. He raised his eyes and looked directly into hers.

"Meals out and walks in the park are fine, but I think we should step it up a gear," he said, as his hand slid across the table settling squarely on hers. He gave her a warm smile and squeezed gently.

"What do you mean, step up a gear?" A feeling of sweet anticipation swept through her entire body. "What do you have in mind?" she asked. In her mind she asked herself, was she pushing him deeper into a relationship that demanded too much of him? Or was he just toying with her emotions? Only time would tell.

For a brief moment his eyes left hers and dropped to her plunging neckline, only to return to where they had been a split second earlier. She knew by this, that his intentions were to go beyond an embrace. As she stared deep into his eyes, her body responded to the involuntary cues sent by his wandering eyes and by the sheer excitement of what was now imminent.

He sat back and adopted a thoughtful expression that filled her with a sense of sweet apprehension.

"I think it would nice if maybe twice a week you and I could spend some time together at my apartment. This would allow us time to get to know each other and we could explore each other's dreams as it were. We could watch a movie and eat some of your Ma-Po-Dou-Fu. We could have breakfast together. Would you like that?" he asked, knowing that such a close encounter could only lead in one direction. He realised that such a suggestion opened him up to absolute rejection or total acceptance. He knew what he wanted, and he knew that paddling around in the paddy fields wasn't going to get him anywhere.

For her, this was not the response she had really wanted, but everything had its price. Should she rebuff him now, she would certainly lose the initiative and end up back where she'd started, she concluded. Accept his proposal and she was probably going to feel obligated to do as he wished, which could end up with her feeling used and manipulated. She reached across the table and held his hand. Although she said nothing, an inner conflict was raging within her as she looked at him, hers for the taking.

Jason closed his eyes and pictured her as she sat there across the table from him, her enduring image etched on his mind. He could picture those dark red lips, her raven black hair and her wide set, long oriental eyes that possessed the kind of fiery passion that was able to burn into a man's soul. Though flawed, she had that certain something that couldn't be ignored. He pondered the consequences of being too forward. It was crunch time; was this now to be their last meeting or the beginning of a love affair that would endure a lifetime?

She looked at his strong masculine features and stern expression. Was this the kind of man to take her away from this land of sorrow and heartache? Deep inside, she knew he probably wasn't. He was attractive and he knew it, his whole demeanour and mannerisms sent out a message that he was a ladies' man. She believed that in time, it was highly probable that he would move on and leave her for someone younger, slimmer and more attractive, and China wasn't short of such women. Still she was, despite these reservations, determined to throw her heart and soul into the relationship. She would show him a side of her that he would be unable to forget. She smiled and gripped Jason's hands inching them towards her.

"I'd like that" she said, knowing she had just put their relationship back on track. After a moments' reflection, she tightened her grip on Jason's hand.

"I need you to remember that I'm your woman, not one of your employees. What I mean is I want to visit you as and when I like, and not just when you feel like seeing me. Do you know what I mean?"

"Look, I'm very busy some nights and I still need to go out and socialise with my staff and other colleagues. I can't just have you just turning up on my doorstep, as and when you feel like it," he explained.

"Got someone else, have you?" she snapped, her eyes narrowing as she recalled the group of eager female students that seemed to hover around him at every available moment. He leaned back and gave her a conciliatory smile.

"There's no one else. Listen, all you have to do is call me first. If I'm not out or with guests, then it'll be fine to come over, okay?" She forced a smile and leaned back, exposing her full figure.

"Okay, can we go to your apartment tonight?" she challenged, with a hint of determination in her voice. He gave her a smile and pulled her close to him.

"Yes of course; what are we waiting for?" He jumped to his feet, grabbed her hand and led her out from the warmth of the restaurant into the cold night air.

An icy wind blew sharp against their faces and penetrated their thick winter clothes. Jeany, whilst holding her coat together with one hand flagged down a taxi with the other. One came to a sudden halt and they both scrambled in, away from the harsh wind and into the warmth of the rear seat of the taxi where they huddled together.

On arriving at Jason's apartment complex, they were ushered in by the compound's security guard, who peered into the taxi to see what kind of visitor this foreigner was bringing home. This embarrassed Jeany, but once they were inside, she relaxed. Jason fumbled in his pockets for his apartment keys, trembling he inserted them into the lock.

As they entered, she gasped in amazement at the spacious, luxurious living room, ornate and decorated to perfection. It was incredibly clean and tidy. There was a subtle fragrance of freshly washed bed linen, a bunch of peonies sat in a large vase set at the centre of a hand-carved classical, rosewood coffee table which dominated the centre of the room. He slammed the door closed behind them and with his arm around Jeany's waist, he guided her to the open bedroom door. Without a word being uttered, he swung her round and threw her onto the huge double bed leaving her puzzled and prostrate. He looked down at her and then slid his body across hers; the passion that was then released rendered their bodies unable to do anything but follow their instincts.

ENTER PEPPER LEE

Although Jeany, to a greater extent, was able to monopolise Jason's time and attention outside the language school, she still relished listening to him talk in class. He taught the most fluent students. Grammar was reduced to an absolute minimum, replaced by role-play and organised debates on social and gender issues. Her English improved in each lesson, though her motivation came from a strong desire to communicate with Jason on a more intimate level.

After just a few weeks in his class, she was beginning to feel a sense of satisfaction, a state of mind that had eluded her since her childhood back in Spring Village. This group of students were all like-minded and eager to expand their expertise in their chosen language, and as such she felt comfortable amongst them. She hadn't felt this kind of attachment to any group of individuals since her early school days, before the Cultural Revolution. In those days, she and her friends would play catch on the dry, dusty playground and later giggle about some insignificant mishap at their primary school.

One member of Jason's class, a Taiwanese lady in her mid-forties, had gone out of her way to befriend her. Jeany had put this down to them being of similar age. The majority of students at the school were girls in their early twenties, with some boys thrown in for good measure. As time went on, this older student, who went by the name of Pepper, began to sit next to her in class, though Jeany had serious reservations about getting too close to her. She came across as one of those women whose aim in life was to delve into everyone's business in order to gossip. Such a woman would need the attention of someone who shared her morbid curiosity about the ins and outs of other people's lives and that wasn't Jeany.

Once in a while, Pepper would ask the odd question about her feelings for Jason. Jeany would ignore the question and change the subject, in order not to offend. Given Jeany's unstable marital background and the sad loss of her son, she was certainly not going to divulge her personal details to a woman like this, whom she didn't know. On one occasion, Pepper asked Jeany about her ex-husband and this startled her, as she had never opened up to anyone before about this episode of her life, only to Jason.

She hadn't even declared that she'd been divorced, although in China having such a sad marital status would in no time have become common knowledge. She didn't openly respond, although she was careful not to show any reaction that would give away any sense of guilt.

Jeany's suspicious nature naturally led her to believe that at some point, she and Jason must have talked about her and the subject of Jeany's past must have been discussed. She gritted her teeth and said nothing, although inside she felt hurt and very angry.

'How dare he talk to that bitch about me!' she thought. As the class continued, the image in her mind of Pepper and Jason talking about her grew and the more she dwelt on it, the angrier she got. After declaring the lesson over, Jason turned to Jeany and smiled.

"How about going to get something to eat?" he asked in a whisper. She just glared at him, her eyes burning with fury. She then stormed out of the classroom without saying a word, and without any explanation of what had made her so angry. He stood there with a puzzled look on his face. Some of the other students, including Pepper, found Jeany's reaction amusing and didn't hide the fact. Rudely aware that he had been placed in an embarrassing predicament, he simply shook his head in disbelief and smiled.

Prior to his attachment to Jeany, the students had been able to talk to their teacher after class. This sudden outburst had suddenly given them back the chance to collar Jason and ask questions they preferred not to air in class. As a consequence of Jeany storming out, Jason was now inundated with students who needed that special time to confide in him, time that had been denied them since Jeany had joined the group.

It was now that he realised that his feelings for her had not only jeopardised his good name but also had a negative impact on his professional performance. This embarrassing episode had opened his eyes to the downside of involving oneself with one's students. He recalled an old Chinese saying that went, 'If you play with dogs, they'll lick your face'.

Jason walked home alone that evening and felt a tinge of sadness at what seemed to be a last curtain call on their relationship. This bitter medicine was duly sweetened by a feeling of relief. From now on he was going to avoid putting himself in a situation where he left himself open to being made a fool of. The more he thought about her display of rejection, the angrier he felt about the whole episode.

Miss Sha Makes an Offer

That weekend they never spoke. Each was convinced that the blame for whatever had split them up lay with the other. Jeany wandered back home, asking herself over and over again if she had jumped to conclusions or if she was being made a fool of. On entering the dark and cold apartment block, the featureless concrete entrance hall compounded her sense of loneliness and despair. She paused for a moment at the bottom of the stairwell and looked up at the ever winding stair that led to her solitary abode, high on the top floor.

Step after step, she trudged up into the darkness, her footsteps echoing behind her. Near the top she stopped and grabbed hold of the stair railing to catch her breath. Her breathing was shallow and rapid. She could feel the blood thundering around the inside of her cranium. Images of her large double bed beckoned her to keep going. As she approached her apartment door, she noticed Miss Sha, the nosey old lady from across the hall. She was standing in her doorway, watching as Jeany's weary steps brought them face to face. Jeany's son had often referred to her as Lao-Niang, which was an impolite name for an old woman. Everyone knew her as Sha. She never used her given name.

"Jin-Mei, they tell me you call yourself Jeany now. Is that so?"

"Yes. Someone suggested it would be a good name for me, while studying English."

"I can guess who made that suggestion."

"It was my teacher Jason."

"Your teacher and more besides I would guess"

"I don't mean to be rude, but I need to get in and rest."

"You look tired and miserable. Maybe it's time you consulted a fortune teller."

"You mean you, don't you?"

"There's no one better. Everyone knows my skills. Even your creepy husband and one of his sluts have used my service. All I need is a lock of someone's hair. It's as easy as that."

"Do I know her?"

"Oh, you mean your ex-husband's belly warmer? That my dear, you don't need to know."

"He can go to hell and whoever he's with. Anyway I thought you were a nurse like me?"

"I'm a pharmacist, but then what single woman can live on such a pitiful wage as mine?"

"I do."

"Jin-Mei, would you like me to predict your future?"

"No. I don't think so. If it's anything like my past, I'd rather not know."

"If I were you, I'd give it a try. Knowledge – be it good or bad – is empowering; ignorance isn't."

"My past is something I'd rather forget."

"No, Jin-Mei, we mustn't forget. During the war, my husband and best friend were slaughtered by the Japanese. Then I was taken by the Japs and you don't need me to tell you what I had to endure. Later the Chinese Guo-Min-Dang troops came and they were no better. I have no time for men. I hate them all and that includes the bitches that suck up to them."

"I'm sorry, it must have been terrible, but I'm sure Jason is different. I really do."

"I'll tell you now and for free, that foreigner you're seeing will bring you nothing but pain. He's no better than that lousy husband of yours. Remember my words. You're going to get hurt."

"Not all men are the same. I just don't want to be alone anymore."

"Jin-Mei, wake up. We all end up alone in the end."

"I really do have to go."

"Think about what I said. We're both suffering in our own ways. The day your son left for Beijing, he took my young niece with him and neither returned. For all I know they maybe both dead, for that I bear you no malice, just think on, you're not the only person here suffering."

"I thank you for that, but I really do need to rest, really."

The old lady touched Jeany's hands, and with a warm and understanding look in her eyes she turned away and retreated back behind her grey apartment door. Jeany entered her room, secured the door and then fell into the large leather sofa giving her scalp a good scratch with both hands, she then sighed. The old woman had never before shown her any kindness. Jeany had always considered her to be a disagreeable old gossip. Maybe this rotten apple had a sweet core; then again maybe not. What was she up to? Jeany reprimanded herself for once more seeing the sinister, where just maybe, it didn't exist.

Enter Jenna

That Sunday evening Jason relaxed alone in his apartment, the troubles of the past now filed in a convenient place at the back of his mind. His moments of tranquillity were to be cut short by an unexpected sharp knock on the door. He tip-toed across to the door and peered through the spy glass, fearing it was Jeany.

The person on the other side was a tall Chinese woman with short hair and glasses, not unattractive, although clearly in her late forties. Jason sighed; relieved that it wasn't who he thought it was and opened the door. As he and the mystery woman stood face to face, he was hit by a subtle fragrance of Estee Lauder. Her eyes were dark and intense, and with a serious expression on her face she stared directly at him. She had a kind of assertiveness and confidence that was refreshing in an Asian woman.

"Jason?"

"Yes, how can I help you?"

"Can I come in for a moment?"

"Yes of course. How rude of me. Take a seat. I'm making some jasmine tea, would you like some?"

"Yes that'd be fine. You've invited me into your home and yet you don't even know who I am, how come?"

"You're a woman! Why should I fear you?"

"Some women can be very dangerous, you know".

"Are you dangerous?"

"No I'm not, but never underestimate a woman's scorn; and never assume pretty means nice."

"I see you know your Shakespeare," replied Jason.

"I've also read 'The Art of War by Sun-zi."

"I'll get you that tea. I won't be a moment." He retreated to the kitchen area, puzzled as to the identity of this sharp witted lady.

"What did you say your name was?"

"I didn't." Jason just smiled.

"Here's your tea." The visitor leant back, sinking into the huge soft armchair and relaxed.

"My Chinese name is Jie-Na, but you can call me Jenna." She then took a sip of her tea. He sat and scrutinized the mysterious caller in the next chair and waited for her to get to the point. After a brief moment of silence, she turned and opened the conversation.

"I work as a paediatrician at the number four Shijiazhuang Hospital, not far from here on Zhong-Shan Road, do you know it?"

"Yes, one of my students is a nurse there."

"Just a student is she?" she asked, with a wry smile.

"Well, not just a student. You mean Jeany, don't you?" he asked, his face flushed.

"I do."

"Has she sent you here to annoy me, or have you come on your own volition?"

"When you have a friend who is upset or distressed, don't you try and help them?"

"Of course I do, but she has never mentioned you."

"Why should she?"

"If you're such good friends, she would have. I had the impression she had no close friends at all."

"That goes to show how much you know. Real friends stay away, when things are going well, and step in when they're needed, dong-bu-dong?"

46

"Yes I do understand. So what is it that aggravated her so?"

"Jason, don't be so defensive. We both want the best for her, don't we? If you really don't know, I'll have to tell you. Won't I? There's no other way to put it. Have you been divulging information about Jeany to one or more of you students, in particular Pepper Lee?"

"Certainly not, the idea is preposterous. I'd never do such a thing."

"Really?"

"Yes, really!" snapped Jason. "So is that's what this is all about? What made her think such a thing? I've only spoken to her in class and never on a personal level. Did Pepper tell Jeany that I'd said something?"

"Not really. Pepper knew something that only Jeany and you did. Pepper somehow knew that she'd been divorced."

"Why doesn't she ask her ex-husband? Maybe he can shed some light on the matter. I'm not the leak, so you'll have to look elsewhere."

"So? What now? Are you going to make up with Jeany or prolong her misery?"

"That's up to her. I mean I'm the accused person here."

"You're right Jason. The information could have come from anywhere. You'll have to forgive her, she's been hurt and it's hard to rebuild trust in relationships once it's been damaged in a previous involvement."

"I'm not having her embarrass me in class again, not now and not ever. She has to understand that or this relationship is going nowhere."

"Look, thank you for seeing me. Here's my card. Give me a call sometime and we'll make it a threesome,

47

okay?" Jenna stood up, placed her cup on the coffee table and left, leaving Jason to ponder her words.

MISUNDERSTANDINGS

The following evening Shijiazhuang was at the centre of a torrential downpour. Despite this, the class was well attended. As he glanced round, he noticed that the chair where Jeany used to sit was vacant. She had left in a huff and everyone knew it, and now she was evoking memories of that soured lesson by her continued absence.

Jason's brow furrowed with displeasure, but he had a job to do and one he loved. He reminded himself that he couldn't have wished for a nicer group of students. Wet and cold, they sat down, in preparation for his class.

Just as they were settling, Pepper Lee burst into the room.

"Am I late? It's raining dogs and cats out there."

Jason smiled to himself.

"Its cats and dogs, Pepper," he said, with a hint of amusement in his voice.

"I know that," snapped Pepper, as she spun around into her chair, slapping her note book down onto her lap. The lesson proceeded as normal with open discussion, but on this occasion, the subject of the 'Cultural Revolution' came up. Jason asked the class,

"Was it the fear of another Cultural Revolution that forced the authorities to clamp down on the June 4th Tian-a-men Square students?" By asking this, he had unwittingly slated Li-Peng, the man who had given the army the go ahead to crush the pro-democracy movement that day.

"You've no right to criticise our leaders," proclaimed Pepper in a stern voice. A fearful silence descended onto the class. They were all well aware that such talk could stir the wrath of the Red Guards. Jason tried to brush over some of the remarks which he had so freely expressed. He was taken aback by this woman's sudden outburst.

"I'm sure Mr Li Peng's heart was in the right place. I mean he placed his country and his duty above the needs of the protesters, didn't he?"

"He had to do it for the party. Those protesters were troublemakers and got what was coming to them. Does anyone disagree?" Pepper asked, as she stared at each in turn. Silence continued and Jason gave up trying to use his western logic and joined those who had opted to stay quiet. Pepper got to her feet and as she was leaving, Jeany arrived at the doorway. Without an 'excuse me' Pepper barged past her and stormed down the corridor towards the foyer and out into the street.

Jeany stood there with an amused look on her face. Jason was relieved to see her back to her old smiling self. As she looked into his eyes, tears welled up from deep within. Words stifled by emotion were barely able to seep out.

"I've missed class, I'm sorry." she said as she wiped a tear from her cheek. The lesson proceeded, with the students quieter than usual. When the class was over the students, one by one and in silence, donned their coats and drifted out of the classroom, still smarting from the shock of Pepper's outburst.

Pepper turned up at the next class, as if her rude outburst had never happened. The group, though still cautious about her explosive temperament, were happy to see her back although still apprehensive about her volatility. Jason was also pleased to see things return to normal, but he'd learnt a bitter lesson about debating political issues in China; he shouldn't do it. Though lessons continued, the group stayed well away from contentious topics that could offend party members.

In China, divorcees and older single women usually found themselves with few friends. These individuals were generally looked upon, as not being quite normal – social outcasts. They were also seen to be plagued with bad luck and that this fate would befall anyone who consorted with them. With few real friends, Jeany welcomed the friendship of Pepper and at times, when she was unable to meet with Jason, she and Pepper would take time out in the school cafe.

Though Pepper was Chinese, she wasn't a mainland Chinese citizen, having somehow landed in China from Taiwan. She claimed she was from a city in central Taiwan called Tai-Zhong. She explained that she had a connection in the Shijiazhuang police department, which enabled her to stay, despite having no legal papers to that effect. How she had got into China without them, she refused to say. Most, including Jason, found it odd that a Taiwanese citizen should defend the Communist party line, when she would have been raised with a diametrically opposed opinion.

The fact that Jeany was associating with a known illegal immigrant, made her feel uneasy. Having been married to a policeman, she was aware of the institutional cruelty amongst the rank and file. Suspicion and hatred was targeted at anyone who was seen to oppose the status quo and towards those who were deemed guilty of offences against the state. These people forfeited any rights they may have had prior to being accused. Though she smiled and chatted with Pepper, she was not prepared to expose herself to any more risk than she had to. She would see Pepper only at class and never outside the school. On one occasion, when Jeany had met up with Pepper in the school café, Jeany noticed that everyone seemed to be looking at them, a sudden hot flush rushed through Jeany's body.

"Is that the time, sorry Pepper I've got to go. I'll see you at class on Thursday." And with that she hurried out of the cafe and onto the bustling street, as sweat ran down her face.

There was something strange about Pepper that Jeany couldn't quite work out. She was tall, elegant and wore make-up that set her apart from the local women. She had a self-confidence that seemed to sweep away any of the fear she should have had. She dressed in distinctive black lacy clothes, with short skirts and high heels which made her stand out from the crowd. She wore her hair up with a black ribbon that hung down the side of her face.

She never even tried to hide her strong Taiwanese accent in public. As conspicuous as she was, she showed no fear at being recognised as an outsider. She had beautiful smooth skin and a perfect body shape. Jeany asked herself, 'shouldn't such a woman have men pursuing her, or did she have a man she was keeping quiet about?' She was also curious about this sudden interest in herself. Was she married, divorced or was she having illicit meetings with some married man? Maybe she was gay! Jeany quickened her walk as she headed for home, her mind churning over the many possibilities but nothing made much sense.

Jeany decided that she was probably gay, but then Jeany was no pin-up girl, far from it. Why then did this attractive woman latch on to her so? It was as if Pepper had set out to befriend her, but why? A shiver ran up and down Jeany's back, as she thought back to Pepper's eagerness to be close to her. How could she have not realised that Pepper had been grooming her for her own sexual needs?

Her brisk walk home broke into a trot, as she approached the safety of her apartment. On her arrival, she dismissed her interpretation of Pepper's affections towards her as erroneous. She knew that she and Jason were an item. Still, the idea had been quite titillating she thought, laughing it off as pure fantasy.

Sprawling across the double bed, her mobile sat silent on the table. Time drifted by and the expected call from Jason didn't materialise. It was at times like these, that her colourful imagination got the better of her. Should she ring him? Where was he and what was he doing that was so important? There were times when her suspicious mind took on a sinister personality of its own. A week earlier she had followed Jason just to see where he went when he wasn't with her. She'd been let down and lied to so many times before; she knew only too well the feeling of being left hollow and worthless. It was hard for her to imagine anyone being any different. She hadn't been let down by Jason, not yet anyway. Maybe the idea of her being with another woman wasn't so bad after all, she thought.

'Jeany, what on earth are you thinking?' she mumbled to herself. She picked up her mobile and shook it and then threw it against the far wall, where it dropped behind her bedroom cupboard. She got to her feet and began to get ready for bed, but as she did her phone began to ring. Unable to get at it, she threw herself back onto the bed and covered her ears with the pillow. Frustration and jealousy had eaten into her very soul.

She kicked her legs against the mattress, she felt wretched and angry at her own ineptness. The phone eventually stopped ringing and Jeany, now having shifted the cupboard, retrieved it and retired back to her bed in an attempt to sleep off her pent-up anger. The missed call had been from Jason.

Once in bed, her inquisitive and suspicious mind drifted in the direction of Pepper Lee, who had been so keen to befriend her. Despite long conversations alone with her, Jeany was no wiser as to her personal life although she was convinced that Pepper knew more about her past than she would have her believe, and that continued to trouble her.

Dinner with Jenna

The next morning, as was her habit, Jeany set off to walk to work. As she made her way down Yu-Hua Road, her mind continued to ruminate over the many unanswered questions that refused to lie still. How did this Taiwanese woman get into China in the first place? And what enticed her here anyway? There were no pots of gold in Shijiazhuang, that was for sure, and no-one in their right mind would have described the city as beautiful or idyllic, far from it. This was an enormous sprawling industrialised city, with very little to entice the tourists, even the odd foreign backpacker that drifted into its concrete tentacles, looked and then kept going.

She struggled to make sense out of what she knew, as she walked past the language school towards the hospital where she worked. Then something entered her head that made her smile.

'I may not know where she lives or anything about her, but I know someone who does,' mumbled Jeany to herself. She felt a warm glow of satisfaction as the realisation sunk in. At once there was a spring in her step and a smug smile across her face.

By chance, Jeany bumped into Jenna as she entered the paediatric ward.

"Jenna, how have you been?"

"I'm fine; did you get your problems sorted out with Jason?"

"Yes, it was just me over reacting as usual. Thanks for talking to him; we're alright now. I don't know what got into me, really I don't. I feel so stupid."

"We all do at times, don't we?"

"Of course you're right, you always are." Jenna gave Jeany a warm reassuring hug and a peck on the cheek.

"We'll have to meet up one evening."

"Yes I'd like that. I'm free tonight, how about you?"

"I'm off tonight and I guess it wouldn't do Jason any harm to be on his own once in a while," said Jenna glancing down at her watch.

"Will 8 o'clock at your place be alright?" Jeany asked conscious of Jenna's need to attend to her patients. Jenna smiled and then dashed off to her allotted ward.

Later that evening Jeany arrived at Jenna's apartment carrying a bottle of sorghum wine. Under her large winter coat, she wore her new red dress that flowed out from the waist line and dropped just below the knee. With her long black hair, low cut neck line and red lips, she looked and felt young and exuberant.

Jenna opened the door and greeted her with a warm embrace. On entering the living area she was bowled over by the fresh aroma of salmon dressed in a rich double cream sauce, sweet potatoes and broccoli.

"That smells so good, it must have taken you hours to make," remarked Jeany, as she looked around at the expensive décor, the burgundy coloured drapes and the precise layout of the dinner table, set for two.

"Nothing's too good for a special friend. Mind you I'll expect you to return the favour and invite me over to your place one day."

"Oh yes, that'd be a pleasure, truly," she said as Jenna helped her off with her top coat.

"That's a beautiful dress, I haven't seen you look so beautiful, it beats your all-white nurse's uniform hands down, doesn't it?" Jenna said, as she manoeuvred the chair for her guest to sit down at the table.

"I bought it to impress Jason. I like my black dress but I tend to wear it a little too often."

"Well, I don't care what you wear; you'd look good in anything. Now let's eat and forget men for a while."

After every last morsel of food had been consumed, Jenna broke open the wine that Jeany had brought. As they sat on the sofa, they enjoyed a mutual feeling of contentment.

"Tell me about this Pepper Lee woman. Is she a threat to you in any way?" Jenna asked, curious to know if Jeany's jealous nature was at the heart of the problem.

"No she's no threat to me, not really. I find her extremely mysterious. I mean she never talks about herself and for the love of me, I can't work out why she should risk life and limb to slip into China from Taiwan. It's not safe, it doesn't make sense."

"She's friendly isn't she, and she's done nothing bad to you, has she?" Jenna quizzed.

"You're right but what seems strange is that she's gone out of her way to befriend me and with such eagerness. She's from a wealthy country and she's attractive, this kind of person isn't drawn to people like me."

"People like you?"

"Yes, you know the type, one of life's ugly ducklings that never quite blossomed, a Christmas cake in January, do you know what I'm saying?"

"Why do you always put yourself down, you're as good as anyone. Jason loves you, doesn't he?"

"Yes, he does, but sooner or later he'll be snapped up when someone prettier and younger comes along."

"There's nothing you can do to keep him, if he chooses to run off with some disreputable woman. You do your best, that's all you can do. Take care of his body and encourage him to take care of your mind. Remember kindness and lies are worth a million truths."

"You make it sound so easy."

"It is, Jin-Mei, it is."

"Then what about you, you're still single aren't you?" Jeany asked. Jenna looked up at her and smiled.

"More wine?"

"To be quite honest Jenna, she was so friendly that I had convinced myself she was one of those lesbians."

"Would that have been so bad?"

"Oh yes, I'm not interested in women that way, oh no, that's not nice."

"So you don't like such women then?"

"I'm just not like that, that's all. I don't care what other people get up to. I'm just not that way inclined," argued Jeany, irritated somewhat by the inquisition.

Suddenly, Jenna reached across and held on to Jeany's wrist and stared into her wide eyes. Jenna was tall but delicate and very slim but despite her wiriness, her grip was firm and unwavering. Now being alone with Jenna was no longer a shallow pleasantry. Jeany felt a surge of incongruous sexual attraction gushing within her that shocked her. She tried to pull her arm away, but Jenna's grip tightened.

"Why is your pulse racing so fast?" Jenna asked in a soft voice.

"I don't know" said Jeany. Jenna released her grip of Jeany's wrist.

"I know," declared Jenna smiling, "you're afraid of your own feelings."

"My feelings, towards you?"

"Yes and why not?" For a brief moment, silence descended on the couple. Jeany stood up. She brushed down her dress, as if sweeping crumbs from her

58

clothing. When she sat back down, she positioned herself at a different angle from Jenna, although not far enough away to be offensive. Jenna once again reached for Jeany's wrist, but this time she allowed her to feel her pulse.

"That's better, you're much calmer now" said Jenna as she gave her a warm smile.

"What now?" Jeany asked. Jenna just shrugged her shoulders and gave her a smile.

"Nothing," said Jenna as she picked up her glass and took a slow sip of the blood red wine. "Jeany, you're an attractive and desirable woman, don't let anyone tell you otherwise, and don't forget it."

"I can see myself. I'm not daft. I have small slanted eyes and buck teeth. I'm not what men would describe as beautiful, am I?"

Tears welled up in her eyes, as she felt life for other women was so much better than it was for her.

"You're slim and you have a radiant personality. Those cardboard cut-outs in the movies would give their right arm to be as charismatic as you," said Jenna in an attempt to comfort her friend.

"Anyway I'm not gay," insisted Jeany.

"I know," said Jenna with a smile. "I promise not to jump on you, okay?" With that, both women began to laugh, allowing the conversation to return to the subject of Pepper. Jenna took one more sip of her wine and leant back.

"Have you thought of asking Jason about her?"

"Yes, that was on my mind earlier. I mean he must know nearly everything about her – where she lives and her motivation and so on. He interviewed her didn't he?" Jeany reasoned. Jenna looked puzzled.

"Why is it so important to know everything about her, why?"

"I think she has latched on to me for a reason, I'm sure of that. After each class I talk to Jason, every time I do, she slides up beside us and behaves in a flirtatious manner in front of him. She smiles at him and pretends to be cute, maybe she's trying to get to him through me, what do you think?"

"I don't know. Does Jason like her?"

"She's slim and very trendy, she wears a lot of make-up, so I guess he's attracted to her," replied Jeany

"Don't be so hard on her. Before you came along, everyone was able to get to talk to their teacher, now you're monopolising him. You'll not be doing yourself any favours doing that for much longer. Maybe her needs are simple. Maybe she'd like to talk to her teacher, and it's her right to do that. Maybe she likes his attention or maybe she's already got a partner somewhere out there. Who knows?" Jeany grabbed Jenna's hand and gave it a squeeze.

"I'm going to find out" said Jeany, "I'm going to find out everything."

JEANY GETS JITTERY

The following week Jason's class assembled as usual, the students were awaiting their teacher's appearance. All were present, except Pepper, who was conspicuous by her absence. This in itself encouraged the class to tell Jeany about Pepper's outburst in their last lesson, which Jeany had just missed due to her late arrival in class. Despite her feelings for Jason, she was annoyed at his thoughtless and outspoken criticism of Li Peng's involvement in the 'June 4th Incident'.

That year there had been a purge on the followers of the student's democracy movement and on the supporters of those involved. It had suppressed open debate and stifled talk about democracy in general. Suspicion and distrust was endemic following the incident. Informants were able to endear themselves to the authorities, by supplying information on dissidents and those deemed to be enemies of the party and of the state. With this in mind, a cold ripple of fear gripped her as she sat there and listened to the way Pepper had reacted. She left the class and intercepted Jason before he had a chance to enter the room. She grabbed his arm, stopping him in his tracks.

"Jason, whatever you do, don't talk politics, and never criticise our party leaders. You don't know what you're talking about and you never know who is listening. They can stab you in the back. It's dangerous, and I mean really dangerous," she whispered.

"I know, don't worry I've learnt my lesson," he admitted holding up his hands.

"That Pepper can be a real bitch. Listen; don't let her know you don't trust her. You can smile at her all you like, but you'd better guard your tongue, if you know what's good for you," she said in a forced whisper. She was now no longer worried about Jason's feelings for Pepper. For whatever chances she had had with Jason, they would now be well and truly dashed after her brash and embarrassing behaviour. A warm glow radiated from deep inside her, as the feeling of gratification sunk in and blossomed into a self-satisfied smile.

Pepper arrived late for class and was greeted by a full complement of her fellow students, all smiling politely in her direction. Though puzzled, she reciprocated, by returning a pert smile and lowered herself back into her usual place next to Jeany. After class, Jeany suggested that she and Jason went out for a bite to eat. The fried chicken restaurant they frequented often was just opposite the museum that backed onto the school, a mere five minute walk away. Jason was slim and muscular, yet food was one of those things that he rarely turned down.

The dark evening streets were sparsely illuminated and quiet as they strolled towards the restaurant. An icy cold mist drifted around them, as they made their way along the uneven sidewalk, her arm tight around Jason's waist. Although she felt safe walking with him, she sensed that something or someone was following them. On looking back, she noticed a slim figure some fifty yards behind them. She wasn't sure, but she thought it was Pepper. Through the mist she could make out a lone silhouette, barely visible through the dimness, ambling along the far side of the mist shrouded street. She turned to her front and smiled up at Jason, ignoring what she believed was on their tail. When they arrived at the restaurant doors, she swung around and looked back but there was no one there.

Once inside, she continued to stare out of the window, expecting to see Pepper appear from out of the cold night air, but the slim, dark silhouetted image never materialised.

"You seem a little distracted. What are you looking at?" Jason asked, with a hint of irritation in his voice.

"I'm sure someone was following us." He shook his head and smiled.

"You're beginning to imagine things; who on God's earth would waste their time following us?"

"Jason, this is China, I love my country but really bad things can happen here and to ordinary people like us, believe me," she whispered, as she looked around to make sure no one had heard her. "Since that woman's outburst, we won't be able to relax. One word to the authorities and I could end up in prison. They're nothing like your cosy English prisons; I could end up being stripped naked and thrown into a male dormitory and raped over and over again, and you wonder why I'm scared?"

"I didn't realise that kind of thing happened in China. I'd rather not see you again, than risk you going through that," he said, shocked at her stark disclosure.

"My friend Mao lost her job at the soap factory for getting pregnant a second time. She'd had twins the first time, so this was her third child. This was in contravention of China's family planning regulations. She ended up in a psychiatric institution. You can't mess around with these people. All I ask is for you to keep your mouth shut on these issues and promise me one day we'll leave here, at least until things change." She looked long and hard at him, her moist, sad eyes pleading for his understanding.

"You don't know what you're asking. Are you suggesting we get married, so you can escape the country you were raised in, is that what you're asking?"

"Yes," she admitted, aware that the proposal didn't really make a lot of sense to a foreigner like him.

"For a start, you don't really know me. I've got skeletons in my cupboard you'd never believe and things I couldn't possibly tell you about myself. I can't stay here indefinitely and even if we decided to leave, you'd have visa troubles. Exit visas for China and resident visas for England – it's a lot of hassle, believe me."

"Skeletons, do you mean dead people?" she asked, horrified as to what kind of past this man of hers had been keeping secret. Jason just laughed.

"No I mean like family secrets, you know things that we'd rather leave buried. Like dead bones, just left alone."

"Talking of secrets, has Pepper ever told you where she lives?" He folded his arms and adopted a rigid posture.

"And why do you need to know; she's a friend of sorts, isn't she? If she wanted you to know she would have told you. Why not try asking her?"

"I'm not asking her, I'm asking you."

"All I'm prepared to say is that she lives in the same apartment complex that I live in, next to Century Park, not the same block but thereabouts."

"So when we go to Century Park on a weekend, she could be watching us?"

"I suppose so," he replied shrugging his shoulders. "What's the big deal? We generally sit by the water feature, don't we? No-one can see us from the apartments. You know that. Actually I've seen her occasionally with some man, usually in the evening down on the main street."

"Really, how old is he?" she enquired with a glimmer of excitement in her eyes.

"He's an older man, maybe he's her father or an uncle, more than that I don't know and I don't care, okay?"

She smiled, for now she had enough information to go on. She now knew she wasn't a lesbian or after Jason, and somewhere out there was a mystery man. All her dark suspicions about Pepper were dissipating fast and she felt a slight sense of embarrassment at her previous presumptions. Still, there remained a problem with her outburst in class. Did she possess a dangerous ideology or did she have a link with the politburo or the Red Guards? If so, was this situation a powder keg waiting to explode?

"No more talk on politics or criticisms of the Chinese system, okay? We've been there before; we'll talk food and health from now on," promised Jason.

"Yes. Food, are we going to order some or not?" Jeany asked as she stared at the empty table in front of her. Jason jumped to his feet and joined the queue, returning with a portion of fried chicken minutes later.

"I received an email today from an old colleague who said he'd be in Beijing tomorrow. I need to meet him at the airport. I should arrive back in the evening some time." Jeany's eyes lit up.

"We can go together, do some shopping and spend some time in Bei-Hai Park, what do you think?" she asked with a glimmer in her eye.

"No Jeany, we're going to be talking most of the day. We'll be discussing business. I think you'll be in the way and I mean that in the nicest way. If I'm to help you in the future, I'll need some better way of making money, okay?" Jeany's face dropped.

"If that's what you want, I'll stay here and read."

"Yes do that, I'll call you when I'm done." Her thoughts immediately went back to those lonely hours waiting by the phone for her husband to call, something he had often forgotten to do.

"So what's your friend's name?" she asked, curious about anything connected to Jason.

"Douglas. He's retired now but as active as ever. I met him when I lived in Galveston. He used to work on the NASA base there. He's a good man."

"Will you bring him here?" she asked, eager to meet anyone she could practise her English with.

"If he has time, I'm sure he'd like that. He can always stop over with me if need be. I suggest you touch base with Pepper and make your peace with her," suggested Jason with a patient expression on his face.

"We haven't fallen out, but I know what you mean. I've read 'The Art of War' by Sun-Zi too." Jason laughed, leaned over the table and kissed Jeany.

"I do love you – you're not only pretty, but you're smart too," he declared. She felt a great surge of warmth inside to be praised in such a way. She knew he wasn't the kind of man to dole out meaningless flattery. Although they hadn't reached that defining moment in their relationship, where they had made promises and expressed commitments to each other, she was sure that would come in the days or years ahead.

ENTER DOUGLAS

The following day Jason's taxi arrived on time. As he sat in the back, on his way to Central Station, it amused him to see how all the taxi drivers had metal cages welded around their seats, presumably to dissuade robbers or carjackers. Jason thought that these crude cages would be of little use against a persistent customer with a long sharp knife or a gun. He reprimanded himself for his habit of comparing China to England.

On his arrival at the station, he slipped the driver the required amount of Ren-Min-Bi and stepped out into the cool morning air. The station forecourt was at least the size of two football pitches, with concrete steps leading up to the main frontage. Despite its enormous size, the area was jammed packed with travellers, many being migrant workers leaving, returning home or entering Shijiazhuang to seek whatever migrant job opportunities were available. They were all seated along the steps like a colony of sea birds, up against the main building, all across the paved area and right down to the roadside curb. Many looked as if they had been there all night, having slept on the cold hard concrete. Others looked like they had been there since the station was built.

There was an overwhelming sense of weariness, as the crowds continued to wait in silence enduring the bitter cold air and without complaint. As he waded through the multitudes, he was scrutinised at length, for many of those waiting had come from remote parts of China and had rarely seen a foreigner, if at all. He had got used to being stared at. He'd been in Shijiazhuang almost a year and still the apparent novelty of his presence had not been exhausted.

Once allowed onto the platform, he boarded the huge double-decker train bound for Beijing. He politely squeezed his way along the crowded aisle, as they stowed away hordes of luggage that everyone seemed to be carrying. Just as he sat down, the train began to pull away from the station commencing its three hour journey to Beijing. He managed to block out all of the chattering around him and drift into a world of his own.

He recalled the early seventies, when Douglas Murphy had been his Commanding Officer at RAF Wildenrath in Germany. They had worked together on number four squadron Harriers from 1972 until 1975. Jason was then a young pilot officer in his mid-twenties. Following his Royal Air Force career, he had headed off to America, where he ended up working for NASA until 1986. Once again, to his delight, he bumped into Douglas. He hadn't seen his old commander for just on twelve years.

He was puzzled as to how he had acquired his contact details, and even how he'd known that he was in China. What was so important for him to have gone to all the trouble of tracking him down? He'd obviously gone to great lengths in order to meet up with him again, but why?

As the huge iron dragon pulled into Beijing Station, chaos erupted along the carriage as almost everybody scrambled to get their luggage to the doors first. Some clambered down the spiral stair from the upper deck, while those below appeared to be intent on being obstructive. He decided to sit there until the frantic passengers had all disembarked.

On stepping down from the train, he was engulfed by the throng and swept along the platform like a minnow in a fast flowing stream. In likewise fashion he left the station, only to find himself at the rear of yet another queue, but this time for one of the many taxis ferrying passengers from the station to central Beijing.

He had been sent confirmation of a VIP superior room booked for him at the Grand Mercure Hotel in the Xi-Dan area of the city, just west of the shopping area of Guo-Mao. As he arrived in the hotel lobby, his mobile rang.

"Where are you?" Douglas asked in a deep, hoarse voice.

"I've just arrived at the hotel, where are you?"

"Right behind you," replied Douglas. He then heard the eruption of throaty laughter against the back of his neck. Jason spun round to come face to face with his old comrade. Douglas immediately threw his arms around him and gave him a manly squeeze.

"You old fox."

"It's good to see you again. Jason, what's with the grey hair?"

"I'm not surprised I've got grey hair, you nearly frightened me to death, you old sod," he replied as he wiped the sweat from his brow.

"Sorry old chap, I just couldn't resist it. Go and get your luggage checked in; then we'll have a nice cup of strong coffee, my treat of course."

Jason did as Douglas had suggested and joined his old commander for a relaxing drink, in a discreet corner of the hotel lounge.

"It's really great to see you again, but how on earth did an old fox like you manage to find me out here in the middle of nowhere?" Though at the back of his mind right now the 'why' was far more of an imposing question than the 'how'. Douglas gave Jason a wry smile.

"Come on Jason, you know I'm a professional when it comes to this kind of thing,"

"Well go on then, what's your secret? How did you find me?" He demanded, annoyed at the way Douglas was holding back on him.

"Well young man, do you know that drop dead gorgeous woman you've been chatting to on that social networking site?" Jason plonked down his cup of coffee on the glass topped table.

"Don't tell me she's one of your operatives? I don't believe it," said Jason, as his pallid face drained of blood. His sullen complexion flushed as the realisation sunk in that he'd been had.

"She located you on the net and the rest is history," said Douglas shrugging his shoulders.

"How did you know I'd be on that site?"

"We've had your personality profile on record for years. You're single now and at large. You were sure to be hunting a fresh kill, so to speak."

"That's a bit crude, but I guess you guys know me better than I know myself," he admitted.

"What are you doing now? You're not MI6 anymore are you?" he asked as he poured himself another coffee.

"No I'm a civilian now."

"MI5 then?"

"Yes, but we're the nice guys."

"Really?"

"Yes, as always we aim to keep the peace. That's enough about me. I'm sure that what I have to tell you should help to liven up your dreary stay in China. At least it'll make this tour of duty a memorable one. Anyway, how's your love life, as if I didn't know?"

Douglas asked as he dunked his custard cream into his coffee. Jason just smiled.

"Up and down as usual, so what brings you to this neck of the woods? I gather it's not a social visit."

"You're right it's not, but that doesn't mean it's not great to see you again," he said as he turned and gestured to one of the waitresses.

"I'd like the same again and could you give my friend one of your te-bie-de coffees please?" Douglas asked, as he handed her a tip. The waitress gave them both a broad smile and returned to the serving area. Jason watched her exaggerated walk that was impossible to ignore.

"Now that's one drop dead gorgeous woman," Douglas remarked, noticing Jason's attention drift in her direction. "You haven't changed much have you?"

"What do you mean?" retorted Jason.

"You were always a soft touch for a pretty face," said Douglas, with a snigger.

"I enjoy female company, but I like to think that I'm the one in control." Douglas shook his head.

"We all come to a point in our lives when we have to allow others to take the reins. You'll see. Trust me," he said with a wise, whimsical expression on his face.

"Okay, enough of the blarney, why are you here?"

"Jason, I'm here at the behest of her Majesty's Government. We need your help, not just for ourselves, but for China. We know you love China and we'd never ask you to do anything that would damage your right to stay here."

"So what is it you want me to do?" Jason asked, still none the wiser.

"It's nothing really. We want you to pick up some tapes from our contact here in Beijing and get them back to GCHQ. No hurry of course – deliver them as and when you arrive back in the UK. Your visa runs out in the New Year doesn't it?"

"You tell me Douglas, you seem to know more about my dealings than I do."

"That's my job old chap, and a well-paid job it is too," he said, reassuring himself that his wallet wasn't lost.

"What's in it for me then?" Jason asked, even though money had never been a primary motivator. He thought, rather than be used and abused for nothing, he'd ask for some recompense to cover the risk and the inconvenience.

"Okay, we'll double your Home Office pension with effect from next April, 1990, okay?"

Jason didn't need to ruminate over such an easy job, he would have done it as a freebie, but to have his pension doubled was a gift he couldn't refuse.

"As you've come so far to get me to do this, I'll do it." The attractive looking waitress returned with the coffees; a cappuccino for Douglas and an Americano for Jason who took one sip.

"This is just a regular coffee. I thought you'd ordered a special?" remarked Jason. Douglas just shrugged his shoulders again and raised his cup.

"Cheers Jason," he then polished off his cappuccino in one gulp. Jason sat back and savoured his; he enjoyed the surroundings and the upmarket ambience of the hotel.

"These tapes, where are they now?" Douglas pondered for a brief moment.

"We don't have them yet. We know where they are but the man who has them is currently under house arrest."

"Let me see if I've got this right – you want me to sneak in and get these tapes from under the Politburo's noses, right?"

"No, no, not at all. We have an inside agent who will hand them over to you. No risk." Douglas smiled and shrugged, "Couldn't be easier."

"Listen, I used to stick my neck out a lot for you guys, but now I'm an English teacher, so why me and why now after so long out of the business?"

"It's easy to work out Jason; we know you can be trusted. You speak mandarin which may be useful and we need this doing now. The tapes are for documentation purposes and are destined to go into our archives for years. Even if published now, they would vilify some and malign others, we're just gathering data, that's all," explained Douglas.

"What's this person's name or aren't you allowed to say?" Jason enquired, not expecting a straight answer.

"Let's just call him Mr Z for now" replied Douglas.

"How do you communicate with him? It's not safe to use transceivers and the like, and phones are definitely out of the question, so you must have someone on the inside, right?" surmised Jason. Douglas smiled.

"I've already told you that, but yes you're right. If you can work it out, so could someone else. That's why we need the tapes, and as soon as possible. Should they get into the wrong hands, someone you don't know will suffer terribly.

"I take it this insider will contact me about the assignment, yes?"

"Yes, she knows all about you and that you'll be doing this for the good of China. In fact, I've arranged for her to meet you outside the panda enclosure tomorrow at the Beijing Zoo. She'll be there at midday.

She knows what you look like and she'll approach you. Just behave normally," explained Douglas.

"Tomorrow's no problem."

"Jason, we go back a long way, it's not a big thing we're asking, but don't let us down. Big it isn't, important it is, okay?"

"So what do I call her?"

"Her nickname is Bunny. That's all you need to know."

"How did you know I would take on this job then?" Jason asked.

"Remember, we have your personality profile and to be quite honest, I thought you'd jump at the chance to involve yourself again. I mean you've done everything haven't you? You've flown in the air force, worked for the Home Office, travelled widely. Now look at you? Few people here have any inkling about what you've done and the majority only understand half of what you're saying. How could anyone here ever really understand someone like you, but we do," he explained.

"What do I do with these tapes when I have them?"

"Call me, then I'll get them to where we can copy and analyse them. I'll expect you to keep in touch, but only after I've left China, next week. And even then, be cryptic and don't mention what you're carrying, you know the protocol as much as I do," said Douglas, as he took a sly look around the lounge.

"Bunny has a few copies of the tapes and the one she'll give you is the first attempt to get them out of China. Should anything happen to her, I know where to find the others. If the Chinese authorities find the tapes, Mr Z will die and our supply of information on the politburo will die with him. And maybe you'll join him," whispered Douglas, as he sat back in his chair and smiled.

"Thanks a lot," jested Jason. Douglas took out his mobile.

"You know I have your number."

"Now there's something. How did you get it? You're a crafty old sod!"

"Never mind that Jason, you now have mine. You can call me while I'm in China, then I'm dumping it."

"How did you get my number?" Douglas smiled smugly.

"Remember Erica, the drop dead gorgeous blonde? Didn't you give her your number, ah? but she didn't call, did she?" Douglas laughed.

"Queen and country and all that," snapped Jason. Douglas stuck out his bottom lip in a comical gesture of ignorance.

"I suppose this Erica is a wrinkly old lady that does this sort of thing for a living," complained Jason.

"Oh no not at all, she looks just like her photo, in fact much better, and believe it or not she's single," said Douglas, smiling.

Just then Douglas's phone rang; he glanced down at the display window and excused himself from the table, ambling across the reception area as he whispered into his phone.

As Jason sat alone, his mind drifted back to Jeany. If she knew that he was meeting up with a strange lady at the zoo, what would she surmise? Though Jason's intentions were wholly innocent, the green-eyed monster, that was her permanent tormentor, would surely get its claws into her. For practical reasons, he was going to keep his comings and goings to himself. He was good at secrets and this one was well worth keeping.

Douglas had come along and shaken him out of his comfort zone. He had to admit that he'd been bored with the absence of excitement and the lack of stimulating conversation. He cherished the love of Jeany and would find it hard to live without her, but what he didn't want was to be forced to make a choice. Still, it was so refreshing to be back in the company of one's brethren.

Whilst Douglas continued his phone conversation, the waitress once again approached the table.

"More coffee sir?" she asked. Jason looked up; her eyes bright and radiant exuded warmth and there was a hint of seduction in her voice.

"Yes please," said Jason still staring into her eyes.

"Americano, yes?" She stood there, as if enjoying being close to him. Jason caught a hint of a sweet fragrance. Such a perfume and at such close quarters was both enticing and distracting.

"Make it two coffees will you?" Jason asked. The waitress gave Jason a warm smile, turned around and made her way back to the bar area. As she did, she exaggerated her walk, swinging her hips as if she were on a Parisian cat walk. Both Jason and Douglas stopped what they were doing, as they watched spellbound as the pretty waitress strutted across the lounge in her inimitable style.

"Ah, coffee that's a good idea. Listen Jason, good news and bad. The bad news is I have to shoot off now and get some work done. The good news is you can now go on up to your room and relax. Tomorrow will be a long cold day; they reckon it's going to snow. Oh, and by the way, that waitress was eyeing you up. I don't think you'll be too lonely tonight. Maybe you can ask her out later. In the meantime, you need to conserve your energy for tomorrow," suggested Douglas, with a hint of humour in his voice.

"Douglas, don't you think you have complicated my life enough without adding to it; another problem I don't need and certainly not another woman, no way," he said shaking his head.

"Don't worry about money. I'll pay into your account some appropriate expenses, but remember to cancel your bank account before you leave China." Jason began rummaging through his wallet.

"Here's my card and this is my UK bank address," he said.

"Thanks Jason, I'll get that sorted. We'll meet in London, soon, yes?"

"Yes we will. Good to see you again, truly," replied Jason. Douglas stood up, shook Jason's hand, scooped up his suitcase and left.

Jason ruminated over all that had been said. The waitress had passed by and had smiled at him twice, but for some reason he didn't respond. Jason was beginning to feel drowsy. He left the lounge and went to his room in the lift. He took a quick shower and retired to the large king size bed. The room was warm and immaculately clean. The bed linen was fresh and soft against his skin. He laid there and prepared himself for a night of untroubled slumber but try as he might, he couldn't quite get that saucy waitress's face out of his mind. His body began to sink into the mattress, he felt heavy and limp. The room's hazy magnolia painted walls seemed to mingle into one. It was as if he were tied to a raft that was drifting into a long dark tunnel, its walls echoing every sound, the darkness forever closing in on him as he entered the deep - the only image left was her face. Despite a feeling of being possessed, he managed to drift into a drowsy state of sleep.

A VISITATION

A while later he awoke. He still felt very drowsy but he managed to sit up in bed. Something had brought him for a brief moment to the edge of consciousness. He was totally unaware of the time of day. He wasn't even sure if it was early evening or the next morning. All he knew was that it wasn't time to get up. Just then he heard a discreet tap on the door. He managed to drag the bed clothes to one side, and totter across to the door, oblivious as to his state of dress. From behind the door a blurred image of a strangely familiar face appeared – it was the waitress he had seen earlier in the lounge.

"Let me in," she whispered. Jason felt so groggy that he said nothing, just opened the door allowing her to slide in, she then shut the door without a sound behind her. Then, with his eyes still closed, he staggered back to his bed and climbed in between the sheets, unaware of her continued presence.

She was wearing a black one piece dress that buttoned down the front. Her hair had been unfastened allowing it to hang long and loose. She had applied lipstick and eye make-up. All this was beyond Jason's comprehension, although he sensed she was there accompanied by her unmistakable fragrance. He felt the sheets being rolled back exposing his flesh to the air. The bedding discarded lay on the bedside rug. Long painted finger nails hooked round his waist band and dragged down his underclothes leaving him exposed and vulnerable.

With great stealth, she knelt astride him. He could feel the soft, warm skin of her inner thighs. She grasped his wrists and raised them up, pinning them against the pillow. He looked up into her bright eyes and froze, allowing her hands to gravitate towards his chest and upper arms. Without a word being said she kneaded his chest and shoulders, her sharp nails biting into his flesh, leaving reddened trails in their wake. She lowered her face next to his and with the gentleness of a predator, bit Jason's lip. Blood oozed across her ruby lips and into her mouth. Her eyes widened with excitement, her lips then met his in a tentative kiss. Now aroused, her hands delved down towards his inner thighs and responsive genitalia. Like a snake she manoeuvred her body all the while voicing gentle words of encouragement, impatient to do what she had come to do. As she mounted him, she continued to talk, to keep him conscious for as long as necessary.

"My name's Bunny. Don't forget my name. Bunny, do you like it? It's a nice name isn't it? Jason you're going to love me, like it or not. What Bunny wants Bunny gets." Though semi-conscious and aware in part, his heavy limbs felt limp and helpless. Her voice sounded like a deep echo, as she rocked and rolled above him. Her body was hot and incredibly smooth, he wanted to grab hold of her but he couldn't. He was clearly under the influence of some powerful narcotic; despite this he was still able to perform the desired function.

She moved her body in a slow rhythmic motion, backwards and forwards over his prostrate torso. She moved faster and faster, deeper and deeper and all the while her nails digging into his flesh. The bed frame creaked and twisted under the force being exerted from above. On sensing his climax approaching she raised the tempo higher still, forcing him into completion. He achieved orgasm and though he was aware of what had transpired, he drifted back into a narcotic induced slumber. After dismounting, she rolled him over onto his front and with a laugh gave him an almighty slap on the buttocks. She took a hot shower and got dressed. She covered Jason's prostrate body, and departed with as much stealth as when she'd arrived, vanishing down the hotel corridor like a wisp.

An Involvement

The following morning Jason woke up with a stiff headache and sore arms where fingernails had dug deep into his wrists. Bloody scratch marks covered his chest and upper arms where her sharpened claws had kneaded at his flesh. His lip had a swollen blister where feline teeth in a moment of passion had broken the skin. He swung his legs over the edge of the bed only to feel his heart pounding deep inside his chest.

He grabbed his towel and staggered over to the shower to recover from the drowsy intoxicated feeling that had taken over his body; he felt as if he were half there and half somewhere else. As the hot steamy water gushed over his body, he noticed the reddened impression of a hand print that had somehow imprinted itself on his now painful rear end.

As the previous night's sexual episode came flooding back to him, he closed his eyes in disbelief. The bed linen was in disarray and all his clothes were strewn around the room. This was no dream and this woman whoever she was, had been no succubus; she was real.

Once back to his senses, he made his way to where his coat hung and searched for his wallet. It was there and intact, he fingered through its contents and although his train ticket and credit cards were all present and correct, a sum of two hundred ren-min-bi had somehow disappeared.

He smiled to himself for he hadn't really been robbed, far from it. He took a large drink from the water receptacle and mopped his brow with the back of his arm.

"Wow what an experience," he mumbled to himself. A hot sensation swept through his body as he considered the likelihood of her still being in the room. Without a sound he glanced into the wardrobe and then behind the large velvet curtains just in case she was in hiding, but to his relief she had gone.

With his mind still in a whirl over what had transpired, he changed into some decent clothes and headed down in the lift for breakfast. On his way down, he kept wondering what he would say, if he were to bump into her en route to his breakfast table. As he strolled through the lounge, he stopped a waitress.

"Excuse me, where's the young lady that was on here last night. She was very slim and wore a red ribbon in her hair?"

"Oh, she doesn't work here often, maybe just once a week. I know her. Can I give her a message?"

"Well yes, just say that Jason said thank you. She was very kind to me yesterday." The waitress smiled politely.

"Yes I'll tell her next time I see her." He couldn't resist asking.

"Sorry to be so inquisitive, but what was her name?"

"Oh that's Bunny," she said, as she turned to get on with her work. His heart sank; she must be the operative Douglas had told him about. Then again this similarity of names could be a coincidence. No, it couldn't be, he thought, that just didn't make sense. If that was her then he'd soon know for sure later that day at the zoo. He didn't believe in coincidences and surmised that she must have known who he was, and come to think of it

Douglas should have recognised her, if she was one of his operatives.

He was beginning to feel duped again, but then why did she rape him? She didn't need to. Why didn't she just give him the tape there and then? But then this logic didn't quite fit with what had transpired. He had every intention of finding out the truth later that day, but for now breakfast was calling.

Full of apprehension, he made his way to the bus station not far from his hotel. As he walked through the city street, reoccurring memories of the night before kept flooding back to him. At times he had to stand still to compose himself, as the mental re-enactment of what had taken place had a distinct tumescent effect on certain parts of his anatomy. Despite this pleasant sensation, he felt guilty about his involuntary involvement with this strange woman and for not contacting Jeany, but at this moment, Shijiazhuang seemed a million miles away.

The morning breeze was dry and bitterly cold. He'd put on a thick top coat, but it provided no protection against the cold penetrating winds that swept down from the Mongolian steppes, like the marauding warriors of old. With his ears and nose a conspicuous red, he stood there motionless reliving the events of the last 24 hours. As he did, the pleasurable thoughts that were cascading through his mind forced a smile to appear on his frost bitten face.

It was then that he became aware of the crowd which had materialised around him. Each individual at the bus stop seemed to be grinning at his incongruous smile. Upon realising he had attracted all this unwanted attention he cleared his throat and adopted a more business-like demeanour. He was puzzled, had it been his arousal that had attracted so many onlookers, or was

84

it his self-satisfied smile which had been so alluring, as to have attracted all these people at the bus stop to admire it?

At last the bus heading for the zoo arrived. He approached the opening door and was swept up in the mad rush of people clambering to get on board first. The crowd that had been so enthralled with his strange demeanour had all boarded with him and were now being thrust against him tighter and tighter as more passengers attempted to squeeze on board. The ride was bumpy and somewhat undignified, as an assortment of passengers struggled to get off the bus at various points along the route.

"Beijing Dong-Yuan," shouted the driver, as the bus pulled up directly in front of the zoo gates. The doors opened and the crowded bus spilled out its contents all over the pavement and he along with it.

The wind had picked up and there was a slight dusting of snow in the air. As he entered the zoo gates he was mindful of the time, he'd arrived two hours ahead of the arranged rendezvous. He noticed that the panda enclosure and the cafe were both signposted in the same direction and so he decided to sit in the cafe until midday.

He stepped into the dismal looking café that was occupied by two elderly gents playing ma-zhong and a lone cafe assistant who sat engrossed in a book. He ordered a coffee, after which he retired to a corner table that was nestled next to a hot cast iron radiator. 'Ideal for a two hour sit,' he surmised.

After a spell of just ten minutes, a young woman walked in; she seemed familiar. Though he thought she was the same girl who served them in the hotel, he wasn't sure. She wore an embroidered white blouse with a plunging neck line and a short red tartan skirt with long black stockings that reached just above the knee and patent leather three inch heels. Her dress and demeanour was that of a street girl, the kind that would love you by the hour. Jason wasn't sure. Maybe this was just a front, and after all if she was one of Douglas's operatives, anything was possible. He stood up in order to make himself known to the young woman, in case it was her.

"Bunny, is that you?" he whispered. The girl spun round and faced him, her long black hair swirling round obscuring her face for a moment as she did. She gave him a broad smile and then laughed. It was her. Instead of going over to the counter, she came across to where he was and sat close beside him.

"We meet again," she said, confidence and exuberance radiating from every gesture. "Do you smoke?" she asked.

"No filthy habit, do you?" he replied.

"Oh no, disgusting," she said and then then began to laugh. "I know what you like, don't I?" she said, as she placed her hand over his and stared deep into his eyes.

"It's not brain surgery," he said. "I mean anyone with a modicum of common sense knows what she has to do to make a man happy. Last night; now that should have been a mutual decision. You never even asked me what I wanted, did you?" he asked, as if he really cared.

"No. I take, I don't give," she said as she squeezed his hand, till he winced in pain. She smiled, lifted his hand and kissed it better.

"Sorry about that, Bunny's sorry, very sorry," she said as she returned to her sweet feminine self. He was more than a little fascinated by this exciting woman and would have relished more time to spend in her company, if it were possible. He had but one day to initiate Douglas's plan.

"Do you have something to give me?" he asked in a businesslike manner.

"Yes, I have a few items you need to accept as gifts," she stated.

"What items? Douglas said..." She cut him short.

"Never mind what Douglas said, you come with me and I'll show you what these things are," and with that she jumped to her feet. "Lai-lai, come." She then grabbed his wrist and pulled him up onto his feet. She seemed eager to get him back to her place; it was as if she was in a hurry. With his wrist still in her grip, she led him out of the café.

Once outside, she linked her arm through his and arm in arm they headed for the zoo gates. As they left the zoo, the ticket lady at the gate waved at them and burst into laughter.

"What's she laughing at?" he asked annoyed at being mocked in public.

"It's not you; she thinks you're a client of mine. She's laughing because it only took me five minutes to find someone who wants some business. Of course she doesn't know we're such good friends," she said as she waved back.

"Me! Your client?" he croaked, struggling to get the words out.

"Yes, you're a foreigner – a good catch I think," she then looked up and gave him one of her 'kiss me now' looks and squeezed his arm, hugging herself close, as they walked out of the zoo gates. After a five minute stroll, they arrived at her apartment block.

"Come up with me; we can talk in my room," she said, as she put her arm around his waist. There was a spring in her step, giving him the impression that she thought they could have a future together, but he wasn't going to be around that long, that's what he thought. Once inside her room, she dived onto the bed that was smothered in pink silky bedding and rolled over, like a cat awakening from a long sleep.

"Bunny," he whispered. "Where are the things? Stop playing around will you?"

"Jason be patient. I don't do anything I don't want to. I take what I need and only when I need it. Come lie down with me, then I'll tell you what you need to know. Lai-lai," she pleaded with her arms outstretched. He knelt on the bed, but she had other ideas, as she pulled him down next to her.

"Kiss me," she demanded, as she held onto his hair with both hands, pulling his face towards hers. Her red lips met his and he yielded to her wishes, but mid embrace he pulled his face back from hers and frowned.

"Bunny you're playing with me, aren't you? That's not fair," he said. He then closed his eyes tight, like a man struggling with a powerful addiction. Try as he might, he wasn't able to shut out that sweet perfume and the heat of her presence that without abate seeped into his every pore. Once again, he felt her hot lips touch his. This time it was his turn to pull her into him and they wrestled in one long passionate kiss.

"I shouldn't do this," he protested, as he rolled away from her.

"Why not?" She argued as she began to unbutton his shirt.

"Are you married?"

"No, I'm not," snapped Jason.

"I knew that already," she said with a smile.

"How did you know?" he asked, as he tried to re-button his shirt, but she was far more skilled at the undoing of his buttons, than he was at doing them up.

"I know everything about you. I know about Jeany and her lesbian friend..."

"What lesbian friend?" he asked, in a surprised voice.

"Oh didn't you know? Your Jeany's friend Jie-Na is as butch as they come. I thought she would have told you. Anyway we all have our little secrets don't we? There's no harm in that, is there?" she asked, as she undid his last shirt button.

"Who told you all that rubbish? It wasn't Douglas was it?"

"Oh yes it was, and I know you'll be going home to her today, so where's the harm in spending a little time alone with Bunny? Go on Jason; don't be so mean."

By now she had undone his belt and his top trouser button. This had the desired effect. Any resistance that he had left soon dissipated. He at once stood up, shook off his trousers and dived into her warm embracing arms. She sat up and pulled the clean white linen sheet over her shoulders, as she knelt astride him, pushing him down into the soft mattress.

"Bunny," Jason protested.

"Don't move − I'll do it," she commanded, as she stared down into his grey blue eyes. "Do you need one of my pills?" she asked.

"No Bunny, I don't think that'll be necessary. Not today." He stared past her long black hair that hung down on either side of her alluring face, to the rotating electric fan that swirled around above them as he lay there under her spell.

"Close your eyes and relax; Bunny will do the rest. Then we'll talk business," she whispered. The hustle and bustle of the morning rush hour traffic outside didn't detract from his intense pleasure. In fact, it enhanced it. 'Where else in the world could one make love against the back drop of a big city's chaotic rush hour at its peak?' he thought. The chaotic background noise; the swirling ceiling fan; her long black hair stroking against his face, the rhythmic motion of her warm firm thighs bearing down hard on his groin and her long sharp finger nails biting once more into his biceps – all added to this superb erotic moment.

As soon as he had climaxed, she dismounted and sprung to her feet.

"That was already paid for. You can thank Douglas for that one," she said, as she laughed and clapped her hands with childish excitement.

"Did you enjoy that Jason?" she asked playfully. He didn't answer he just smiled, laid back and savoured the moment.

"You stay here. I'm going to get some food. We can talk when I get back, okay?" And with that she pulled on her one piece dress, buttoned it, grabbed her bag and left the room.

Jason rolled over onto his back again. Whoever she was, he thought, she was certainly a key player in Douglas's plan. He looked round the tiny room; a small square table sat to one side of the large window that opened up to a veranda overlooking the city street below. She had a fine array of clothes; many were seductive and outrageous, and designed to impress. He had no doubt as to how she made her living. She was able to excite, he had no doubt about that; she was good with people. He had to admit, he couldn't see anything wrong in what she did, although it did worry him that he'd just had unprotected sex with 'a woman of ill repute.'

The first time with her was wholly excusable, but the second time wasn't. Jeany had told Jason that 'kindness and lies were worth a million truths.' He made a promise to himself that this little episode with Bunny, exciting as it was, wasn't worth losing Jeany for. He would draw a line under the whole affair and pretend that it had never happened.

The tranquillity of the bedroom was soon broken by Bunny bouncing back into the room, with two portions of egg fried rice, soy mince and chilli sauce. She threw herself onto the bed next to Jason and presented him with his share of the refreshments.

"Eat now. Do you like Chinese food?" she asked, as if she had made it herself.

"Yes, it smells good," he replied, as his mind drifted from aroma to fragrance, secretly wandering what kind of perfume she wore. He would never forget it. Then again, he was far too concerned with the hot succulent food in front of him to ask. Together they sat and ate in silence like an old married couple. Her confidence and sharp wit made him feel relaxed and at ease. It was as if they had known each other all their lives. Tactile and intelligent, she would have been able to do anything and go anywhere, had her circumstances been different. A ripple of sadness swept through him, as he pondered her precarious future. What was she to become? and how would she manage, when her youthful exuberance eventually dwindled and the sex wasn't saleable anymore?

After they'd finished eating, she sat by the small table next to the window.

"Jason lai-lai, can you see those pigskin shoes at the foot of the wardrobe? Inside the heel is a cavity where the mini tapes are concealed. Both shoes have one tape in each heel. Whatever you do, don't take those shoes off outside your home." He stood up and examined them; they were finely tailored and intricate in design, and just his size. "You'll need to cut up the shoes to extract the tapes," she said. "Douglas had them made especially for you, so cherish them while you can. Oh – and I have a present for you. Open the cupboard and reach out the black leather jacket, the one with the studded pattern on the arms." She pointed to the bulging wardrobe, bursting with garments of every shape and colour.

He pulled out a thick, black leather jacket, its arms copiously peppered with chromium studs. It was lined with red silk, which contrasted sharply with the heavy black leather. He tried it on – a perfect fit.

"It fits," he exclaimed.

"Yes of course, I bought you the jacket myself when Douglas said you were coming to see me. I want you to take it back to England to remember me. Will you?" Her face was a picture of admiration as she looked up at him in his new 'look tougher' outfit. He glanced at himself in the wall mirror.

"Yes I like it. It's so reminiscent of the sixties." It evoked memories of his nearly forgotten 'Rocker days.' He smiled – such a coat should last him a lifetime.

"Thanks Bunny, I'll keep it always." He said while still posing in the mirror.

"There's a mobile in one of those pockets. It's all charged up and it's got enough credit for what you need it for. Use it only in emergencies, and get away from the area once you've used it. If you call Douglas on it, he'll think it's me calling, but so will the Politburo, so don't use it unless it's a must, okay?" He nodded as he felt in the pockets for the phone.

"Actually, if you have a real problem, just pay someone to use their phone and then clear the area. For a few ren-min-bi you'll be able to use anyone's phone for a quick call," she explained. He was well aware of the dangers in using phones; conversations were as a matter of course often monitored by the authorities. He hoped he'd never need to call anyone from her phone. He wasn't on the run, and as far as he knew he wasn't suspected of any wrongdoing, not yet anyway. It all seemed so melodramatic. Maybe there was something she hadn't told him.

"How did you get the tapes?" he asked. She smiled and put her vermillion painted finger nail against her pouted lips.

"I shouldn't tell you, but Mr Z gave them to me personally. His intention was to somehow get them out of the country. These tapes are first-hand evidence that Mr Z and Mr Deng should not be implicated or blamed for the June 4th incident. Others have blood on their hands for this. They know who they are. People like Li-Peng, when the students tried to negotiate with him, he couldn't even look them in the eye. He knew what was going to happen. He's a spineless murderer of young Chinese innocents! History will tell the truth and these tapes will exonerate Mr Z, and to some extent Mr Deng," she said, her fists clenched.

"How come he decided to give them to you?" he asked.

"I sleep with Mr Z and Douglas too. They love and trust me. I'm not a good woman, but I'm honest and I love China. My younger brother died in Tian-a-Men Square with those Pro-democracy children. To hell with

Li-Peng I say!" she snapped. "You like me too Jason, don't you?"

"Yes, you know I do," he replied.

"That's because we bonded in bed. We now know each other, don't we? Like Mr Z and Douglas. Am I right Jason?"

"Bunny, you're always right, but being right doesn't make you bulletproof. You're living a dangerous life. I'd hate to see you come to grief," he said, as he placed his hand on hers.

"You're good at what you do but one day..."

"I know," she cut him short. "I'll be fat and ugly!" she said with a smile.

"That's not what I was going to say! One day, you'll find a good man and become his wife. You'd like that, wouldn't you?"

"Yes Jason and maybe you'll be available when I'm ready," she said, as she looked into his face.

"Maybe, only God knows what the future holds for the likes of us. No one knows Bunny, no one," he said in a solemn voice. He was anxious to discover more about Douglas's plans and if there were any more surprises in store for him. Like the odd inconvenient minor detail that may have been brushed under the carpet, only to reappear later and place his life and liberty in jeopardy.

"So whereabouts in Beijing does this Mr Z live?" he enquired, conscious of the fact that he really didn't need to know the exact location of this man, or even his name. She gave him a stern look and shook her head.

"He's been under arrest since the incident in Tian-a-Men square. That's when his so-called comrades realised he had pro-democratic sympathies. Anyway, I clean his house twice weekly and cater for his emotional needs. He pays me well for what I do, if you know what I mean.

94

He's a great man and the people of China should know it. That's why you mustn't lose these tapes. If you do, he's a dead man. He trusts me implicitly and I believe in what he is trying to do, to set the books straight once and for all."

She stood up and straightened Jason's black leather coat, then knelt down and fastened the laces of his newly acquired pig leather shoes.

"Never let these out of your sight, and don't get them too wet. They should be okay, but it's better to be safe than sorry." She stroked the smooth leather garment, as she leant back and admired the fit. On the right sleeve he noticed an embroidered rabbit motif. She laughed.

"That's me, Bunny," she proclaimed proudly. "I hope you'll look after the coat." she said it as if it were her heart and soul she was giving him to cherish. He opened his arms and gave her a hug and looked directly into her deep, dark eyes.

"I'm sure we'll meet again," he said, as a strange emotion welled up inside him, forcing tears down his cheeks. He realised then that he had really taken this wild and outrageous woman into his heart, but he also knew that he had to go. Any future with such a wild spirit would be unendurable. She just smiled.

"If you ever need me, I work at Mr. Z's on Wednesday and Friday and at the Xi-Dan Hotel on Mondays. At other times you can find me doing my rounds at the zoo. All I ask, is that you deliver the tapes and not to forget me, okay? I'm sure we'll see each other again, now go." Jason grabbed hold of her and gave her a long slow sensuous kiss on her lips. Then with his eyes partially closed, he pulled away.

He left her apartment and stepped out into the kind of fresh, sharp air that makes one feel alive. He zipped up his leather jacket and smiled, his spirit rejoiced in having experienced a mind changing erotic experience.

Though bitterly cold, he decided that he would walk back to the zoo gates where he would pick up his bus. He glanced around to see what number her apartment was, but there was no number on her door. Despite this, he was sure that he would remember the floor and building as well as the view from outside her apartment. He turned and with a spring in his step, made his way down the stairs to the street.

He spent an hour ambling around the zoo before catching his bus back to the hotel. He thought there was a chance he may be able to catch a glimpse of her again inside the zoo, but it wasn't to be. He went back to his hotel, gathered his few possessions and got a taxi back to Beijing Central Station. Trains to Shijiazhuang were frequent, so it wasn't long before he was on one, bound for Jeany.

He felt in his pocket and pulled out both mobile phones, the one Bunny had given him that was switched off and his own, that he hadn't looked at since leaving Shijiazhuang. He scanned his messages. There was one from an unidentifiable number. It read: 'Text me the time of your arrival. I will meet you then, Regards Harry.' No doubt one of Douglas's surprises he thought. He texted his arrival time back to whoever it was. Only time would tell if this was from a friend or a foe he thought, unaware of the trouble brewing ahead.

THE ATTACK

At the very moment Jason was boarding his train to Beijing, representatives of the Politburo were visiting his apartment, led by the Chief of Police, Liu Bo-Cheng. Having acquired the master key from the complex's security staff they entered Jason's living quarters, intent on provoking him into any action that would render him liable to being incarcerated. Bo-Cheng's office had received incriminating information from a person close to Jason. The source implied that he had actively sympathised with members of the pro-democracy movement and that he had openly condemned Li-Peng for his role in the June 4th crackdown in Tian-a-Men Square.

An unfortunate sequence of events was now unfolding, for the Chief of Police, Bo-Cheng, was none other than Jeany's ex-husband. He was constantly updated as to the activities of this bourgeois foreigner, who had clearly overstepped the mark, as far as Bo-Cheng was concerned. Not only was Jason considered to be an enemy of the party, but he was also dabbling in the personal affairs of the Chief of Police, an unforgivable act of audacity.

Jason's already precarious position was further exacerbated by the fact that he was known to be bedding the Chief of Police's ex-wife. Bo-Cheng considered that he now had enough of an excuse to put an end to this foreigner's philandering once and for all. Although well and truly estranged from his ex-wife, he still regarded her as his property, and as such to have some smart alec westerner seduce her with his money and promises of a better life, enraged him. Such a shameful exhibition of depravity dug deep and painfully into his psyche.

One way or another he was determined to eradicate this scourge on his manhood. The foreigner had dragged his ex-wife down into the gutter and brought shame on her family. She had shared what was once their family bed with an enemy of China. He considered her to be as guilty as the foreigner, and by association they were both enemies of the party and the state. The Politburo drew little or no distinction between genders, when it came down to those who were deemed to have betrayed their country. Whatever it took, Bo-Cheng was going to have his pound of flesh.

Apart from a few items that were deemed un-Chinese or overly bourgeois such as glossy magazines depicting women in various states of undress, some aviation magazines and a spare mobile phone, they found nothing incriminating.

Bo-Cheng himself initiated and accompanied the search team as they tore the apartment apart. He stood there in his ex-wife's lover's apartment seething with hate. Images of the two on that bed flashed through his consciousness. The hostility he felt for both of them bubbled up inside him as he stood there staring at Jason's possessions. His teeth ground as his stifled inner rage twisted his stomach. Such was his animosity that he couldn't resist the urge to destroy or deface anything that seemed to have any value at all. The pillows were cut open and searched and sugar from the kitchen area was strewn across the floor. Jam was dug out and smeared everywhere in the search for any illegal substances. The entire apartment was violated.

Bo-Cheng felt bitter and aggrieved, not to have found anything more incriminating, and even angrier that he hadn't been able to confront this despicable foreigner face to face. He would have enjoyed provoking him to such a point that he would have had to react, and in so doing commit an assault against a police office, a crime he would live to regret but not for long.

After the search team had exhausted their destructive energies, Bo-Cheng took time out to think. He concluded that Jason should have been at work, but they had called the school earlier and confirmed that he wasn't there. Maybe he was out somewhere doing the tourist thing. Bo-Cheng turned and leant against the kitchen sink gripping the edge in frustration, but as glared down, he noticed a pair of pink washing up gloves neatly placed behind the taps. He grabbed them and spun round to his men.

"I know where he is," he declared as he threw the gloves onto the jam smeared floor. Once again images of the two lovers together re-emerged in his mind. 'They're getting cosy in our marital bed,' thought Bo-Cheng.

"He's in her apartment," he said loudly.

"Who's apartment?" one of his men asked. Bo-Cheng thought for a while.

"That whore's place, the old whore he's been seeing. Follow me; we'll catch them at it and God help them if they resist arrest. Let's go! I know exactly where they are."

As he made his way down the stairwell he was followed by his four eager subordinates. The three cars, led by Bo-Cheng's, sped through the busy morning traffic en route towards Jeany's apartment near Shijiazhuang's central station. It wasn't long before the group were stealthily on their way up the concrete stairwell towards her apartment.

On their arrival outside her door, they stood for a brief moment to compose themselves. Bo-Cheng whispered to his men to stand back while he searched his bunch of keys for a familiar shape. In silence he inserted the key and without a sound released the lock on the door. He opened the door a fraction and then stood back. As if possessed by the devil himself he gave the door an almighty kick. The door flew open crashing against the inner wall as it did.

Jeany had been busy trying on clothes for that evening when the sudden shock of her door being kicked open startled her and sent her scurrying behind the bed. With no time to make herself look decent, she pulled the bed linen from off the top of the bed to cover herself. From behind the bed, she recognised the intruder as Bo-Cheng; she had no doubt as to his motives and was well aware of his capacity for inflicting pain and suffering. He stood there with disgust etched across his hardened face as he looked down at her partially undressed and cowering behind the bed.

"I'm told we have to call you Jeany now, your Chinese name not good enough for you, is it?" he snapped, swiping the porcelain bedside lamp so that it impacted against the wall breaking into many fragments as it did.

"What I call myself is of no concern to you anymore," argued Jeany, but his heart had hardened to such an extent, that she would have better spent her breath in prayer.

"I'll decide what my concern is and what it isn't. At this moment, your life and that of your lover boy is of no concern to me. You are nothing more than a common

100

whore and women like you are only good for one thing," he said as he glared down at her, contempt written all over his red and bloated face. Bo-Cheng turned to two of his four men and pointed to the living room.

"You two, take the room apart and leave nothing unturned, and I mean nothing. Slash the furniture and shred the curtains, take the cupboards to pieces and when you've done that, help these to finish off in the bedroom," he growled through gritted teeth. It wasn't often that they were given licence to ransack the home of their boss's ex-wife. They would obey in silence whilst secretly they felt a rare sense of satisfaction in following these most unusual orders. Bo-Cheng turned to the other two men.

"You two search this bedroom and take it apart and then you can do what you like with that whore. I don't care in what order you do it but do it. You know what whores like, so give her plenty and then some more," he ordered as he spat at her. The two men in the living room began to snigger.

Bo-Cheng then left the room his footsteps could be heard as he descended the concrete stair well. The four men waited for a moment until the footsteps had faded and then they inched their way towards Jeany as she cowered behind the bed linen. One of the men was her best friend's husband, a pig of a man called Fei-Liao. He had large, bulging watery red eyes that were now focussed on her.

Her heart sunk deep inside her chest for she knew that Bo-Cheng had the authority to do with her as he wished. She was aware that she had no rights at all and no recourse to justice, certainly not in China. She could feel her heart pounding inside her chest as perspiration seeped out of her pallid skin. One of the men, unknown to her, had made his way around the bed end in her direction, his unblinking eyes fixed on her, like a wolf stalking a lamb for the kill.

As she watched him edging closer and closer, Fei-Liao dived across the bed and grabbed her hair with both hands, pulling her towards him across the bed. Her heart almost audible pounded faster and faster. Her breathing became strained with her face thrust down into the mattress. She managed to position her face in a sideward slant so that she could breathe.

She could feel the other man pulling at her legs tearing what little underwear she had been wearing from her body. As panic took hold of her she struggled but the more she did, the more the faceless man behind her beat her from behind, punching and slapping at her buttocks until they stung. Hurt and exhausted, she gave in and lay limp, trying to block out what was happening. She couldn't fight anymore, breathless and beaten; her physical body had all but given up the struggle.

Behind her, the man who had ripped off her underclothes and had been beating her, now unbuckled his belt and dropped his trousers to the ground kicking them to one side. He pulled her by her hips up to his body and entered her, his nails digging into the flesh on her waist. She wanted to scream but she hadn't enough air in her lungs to cry let alone scream. For her, time seemed to stand still as one by one the men took it in turns to rape her. For some reason one of them took pleasure in inflicting her with more pain by slapping her face whilst she was being held down, unable to move and defenceless.

Fei-Liao, who had held her down by her hair for what seemed like an eternity, suddenly pulled her head up and began to pull down his trousers, exposing his genitals. At last she could breathe and as she gasped for air, it was obvious to her what Fei-Liao's intentions were as he moved closer, nudging across towards her on his knees, settling within a few inches or so from her face with his knees astride. It was then that she lunged at the soft tender skin of his inner thigh and bit harder than she had ever bitten before. The blood in her mouth made her want to retch. He screamed like a woman giving birth. One of the men to her rear struck her a sharp blow on the back of the head. She lost consciousness. As she lay there bleeding and motionless, the men fell silent.

"The filthy whore bit me," he said as he tore a strip off the bed sheet twisting it in his hand to form a taut ligature. He grabbed her hair, pulling her limp body towards him. He lifted her head and proceeded to wrap the ligature around her blood soaked neck.

"I'm going to strangle the bitch." He knotted the rope around her throat and pulled it tight. Just then Bo-Cheng walked back into the room, only to see his men in various stages of undress, one bleeding profusely and what appeared to be a badly beaten body lying across a blood soaked mattress. He cared little about what they had done, but he was repulsed by the clumsy way they had perpetrated the assault.

"What a bloody mess! Get dressed and get out, and I mean now," he bellowed, kicking at the men, as they left. He loosened the ligature that had dug deep into her neck and gave her a slap in the face. She coughed as the blood in her mouth made her retch. She opened her eyes and looked up at her ex-husband. Furious, she spat blood at him.

"So the whore still lives," he said smirking as he looked down on his bruised and battered ex-wife as she laid there naked and barely able to move. Her legs were blackened and raw from the constant beating.

"God has eyes," she said, defiantly as she wiped the blood from her mouth.

"Where's your precious God now? You've got a lot more praying to do, for I haven't finished with you, not yet. You already know what women like you get when they end up in a male prison. What you got today would be nothing compared to what you would get in such a place. Both the guards and prisoners, they would all have you. You know I can do it."

"Then why don't you?" she retorted.

"Don't tempt me, I'll do it bitch and you'll die in there; I'll see to that! You'll never see that foreigner again, do you hear me? If you do, we'll do this again and again. My men don't care if you live or die, and frankly I don't either. Prisoners often donate vital organs to needy party members. Sadly they don't last long. Then we have our stun guns – always fun when we get a nuisance bitch that's too ugly for what you'd be getting. Am I making myself clear?" He then grabbed her hair, making her yelp in pain.

"You don't need to come back. He's gone away. He won't be coming back," she said wincing from the pain. He released his grip of her hair.

"Now you're making sense. If I do see him around here, you'll both wish you were dead, believe me," he said his face only inches away from hers. The foul odour of stale tobacco repulsed her. He then stood upright and walked into the living room that had been theirs. For a moment it seemed as if he were reminiscing, as he stood there in the middle of the room. He then unzipped his trousers and urinated on the carpet. He re-zipped his flies, turned in her direction and smiled, he then left leaving the door wide open behind him.

The Aftermath

Having heard Jeany's initial cries and screams, Miss Sha her neighbour from the opposite apartment, had decided that she would wait until whatever was going on with the police had finished. Only then would she venture out to find out what had transpired. On entering the living room, the old lady saw Jeany still lying on the blood soaked bed in a state of shock. She sat next to her and took hold of her hand.

"You poor thing, this is what you get for involving yourself with foreigners. Nothing good could ever have come from a relationship with the likes of them. Now look at you. You need to get to a hospital and now." She used one of the shredded pillow cases to wipe Jeany's blood marked face.

"Just leave me alone will you? I'm alright. Please go and shut the door behind you when you leave," she snapped. "I'll get over it. The last thing I need is some busybody invading my space," she said looking away. The old lady stood up and shook her head.

"Get over it, will you? I don't think so," she turned and made for the door. "Remember, I'm just across the hallway, if you need anything." The old lady closed the door quietly behind her. She could hear her footsteps descending the stairwell. She sighed; for she had no doubt that the old busybody would be broadcasting the latest scandal to all and sundry in the tower block.

She rolled off the bed and crawled on her hands and badly grazed knees, across the debris littered floor, to retrieve her mobile that had been thrown against the wall. She was able to re-assemble it and punched in Jenna's number. She then collapsed motionless on the floor.

Jenna responded to her missed call and called her. It was then that Jeany told her that she'd been beaten. Jenna grabbed her medical bag and signed out of the paediatric department and headed for Jeany's apartment.

She arrived only to be greeted by a group of neighbours whispering outside the main entrance. She barged her way through the crowded doorway and up the stairs to Jeany's apartment. Most were afraid of any involvement with the police but Jenna wasn't. She was above reproach, having connections in the Chinese Politburo committee. She also held an intense dislike for Bo-Cheng and everything he stood for.

Once inside the apartment, Jenna helped her to get dressed and packed – just a few items of clothing and some items of sentimental value that had belonged to her son. They both left the building in full view of the gathered neighbourhood and climbed into Jenna's imported car and set off in the direction of Jenna's home, situated in an affluent area on the outskirts of the city.

Within an hour of her ordeal, Jeany was recovering in a deep aromatic Japanese bath, while Jenna rinsed her scalp free of the caked blood that matted her long hair.

The large amounts of blood were from the blow she'd received on the back of her head. Her thighs and buttocks were black and blue with areas of skin breakage that were raw and painful. She remained in a state of shock, saying very little other than incoherent mumblings. Tears rolled down her cheeks, but she expressed no other emotion, no anger, no hate and no self-pity. It was as if she were still experiencing the emotional numbness she had cloaked herself with during the trauma. Jenna dried her hair and dressed her wounds talking to her all the time in an effort to reassure her that now she was safe. She dressed her in a soft cotton night gown and gave her a warm drink and a strong sedative. She then put Jeany in her bed, where she soon fell to sleep.

It was approaching midday and with Jeany being the way she was, Jenna wasn't prepared to leave her alone and so she settled down on the sofa. She had a lot of thinking to do. She decided that Jeany shouldn't go back to her apartment, what with the attack and the possibility of another violation threatened by Bo-Cheng. Though safe now, she wouldn't be safe at Jenna's for long. He knew Jenna was a good friend to Jeany and so she concluded that in time, the authorities would be knocking on her door bringing with them some trumped up charge or allegation. To be safe she needed to go away, but where? She then remembered their old school in 'Spring Village', both women still had connections there. Jenna decided that she would call them from the hospital that evening, if and when Jeany could be left alone.

Aware that both the home phone and mobile phones weren't safe, she decided she would wait until that night shift when she would be able to call from her office on the paediatric ward. Jenna's mind then turned to Jason. If jealousy was Bo-Cheng's motive, then Jason was the next in line for the hate patrol. Jeany had already told Jenna that he'd be arriving the following day, late in the afternoon or evening. If Bo-Cheng was aware of this, Jason needed to be told, to avoid being picked up at the station. She thought about going to his apartment and leaving him an anonymous note, telling him that his life was in danger and to get out. She could do that on her way to the hospital later that day. But tell him to go where? He could go to 'Spring Village', of course. But what if the police or anyone else found the letter? Then they would all be in trouble, she needed a better idea, but what?

She then decided she would text Jason, and make him believe it was from a student requesting his time of arrival and then she would meet him at the station. Then she could pick him up and convey him along with Jeany to Spring Village and comparative safety. Bo-Cheng would of course know about Jeany's home village and eventually go there, but even within the confines of the village they would be able to secrete themselves away until a better plan could be formulated.

She fired up her computer and emailed her colleague asking her to send a text to Jason from her phone, as hers was out of order. She asked her to send Jason a text from 'Harry' saying that he needed to know the time of his arrival in Shijiazhuang Station, so that Harry could meet him. She also asked if her friend could forward his reply back to her as soon as she received it, so she could inform Harry.

Turning her mind to help Jeany, she recalled that one of Jeany's old friends in Spring Village worked at the village hospital as a caretaker. He had a great many vacant rooms at the hospital which was grossly oversized for such a small community, and as such there were many rooms that were always vacant. Few people entered the building unless they were ill. Superstition and prejudice in the tiny community kept the remainder safely at bay.

The afternoon slipped by without incident; with Jeany sedated and sleeping, Jenna managed to catch up on some important documentation she needed to finish.

The radio provided a soothing backdrop of relaxing music while Jenna tapped away on her keyboard. Jenna's apartment was warm, comfortable and luxurious, something which her position as a paediatrician afforded her. Suddenly there was a loud bang on the door.

"I have a parcel for Miss Jie-Na. Shall I leave it outside the door?" A voice bellowed from the other side of the door.

"Okay, I'll get it in a minute," replied Jenna, startled by the sudden noise. Just then, an almighty scream came from Jenna's bedroom. She jumped to her feet and ran in, only to find Jeany cowering behind the bed in the same way she had done back at her apartment. Her watery eyes wide and reddened, stared at the bedroom door, a pallid mask of absolute terror etched across her face.

"The police are here to get me, aren't they? They're back for me. Don't let them take me! Oh God don't let them do that to me again," cried Jeany. She howled as loudly as she could, tears flooding down her face. Her hands gripped the bedlinen so tightly, that her knuckles turned white. Her body trembled as she shrunk behind the bed, still gripping it, as if she were being pulled by some unseen force. Then her cries died down to a sad and mournful whimpering, like a sentient animal resigned to the butcher's knife.

Jenna dashed around the bed and fell by her side embracing her as she did. She looked into her frozen eyes and sensed her fear. Jenna smiled in an effort to reassure her that now she was safe. Jeany gave her a hug that almost squeezed the life out of her; such was her desire for security and someone she could turn to.

110

"It's alright you're with me now. No one's going to come here and get you, not while I'm here," she said trying to offer her some reassurance.

"What can you do to protect me, you're a woman. Bo-Cheng has the Chinese government behind him," she whispered as she trembled in Jenna's arms.

"The Government doesn't know what's going on, but they will one day, believe me. The day will come when he and his Henchmen will wish they were dead. If there's any justice in this world, you'll live to see those animals suffer for what they've done, believe me," she said as she continued to embrace her.

She was too petrified to let go of Jenna and though tired and weary she was terrified of going to sleep in case she was awoken by the door being kicked in. Or she would wake up only to find men standing around her bed, staring down at her and salivating like wild animals. Jenna managed to free herself from her vice like grip and climbed into the bed with her.

"Come lie down with me. I'll stay with you until the morning; tomorrow we'll get in my car and get out of here. I'm going to take you somewhere safe, but for now, relax," said Jenna. They embraced each other until sleep overwhelmed them both.

The following morning, Jenna woke up early and slid out of bed leaving Jeany huddled up asleep in a foetal position, her pillow locked in her folded arms. Jenna slipped on some clothes and began to cook a light breakfast of warm bread and soy milk. She placed a tray on the bedside table next to Jeany and then leaned across and kissed her gently on the lips to awaken her. Jeany's eyes shot open only to find herself staring directly into Jenna's broad dark eyes. In the seconds that passed,

Jeany felt a multiplicity of emotions that fluctuated from repulsion to excitement. She turned her head away.

"Not you as well," she murmured as she covered her face with her hands and burst into tears.

"Jeany you need to be able to discern lust from affection. To love another woman, if you were to try it, is no different from being able to sleep with men you're not attracted to. It's an acquired taste. I'm not after your body, your heart maybe, but please don't compare me with those animals. I'm on your side. I'm your best friend, yes?" Jenna left her alone and went into the living room.

Despite openly rebuffing Jenna's advances, she'd felt a certain desire to embrace her and hold her. How she wished she could hold another human being in her arms and not feel as if they were going to use and abuse her. And where was Jason when she needed him most? She knew he was out there somewhere, enjoying the freedom now denied to her. Jeany's needs at this moment were for the kind of friendship that only another woman could deliver. She felt guilty about being so blunt in her response to Jenna, to what had probably been an innocent, kind and affectionate gesture.

Jenna stood by the bedroom door and smiled at her. Jeany sat up in bed and raised the glass of soy milk up to Jenna.

"Sorry for being such a bitch and you made such a nice breakfast for me too. What are we going to tell Jason? He'll be back tonight. If I were him I'd be on a plane back to England; I really would," said Jeany.

"Leave Jason to me, we're going somewhere safe for a few days until it is safe," explained Jenna.

"But when will it ever be safe? Can anything ever be the same again?" She turned away and drifted into a daydream.

"When you know who is out of China, that's when. He's the problem. Once he's gone we will all be able to sleep safe in our beds again," stated Jenna.

"If he goes, that means Bo-Cheng wins, and I lose. That isn't what I want and I don't think you would expect me to lie back and let him and his cronies control my life and do what they want with me. You wouldn't let them get away with it, so why should I?" Jeany snapped.

"You're right but the reality is that he still needs to be told of the danger. My first concern is for your safety – you need to go into hiding – then we can help him escape from whatever Bo-Cheng has in store for him." Jenna threw Jeany's clothes onto the bed.

"Now get changed and we'll be off, before any one realises we've gone."

"Where are we going?" she asked, as she got dressed.

"Spring Village of course and to your old schoolmate's hospital," came the reply. Jeany gave her a broad smile; for the first time since her ordeal, she felt a ray of hope. She knew who her loyal friends were and knew that they wouldn't let her down.

"Jenna, you do know there are always those in every village that would sell their own kinfolk to the party thugs just to ingratiate themselves. You know that don't you?"

"Yes, that's why we need to go to the village after dark, just to be on the safe side." She pulled back the curtains to see the bright morning sun, its radiant red orb glowing over the hazy industrial skyline of Shijiazhuang.

"I need to be back at work later this morning so as to avoid implicating me in your disappearance. That's why we have to leave now," she said as she finished buttoning up her white uniform. Both crept out of the apartment without a sound and made their way to Jenna's car. Jeany loaded all her belongings into the boot and they drove casually out of the car park in a north easterly direction away from Shijiazhuang and its ghosts. Jeany knew in her heart that even though they were leaving the scene of her trauma, its dark shadow would nibble away at her ability to love and be loved for a long time to come.

After an hour on the Beijing bound highway they turned off and entered a small agricultural town a few miles off their planned route.

"I will have to leave you here until later this evening, but first we have to find you somewhere to rest up. I'll return later and meet you at that coffee shop over there at seven-o-clock tonight. Then we'll get to Spring Village after dark. Will you be alright here until then?" Jenna asked. She felt guilty about leaving her alone in such a vulnerable state, but she had no other choice.

"I'll be alright, but I do need to find a room, somewhere to get my head down. I mean, walking around with these cases will attract a lot of attention," said Jeany, conscious of her bruised face and scab ridden scalp. Jenna drove on a short way, until they found a small hotel where she dropped her off having made sure she had a room, enough money to buy food and something to drink. With Jeany sorted she drove back to the hospital and behaved as if nothing was amiss.

By lunch time the 'what to do about Jason' issue had to be addressed. Jenna knew the time he was due to arrive although she would have to wait at the station for

114

about an hour. She daren't phone him and she had to consider what she would do if they were recognised by the police in the station. Having checked the train times, she decided to go to the station and wait for him to arrive. In the unlikely event that he had decided to return early and unannounced, she decided to drive past his apartment.

As she approached, she was shocked to see a gathering of policemen just visible from the roadside, loitering around his apartment veranda. Troubled by this she kept on driving. It was clear by this that he hadn't arrived yet. Now aware of the danger that he was in, she wasted no time in getting to the station.

On her arrival, she came to the conclusion that the police had no knowledge of his trip to Beijing. She noticed that there were just a few police on duty in the station and those that were there didn't look as if they were interested in looking for anyone. It was now 4.30pm and the train was due to arrive at any moment. She fumbled in her handbag looking for something, anything that would take her mind off these tense moments of inactivity.

Just then the metal barrier gates ahead of her opened and a sea of human bodies flooded in through them as if there were a tsunami to their rear threatening to engulf them. She strained her neck to catch a glimpse of him, to see if he was amongst the hoard leaving the platform. Then she caught a fleeting glance of a tall foreign male, with greying hair and a black leather jacket. She wasn't at all sure if it was him or not, but she had no other choice but to find out. She barged her way through the flow of frantic passengers, to within a few feet of the tall foreigner, before she recognised him.

"Jason, Jason, lai-lai, come follow me," she said as she struggled against the human flow.

"Where's Jeany?" he shouted, his voice lost in the sonorous symphony of sounds that seemed to fill the cavernous station.

Once out into the cold evening air, she wasted no time in trying to explain but kept walking, all the while ahead of Jason. His instincts told him that something wasn't as it should be. Had the authorities found out about his secret task or had something terrible happened to Jeany?

On their arrival at the car, Jason threw his bags into the boot and clambered into the passenger seat next to Jenna.

"What's going on? Where's Jeany? I suppose you're the one who sent that 'Harry' text?" he asked with a stern tone to his voice. She looked at him long and hard.

"Yes that was me. For the time being all you need to know is that she's had some trouble with her ex-husband. For some reason he blames you for her corrupted ideas. He's the Chief of Police and to be quite honest; if I were you I'd take your Christmas break early. It's not safe for you here. Your apartment's been trashed and you don't have a job to return to."

BO-CHENG'S ATTACKED

Jason's heart sank. All he had worked for in China had now been trampled underfoot by persons he didn't know or want to know.

"Is this guy some kind of psychopath or something?" he moaned, he felt tired, barely able to comprehend what had occurred in such a short space of time.

"Yes he is," but then she smiled.

"Let's go and see Jeany, she's staying at a small hotel in Ding-Xian. That's half way to Boa-ding. If we set off now, we'll be there in an hour. Do you want to go and see her, or would you rather stay here and face the wrath of the party machine?" she asked, knowing that whatever decision he made, she would be there for Jeany. He thought for a while and then shrugged his shoulders.

"What options do I have? I knew I would have to leave China one day. You do realise I can't take her back to England with me and neither can I see a future for us living separately. And with all this trouble around, it's going to take a miracle for us to stay together."

"If you love each other, surely you can sort something out? Maybe not now; give it time eh? Right now we have to go to Ding-Xian, she's waiting for us," she said as she started the car. He stared at his glum image in the darkened windscreen. Jenna slipped the car into gear and drove out into the busy rush hour streets of Shijiazhuang.

She headed in a north easterly direction saying nothing as the yellow phosphorous glare from the overhead street lights rippled across her face, as if she were the subject of one of those old time black and white movies. He stared at her, expecting her to turn round and explain everything, but she didn't. As the lights danced across her face, he began to admire her sharp angular profile and intense eyes as she drove on, indifferent to Jason who had been scrutinising her from the passenger seat. The car then joined the main highway towards Beijing some miles before the Ding-Xian turn off; it was then that she seemed to relax a little, which in turn put Jason at ease.

"Now, can you tell me what's going on?"

"We'll be in Ding-Xian in half an hour. We'll discuss the problem when we get there, until then just sit back and relax," she said, her own mind all too preoccupied with formulating some kind of strategy to get Jeany out of this precarious situation. If it meant cutting Jason out of the picture, so be it,' she thought as she drove on, her foot pressed hard to the floor.

Meanwhile back at the hotel, Jeany lay on her bed, with her eyes closed, unsure of when Jenna would turn up, or even if she would turn up at all that night. She had been in that room most of the afternoon, but she didn't mind. Here she felt safe and away from those people and places, that would by their sheer presence conjure up memories of that attack. Her mind drifted into a fantasy world where she pictured herself and Jason walking across Scottish moorland carpeted with heather. She could imagine the feel, the fresh cool breeze mingled with the natural aroma of pine needles and wild lavender. Tears rolled down her cheeks as her heart yearned for better days and the love of her lost son so cruelly taken from her.

Just then a knock on the door broke the silence. Startled she jumped to her feet relieved that Jenna and hopefully Jason had arrived at last.

She dashed across the room and opened the door. To her horror there stood Pepper Lee, with her hands on her hips, bold and as intimidating as ever.

"Surprise surprise, I bet you didn't expect to see me so far from Shijiazhuang. I've been told that you and that foreigner are planning to run away together. Where is he?" she demanded in a stern voice.

"I'm not running away from anyone, or with anyone. I just needed to get away, I've been ill, that's all," she explained. "How did you know I was here?"

"When you and your lesbian friend left your apartment, the police were already watching you. Did you think you could get away from justice? The police have been keeping an eye on her movements too. It's good to know that even at your age, you're still being noticed, isn't it?" said Pepper. "Have you turned gay? Well, I suppose it's better than what you got the other night. Mind you, you asked for it, didn't you?" she snapped, still leaning on the doorframe.

"How can you say that? That could happen to any woman! You should be thankful it wasn't you. Did your friend in the police department tell you I was here?"

"Ah, my boyfriend, I'm glad you asked me. Would you like to meet him? I call him Bo-Bo." Just then the hateful figure of Bo-Cheng appeared, from behind her. He gently wrapped his arms around her, kissing her neck as he did.

"This, my dear Jin-Mei, is my man. And you are nothing but a used up mattress, alone and on the run from no one, heading nowhere." Jeany stifled her anger with a mask of indifference.

"What do you mean from no-one? It's you and your men." Bo-Cheng just smiled and hugged Pepper still closer.

"I've got what I want, you punished and a decent woman to share my bed with. All I need to do now is to rid China of that enemy of the state. Where is he?" he demanded. Jeany said nothing. "Tell me and you can go home and live in peace. That's a promise," Bo-Cheng said in a calm voice.

"He's gone back to Beijing and won't be coming back; that's the truth," said Jeany.

"Bo-Bo, I think she's telling the truth. She wouldn't get far with him in tow and no one has seen him since you searched his apartment yesterday," said Pepper.

"Can I go home then?" Jeany asked in a meek voice.

Bo-Cheng pointed his finger at her forehead.

"Do you swear that you don't know where he is, other than he is somewhere in Beijing?" he said, glaring into her moist eyes as he did.

"I swear it," said Jeany, tearfully. Bo-Cheng turned to one of his men.

"You take this woman home, don't talk to her and don't molest her, or as God is my judge I'll kill you," ordered Bo-Cheng. She recognised Fei-Liao, the husband of her friend and the very same man who had pulled her hair during the attack only a day ago. Jeany now shaking from head to toe backed away from the door and reached for the drawer next to the kitchenette area and pulled out a long serrated bread knife.

"If I'm going on my own with him I want to carry a knife, I don't like or trust him," she growled as the trauma of the day before began to return. Bo-Cheng laughed.

"Yes go ahead and if he touches you, by all means kill the bastard. Fei-Liao looked at Bo-Cheng, seeking some assurance but he was in no mood to be lenient.

"Go now and get her home, and you," he said pointing to Jeany, as she stood there knife at the ready.

"You, sit in the back and don't provoke him, understand?"

Jeany followed the fat police officer, better known as Fei-Liao, out into the cold night air and into one of the waiting police cars still clutching her bread knife. As she climbed into the back seat another police office loaded her bags next to her on the rear seat. She was anxious to get out of the area before Jenna and Jason appeared on the scene. Bo-Cheng and Pepper stayed behind, and as rank has its various privileges, they settled down to enjoying some free Qingdao beers at the landlord's expense.

Meanwhile, en route to the Ding-Xian hotel, Jenna told Jason about the attack, leaving out the rape. Whatever he had been doing in Beijing was now placed to the back of his mind, pushed back by new and terrible revelations. Shocked by the news, his rosy complexion now turned grey and pallid. What else could go wrong he asked himself as he stared down into the dark at his new shoes? As they approached the Ding-Xian Hotel, Jenna slowed down and stopped some way before the hotel on the opposite side of the road. She switched off the engine and the lights, and then waited.

They noticed three police vehicles parked around the side of the hotel. One of the patrol car's headlights came on, it moved to the front of the building and then it stopped outside the main entrance. Jenna and Jason sat there and watched as Jeany was escorted out of the hotel. They saw her get into the back of the police car and her bags thrown in next to her. The vehicle then moved off heading south west, in the direction of Shijiazhuang.

A dark shadow of gloom and despondency descended on the couple as they watched the police car vanish out of sight. Jason wondered who was left behind. He had never met this Bo-Cheng. Somehow the tape secreted in Jason's shoe seemed less important than Jeany's current dilemma. Anything he did now would no doubt impact on Jeany's life, wherever she was. If she was in custody, she could find herself inside a male prison being raped or subjected to electric shock torture techniques.

He sat there and procrastinated; as his anger boiled up inside him, his cool rational self-control dissipated into fury fuelled by the hate he had for this Bo-Cheng. Tears of guilt moistened his eyes as he reprimanded himself for being elsewhere when she was in need. He felt helpless and humiliated, in that he had been forced to sit and watch the police take away the one person he now realised he loved.

A dusting of snow blew in the cold night air. His resolve now slipped into some unknown gear. Without a word of explanation to Jenna, he pushed the car door open and marched across the road towards the hotel entrance. Jenna open mouthed fell silent as he stepped boldly into the hotel lobby.

There at the bar was Pepper Lee and beside her stood an overweight round faced policeman in his fifties, his face reddened with alcohol. As soon as he saw Bo-Cheng he knew he was the culprit. Pepper stood up and pointed towards Jason.

"That's him, Jin-Mei's lover boy; he's come to get you Bo-Bo. He's after revenge, mark my words," she shouted at the top of her voice. It was as if she were trying to rally support from his other three men, who were sat round a small table still clasping their beers. Everyone in the bar got to their feet and stood with bated breath.

Bo-Cheng reached for his gun holster. Jason wasted no time in delivering a pre-emptive strike, kicking Bo-Cheng firmly in the groin. This doubled him up. Jason then grabbed a chair and delivered a hefty blow to the nape of Bo-Cheng's neck sending him to the floor in a bundle. The three policemen who'd been momentarily stunned by Jason's audacity pushed aside the table spilling their beers in the process. Still grasping the chair Jason went berserk swinging it wildly at each and every one. The floor was wet and very slippery and the police men, big as they were, fell like nine pins. For a moment all was quiet. He looked around, his heart beating fast and furiously, his legs felt like jelly, but his assailants were all carpeting the floor. Bo-Cheng's face was a greyish yellow, Jason heart sunk, Bo-Cheng was dead.

A bald headed man's face appeared from behind the reception desk with a delighted look on his face.

"This hotel will be the most famous hotel in Hebei, once every one knows you killed that pig in here, and good riddance, that's what I say. He never paid for anything; as for that bitch of his, she's not even Chinese, she's no different from you, just a foreigner," said the receptionist, as he spat on the body of Bo-Cheng.

Jason looked down and saw Pepper lying there in a pool of blood and felt sick at what he had done. Without checking any of the casualties, he fled out of the hotel and headed back to the car where Jenna was waiting.

"Get in let's go," cried Jenna. Without a word being said, they headed back towards Shijiazhuang.

"What happened in there?" she asked, realising that he would not have been allowed to leave alone had there not been an altercation.

"I killed the bastard," he admitted as sweat ran down his forehead. He sat there with his head bowed rubbing his sore and splintered hands.

"At the next turn off is a Wild Chicken bus station, get the bus to Beijing and hold up there. The police will be looking for you. I can't hide you. Jeany is in custody or in prison. I have a job to go to. Just worry about yourself, as for Jeany and me we'll be okay," said Jenna.

"What about Jeany and me?"

"There is no Jeany and you. From now on, you had better run and keep running until you can get out of China." With that, Jenna stopped at a dark and lonely street lamp.

"Now what do I do?"

"Go to Beijing. This is the 'Wild Chicken' bus stop; they leave for Beijing every hour. There is nothing else I can do. Don't contact me again. Sorry Jason." He gave Jenna a look of disapproval and stepped out of the car and onto the grassy verge. She pulled the car door shut, looked to the front with a heartless expression on her face and pulled away. Jason was left standing alone on the grassy verge of a long dark road.

Empowered

It wasn't long before the 'Wild-Chicken' bus appeared from out of the evening mist. Jason paid his fare and secreted himself alone on the rear seat. A sense of relief washed over him as the sparsely populated bus pulled away from the dark and remote location. Though he was on the move, he knew that he wasn't out of the woods yet. The gravity of what he had done weighed heavily on his mind. The mitigating circumstances for what he had done, albeit justifiable, were not going to wash with the Chinese authorities.

The coach sped through the dark night, stopping at various secluded locations on its way. He was a free man at this moment in time, but for how long, he didn't know. Now, despite being on the run, he felt obliged to cherish the peace and solitude before the inevitable storm that was looming up behind him engulf him. There was only one place he could run to, and that was Beijing, and once there, there was only one person he could turn to for help and that was where he was headed.

Sometime later Jenna arrived back at her empty apartment in silence, convinced that Jeany had been arrested. It was common knowledge that from the many who were arrested in China, few left in the same mental state as they went in. So much so that the likelihood of seeing her again as she was, was very slim. Many of those that were released from prison after years of abuse, were mere shadows of their former selves. She understood the grave danger that her friend was in whilst in custody. She was determined to make a phone call to have her released, or at least to try and clarify the exact charges that she was being held on.

On entering her apartment, she slumped down onto the soft leather sofa. She felt empty. With her eyes tightly closed she could see Jeany in her mind's eye, that infectious smile of hers and her indomitable spirit and energy. She opened her eyes and tried to snap out of the melancholy she was sinking into. She opened her glass cabinet and reached for an unopened bottle of Glenfiddich and retired to her bed, that still bore the crumpled sheets from the night before.

As instructed by Bo-Cheng, Jeany was being taken back to her apartment. As the police vehicle pulled away from the hotel, the solitary fat policeman drove whilst Jeany sat directly behind him, shrunk into the shadows of the back seat. The vehicle carrying her made good headway as it sped along the long dark deserted highway towards Shijiazhuang. She sat there clutching the sharp bread knife that she had been allowed to carry with her for her own protection.

As the journey progressed she began to feel less and less intimidated by the driver, whose only wish was to dump her and forget that he had ever been involved in the despicable act he had been a party to. The night lights flickered past in the dark, she stared at the low life form before her. As she did a strange feeling came over her as the back of the driver's thick set hairy neck was beginning to take on a sinister dimension. She felt a devilish pleasure as she imagined herself plunging her sharp knife into the bulging flesh of his neck.

This man had been the one who had painfully pulled her hair, dragging her across the bed holding her down, pushing her face into the mattress, why should she let him get away with doing that to her? Even now she could smell his unforgettably foul body odour, reawakening painful memories. A cold sweat ran through her entire body, as her assailant sat in front of her, at her mercy. He wasn't human; he was a piece of disgusting meat, waiting to be dissected and now she had the opportunity. The irritation was gnawing at her, as she poked the material at the back of the driver's seat, eventually piercing it with her sharp knife.

As the hypnotic yellow lights of the motorway flashed past her nearside window, reality and fantasy somehow embraced each other. She struggled against the urge to thrust the knife firmly between his shoulder blades and face the consequences. Then again the option of suicide would be preferable to what the authorities would have in store for her. 'How could it have come to this,' she thought as she clenched the knife harder than ever. 'These are not my evil thoughts,' she said to herself, 'it's because of these men, they've contaminated my mind and dirtied it with their evil, damn them'.

Jeany managed to stifle the internal voices and the temptation before her, but instead reverted to shredding the rear seat, just as they had done to her sofa at home. The driver on hearing the sound of his car seats being ripped looked long and hard at her through the rear view mirror.

"You're going to have to pay for that damage, do you hear me bitch?" snarled the fat policeman angrily.

"We will all have to pay for our misdeeds sooner or later, won't we?" she retorted.

"We'll see who has the last laugh," said the driver unaware of how close he had come to being perforated from behind. Fei-Liao's eyes and Jeany's met in the rear view mirror.

"You do know that I know you, don't you?" she asked, curious as to why he had been so unashamed of doing what he did.

"So what?" snapped the driver, as he looked away.

"Yes I know you; you are Zang Fei-Liao. I work with your wife at the hospital. The poor sad bitch, and to think I used to envy her being so popular and all that," she said, as thoughts of vengeance served cold lit up her spirits.

"Shut up bitch," he snarled.

"Does she know you're a fat slimy rapist? Well, does she?" growled Jeany, as she once again perforated the back of his seat with the sharp end of her knife, tantalising herself with the opportunity she was letting pass her by.

"You leave my wife out of this. Do you hear me?" ordered the red-faced driver.

"You had the audacity to call me a whore; I'm no more of a whore than your wife is. In fact come to think of it, I'm less of a whore, she has to bed the likes of you, a fat perverted rapist. She does bed you, doesn't she?" Jeany sneered, cherishing her chance to vent her spleen. "You tried to rape me, I'll tell you this that when your wife hears of this, the only woman who will allow you to bed her, will be the ones you have to pay for. Oh I almost forgot; you policemen don't pay for it, do you? What do you men call it? Ah, freebies, is that what you say?" she said, smirking back at him through his rear view mirror.

"Keep your mouth shut or I'll shut it for you," threatened the driver as he slammed his foot hard down onto the accelerator, gripping the steering wheel as if he were throttling someone.

"Tell me why I shouldn't stick this knife in to your fat greasy neck right now?"

"I've told you once to shut it, ugly bitch."

"Why don't you take a long hard look at yourself? You're a fat filthy pig, who do you think would shed a solitary tear at your passing? Nobody would, and I'd make sure that if I couldn't, someone would stand up at your funeral and tell the whole world you had been a perverted rapist. I'd tell them all just what you did, so God help me I would!"

Fei-Liao's patience now snapped; with his face flushed red he took his foot off the accelerator and pushed down heavily on the brake pedal swerving erratically into the hard shoulder. Without a second thought, she grabbed the fat policeman's greasy black hair as tightly as she could with her left hand and pulled his head back hard against the bars separating his head rest from the rear seat area. With her right hand, she slid the sharp bread knife across the front into Fei-Liao's mouth, its sharp tip piercing the fatty tissue of his inner cheek.

"Drive on, or as God is my witness I'll kill you," she screamed her hand shaking. He could taste the blood as the knife crept towards the back of his throat. "Do as I say or I'll slice you up and don't think I wouldn't," she growled, her body shaking and pulsating. The car never came to a halt but swerved once again back onto the motorway without stopping.

Being unable to concentrate whilst driving was the least of his problems, for the knife in his mouth undulated with every bump in the road etching his inner cheek with bloody marks that made him want to retch. As much as he wanted to throw up, he had to stifle it in order to remain still. His brow ran with perspiration, he could feel the veins in his forehead pulsate. By now, his patience had worn thin as he fumbled around his midriff in search of his firearm.

She saw what he was trying to do and tightened her grip on his hair and then made sure that he could feel the sharp end of her wrath.

"Open the window and throw out your firearm, and I mean it," she ordered, her voice harsh and bitter unambiguous in its intent. Fei-Liao trembling opened the window and dropped his firearm out onto the road.

"Now your ankle sidearm, don't forget I was married to a rotten policeman. Reach down and undo the clip, then throw that out and I mean real slow," she said as she stared down over his shoulder. Her strained breath whisked past his left ear, dispelling any idea he may have that she was not in complete control.

"Now keep driving," she ordered feeling somewhat surprised at her own audacity. She had never taken total control of anything in her life before; there had always been someone in the background pulling the strings. Though she had never gone to such lengths before, she felt empowered and liberated, albeit for a brief episode. She had never understood why certain people rebelled against authority, but now the light flooded in and she was enjoying the sweet taste of payback, and it felt good. Pang-Xi would be so proud of me if he could see me now, she thought.

Despite being in a fair amount of discomfort, Fei-Liao drove on, with Jeany's arm wedged through the bars still holding the knife firmly in place. She was ever mindful of the consequences should she be relieved of her only method of self-defence. Afraid that her grip was waning, she jerked his head back to re-establish her grip causing him to wince with pain.

"You're not going to kill me, are you?" Fei-Liao asked in a feeble voice, barely able to articulate the words from behind the steel blade still in his mouth. She moved her face closer to his ear.

"To be honest I'm not quite sure at this moment, but I can tell you this, I'm seriously thinking about it. Give me a good reason why I shouldn't."

"Because it's illegal," he said in a high-pitched voice as he bit down on the blade.

"So is rape, but that didn't stop you did it?" Jeany snarled.

"But I didn't rape you, did I? It was the others, not me," he said in an attempt to distance himself from the crime.

Jeany's arm was now beginning to suffer from fatigue and was uncomfortable, so she decided to reassign her hold on him, transferring her left hand to his collar, and then she withdrew the knife from out of his mouth and repositioned its sharp point into the nape of his neck in order to re-confirm her authority.

"Thank you", he mumbled as blood soaked saliva dribbled down onto the front of his white shirt.

"Don't thank me. I haven't finished yet. You didn't rape me because you couldn't. It was you who began it and you could have stopped it. You're as guilty as they are," she said, as she pulled at his collar and buried the point of her knife just a little deeper into the fat of his nape.

"You don't know Bo-Cheng. No one refuses an order and gets away with it. You should know better than anyone," said the driver looking at her through the rear view mirror.

"Yes I know him, but I've had the balls to say no once in a while. You men are 'yes-men' you're not real men at all. You're nothing but a bunch of cowards reduced to bullying women and intimidating the elderly. You and Bo-Cheng are going to answer for your crime in a court of law, so help me God you will," she said. "Unless the youth of this country stand up to bullies and implement change we will always get what we've always got. We will be left with this heartless regime and its henchmen, people like you will remain. And so victims like me will always be denied my time in court and denied justice." Fei-Liao stared at her through the rear view mirror, his watery red eyes bulged as his contempt for her boiled over.

"In your dreams bitch," he replied, as he leant forward, in an attempt to break free of her grip. She at once tightened her hold on his collar and advanced the blade deeper into the rolls of fat, just enough to send a sharp unambiguous message. A trickle of blood ran down over the coils of fat onto his white collar that rapidly soaked up the bright red colouration.

"You call me bitch just one more time and so God help me, I will kill you." Fei-Liao remained silent. It didn't take him long to realise that by provoking this woman into some kind of retaliation, he was sure to be the first casualty. He concluded that the whole issue was best forgotten. If he were to report her irrational behaviour, he would also be allowing her to explain and voice her accusations of rape; such accusations would then be brought out into the open. He would then be forced to accept or deny her allegations.

At last the police car pulled in through the high metal gates as it entered her apartment complex and stopped outside the main entrance. Even at that time of night, when most people would be tucked up in their beds, the presence of a police patrol car entering the compound managed to attract a fair amount of attention from the local residents. Jeany gave the driver a sharp tug on his collar.

"Open the rear door," she said sternly. He reached for a switch on the dashboard and the door sprung open, allowing her to stretch a leg out. She grabbed her bag of belongings and slid out of the car door, releasing the knife from his neck at the very last moment. She slammed the door loudly. The noise echoed round the whole complex, alerting the occupants to their presence. She stepped back from the vehicle and stood there defiantly, staring at the red faced policeman. He glared back at her from behind the window. Jeany began to laugh at him. Not only was his brow deeply furrowed and his mouth reddened and bleeding, but his hair remained pulled in a spike at the back of his head. Her laughter angered him so much, that he wound down his window.

"I won't forget this you bitch!" He spat at her and gritted his teeth in contempt. By now the entire neighbourhood had been alerted to the possibility of yet another altercation between Jeany and the police. Inquisitive faces, one by one, appeared at windows and on balconies all around the complex quadrant. With her neighbours as her audience, she once again felt empowered and determined to show the world that someone had to stand up to these bullies. Those who had challenged the authorities before had had their lives cut short. In her current state of mind, she believed that life without dignity wasn't a life at all. And with a voice that resounded throughout the whole estate, she broadcast her response.

"And I won't forget you either! You're a fat ugly perverted rapist. You should be ashamed of yourself."

She picked up a nearby metal trash can and hurled it at the car, sending it crashing into the vehicle's side. The impact created a noise so loud that if the first door slamming closed hadn't woken the neighbourhood, this was certain to.

"Rapist, rapist!" she chanted, taunting him and pointing her finger directly into his face. It was no secret that she'd been raped, for she'd been shunned by most of her neighbours. Now the same people who had avoided eye contact with her, unsure of how to behave towards her, could now recognise the accused police officer as Zang Fei-Liao. The fact that he refused to respond to the accusations and wouldn't leave his car was evidence of his guilt. She now knew that from here on in, the rumours would begin, and circulate they would.

She stood in the dimly lit car park, a lone figure as she watched the police patrol car silently reverse out of the complex gates. She felt good about her behaviour, albeit uncharacteristic. She was sure that her misdeeds of this night would pass without formal retribution. The whole estate, though in virtual darkness, whispered to itself as a multitude of voices behind closed doors, debated her foolishness or her brave audacity.

With a warm sense of satisfaction and a smile to match, she entered the concrete stair and with brisk steps she dashed up to her apartment. She'd barely used the new set of keys but now she needed to feel safe. She could sense the ghosts of past traumas, still nipping at her heels. Despite the newly fitted security, she was anxious to get back behind closed doors, just in case the driver had decided to follow her up the dimly lit stairwell. She reassured herself that if he was behind her, she was well able to outrun the overweight policeman. If the worst happened and he caught up with her, she still had the sharp knife. The idea of using the knife on him remained a pleasurable one. She would retain this fantasy and savour it. 'One day maybe', she thought.

At last she reached her apartment door. She then noticed light emanating from below her neighbour's door. Her neighbour had obviously seen the altercation below. She smiled, for anything the old lady knew about anyone was soon to become common knowledge. Though unsympathetic after the attack, the neighbour would make an excellent witness for the prosecution.

Once inside, she was comforted by the thought that Bo-Cheng himself had told her to keep the knife and use it if necessary. He had stated this in front of his men, although anything was likely to be denied with such 'yes men' as these. Bo-Cheng had probably spoken in jest, presuming that he knew her to be the same spineless female he had been married to and bullied for years. What she had done to the driver would have been beyond Bo-Cheng's wildest dreams.

She stood inside and admired her new heavy solid wooden door. It had iron bolts at the top and bottom and was reinforced with a steel bar at the centre point, to prevent anyone kicking in the door again. She had concealed knives in and around the living area, in the bedroom, such as under the mattress and in the lining of the curtains, mended with great care by Jenna. The tattered remains of her sofa, the bedding and all the contents of her pre-attack home were piled up in the far corner of the living room under the window. The urine stained carpet that had been hoisted out of the window in disgust when Jenna and she had cleared up, had now incredibly disappeared from its resting place far below.

Her mutilated sofa, though in part destroyed, still held a great deal of sentimental value, for it was on this sofa that she spent hours playing with her son from being a new born baby. Six long months had passed since she had heard or seen anything of him now presumed dead. She was determined that at least this one last thread, linking her to her lost son, wasn't going to be destroyed by his evil father.

She sat on the bed and picked up her mobile. She rang her old friend, Mrs Zang, none other than the wife of Fei-Liao, the fat policeman she had just left less than half an hour ago.

"Nan is that you?"

"Jin-Mei, It's so late how can I help you?"

"Do me a favour, can you tell your husband when he gets in, that Jeany called? Could you also tell him, I'm sorry about his neck. I apologise for calling so late. I'll be in touch, tell him that, won't you?" She felt pity for this poor sad woman. She had to remind herself, that what this man and his colleagues did to her, wasn't this woman's fault.

"Alright Jin-Mei I'll tell him. You haven't made a lot of sense, but I expect he'll understand what you meant when I tell him, right?"

"Oh yes, he'll understand. Have a good night," and with that she ended the call. It was far too late to call Jenna, so she texted her, asking her to call when she got up. She curled up on her tattered sofa and caught some well-earned rest.

Jenna had got up to use the bathroom, unable to sleep. She'd spent most of the night tossing and turning, but tranquil sleep eluded her. Thoughts of Jin-Mei being back in the clutches of those animals that had molested her, continued to torment her. After a mug of extra strong coffee, she stood up and strolled back into the bedroom, where she threw herself down onto the large double bed where she and Jeany had lay the previous night. She could smell Jeany's distinctive fragrance. Tears of anger and resentment welled up inside her, as she entertained vengeful thoughts against those who had violated her friend. She buried her face into her pillow and vowed to do whatever it took to put matters right.

JENNA'S CONQUEST

For some reason Jenna glanced over at her mobile sitting on the bedside table and checked her messages. She then noticed an unread text from Jeany, requesting a call back. Even though it was from her mobile, Jenna jumped to the conclusion that it was the police calling her from Jeany's phone, possibly with bad news of her friend's unfortunate demise or worse. There seemed no other option, other than to answer it and face whatever problem there was, head on.

"Hello Jie-Na speaking, you asked me to call you back. Who am I speaking to?"

"It's me, Jeany. I'm home and alright but it can get a little scary and feel I still need to leave my apartment. I'm not afraid to be on my own, but I'd rather not be. Can you come over and pick me up? I don't want to spend the night here alone. I never want to sleep here again. Do you mind?" Jeany asked.

Jenna smiled to herself, this was exactly what she had dreamt would happen.

"Don't be so silly, of course I'll pick you up. I'll be there in twenty minutes," said Jenna with a satisfied smile on her face. Jenna hurried into the bedroom, threw some casual clothes on, gave her hair a brush and then grabbed her car keys.

Jenna sped off in the direction of Jeany's apartment. She felt elated, for with the foreigner out of the picture and Bo-Cheng having had his revenge and presumably now cohabiting with some simple minded Taiwanese bimbo, Jeany was sure to gravitate towards her. After all it was Jenna that had risked all to show her affection and loyalty. Not only this but also because of her position at the hospital, she was well able to provide her with the material things that most other people couldn't.

By the time she had pulled up outside her apartment, Jeany was waiting by the main entrance with her cases and an assortment of boxes. Jenna got out and approached her.

"Are you moving in permanently?" she asked in a quiet voice.

"Yes if you'll have me," replied Jeany, looking back up at her apartment window.

"You can stay with me as long as you like. You'll still have your apartment. Keep it for when you need some space. The new locks we had fitted should have made you feel safer. Don't worry, from now on, we're living together," said Jenna, as she gave her a warm hug. Jeany leant back and gave her a tentative smile of approval. Jenna looked up at the surrounding apartment blocks and noticed faces appearing as curious neighbours peered down from their windows.

The two women hurriedly loaded Jeany's personal belongings into the back of the car and then climbed in. Jeany sat there without a sound, contemplating the complications that were sure to arise from her decision to move in with such a woman. Her skin was cold and clammy; her body was beginning to tremble again. She was exhausted but too afraid to sleep, tormented by the isolation and the whispering walls of her apartment. She felt intimidated by the silent glares of her neighbours and too scared to face their unvoiced condemnation alone. The self-assuredness she had felt the previous day had now faded. At this moment she needed support and was willing to undergo whatever it took to escape from her perpetual fear.

It wasn't until they had arrived back at Jenna's apartment that Jenna sat down and told Jeany about Jason's fracas with Bo-Cheng.

"We'd just arrived at the hotel when we saw you being driven off in a police car. That's when he lost control. I couldn't believe my eyes when I saw him charging across the road and flying straight into the hotel. There were police cars outside so I knew there was going to be trouble. Soon after he'd gone in, I heard a loud commotion from the hotel lobby and then he came running out. He was out of breath and babbling on about how he'd killed Bo-Cheng and the others. What else could I do but get him out of there and advise him to run and keep running? I couldn't hide him and certainly not when you were in police custody." Jeany grasped Jenna's hands.

"Where do you suppose he is now?" she asked her voice sad and mournful.

"I dropped him off at some wild chicken bus stop bound for Beijing. What else could I have done?" Jenna replied. Jeany looked resigned.

"You're right. He's safer away from all this mess. To be quite honest, after all that's happened, I don't suppose he'd want me back, soiled goods and all that," she sighed.

"They can't blame you for what Jason did. You were in police custody at the time of the killings. You're in the clear, so don't worry about that," explained Jenna trying to reassure her of her impunity.

"Anyway never mind about Jason, how did you manage to avoid being imprisoned? We saw you being

140

driven off; I assumed you were bound for the police cells. What happened?" Jenna asked, puzzled.

"Nothing, they simply drove me home and here I am, free and unmolested," she said as she gave out a huge yawn.

"I'm sorry, I'm exhausted. I don't want to talk anymore. All I want to do is sleep," said Jeany her eyes half-closed, as her body, drained of energy began to feel drowsy. Jenna was full of anticipation and excited at the prospect of having Jeany to herself, now that Jason was no longer between her and her objective. As Jeany lay slumped on the sofa, she gestured to Jenna to sit beside her.

"Jenna, I need you to get in touch with your contact in the government and tell them about the rape. Ask them what I need to do to get justice." She squeezed Jenna's hand tight.

"Yes of course I will. But if Bo-Cheng and his men are dead, who's left to answer the charges?" Jenna reasoned.

"There's that policeman, Zang Fei-Liao, the fat slob that drove me home. He's still around. I can't believe that Jason managed to kill them all. He can handle himself, that I'm sure, but that kind of brutality just isn't him. I want advice and justice," Jenna smiled and nodded.

"Yes I'll do that first thing tomorrow. You look so tired. Leave all that for me to sort out in the morning. For now, let's sleep," suggested Jenna, anxious to draw a line under the Jason issue once and for all.

Jenna got up and disappeared into the darkened bedroom. Without a sound she undressed and then slipped her naked body in between the soft clean sheets.

"Are you coming to bed?" whispered Jenna, from the comfort of her bed, making sure she was decently

141

covered. Just then the tall, shapely silhouette of Jeany appeared at the doorway of the darkened bedroom.

"Where are my bed clothes?" she asked in a whisper.

"The bed is so hot, you're not going to need any, trust me," said Jenna, as she threw back the sheets on Jeany's side, inviting her to get in. Jeany wasn't in any state to argue. She entered the bedroom; there in the soft dim light that filtered its way through the window, she gently let her clothes slip to the floor, before creeping into bed beside Jenna, wearing only her bra and pants.

Jeany felt her tenuous state of consciousness drifting into a sphere of sublime relaxation, as the fresh clean sheets embraced her semi-naked body. Unlike Jeany, Jenna's blood was pulsating with adrenaline and excitement as she felt the warmth of another woman's body soft and yielding next to hers. Without a word being spoken, Jenna unclipped Jeany's bra from the front and laid her breasts bare, pulling back the sheets. The yellow street lights that filtered gently through the shuttered blinds, criss-crossed the bed and across the bedroom wall. She was not voluptuous, but was perfect in form; her nipples had become erect in response to the cool night air wafting over her exposed skin. Her breasts were soft and even, as she breathed gently.

Jenna lay there and admired her as she slept. At long last, her recurrent fantasy could now be realised and the focus of her hunger lay prostrate beside her. Her smooth warm hands slid with ease over Jeany's limp body, over her flat stomach and up and over her warm breasts, pausing for a moment in order to titillate her nipples further, causing them to be even more firm and erect than they were before. Jenna moved slowly and deliberately like a recoiling snake; she shuffled down, so that her face hovered over Jeany's breasts. With great stealth she lowered her full lips onto her erect nipple sending Jeany's body into an erotic spasm, as each and every muscle in her body tensed up. Instinctively Jeany's arm curled round the back of Jenna's head and embraced her, a response that sent Jenna's heart racing, for in her mind, this was the sign of approval, and one that she had been waiting for.

With great care not to break the spell she now had over Jeany, she moved her now flushed lips tingling with passion up towards Jeany's. Her body sliding, flesh against flesh, upwards until their lips met. At first the kiss was soft and affectionate, so slight that it was barely a kiss at all. In her mind these were the lips of Jason and to these tender moves she responded. With her eyes still closed, she threw herself into a frenzied kiss, casting aside the bedclothes. They grappled with each other each in their own fabricated reality.

Jenna's hands now gravitated from her upper torso and slim waist down to her thighs, cupping her genitalia in the palm of her hand. Jeany's once limp body, now responded by throwing itself into agonising twisting movements as if her inner parts had minds of their own, writhing, moving as if she were riding on an invisible wave of sheer ecstasy.

Jenna's slender and dextrous hands gravitated with the skills of a surgeon and the stealth of a serpent to stimulate and enthral. Jeany was rendered powerless to resist Jenna's wishes. For Jenna her long held dream had taken over and the fantasy she had been nurturing was now unfolding as she had dreamt it would, and no level of restraint was able to stem the flow. Jenna swung her body around bringing her face up against Jeany's nether regions, burying her face into her groin. The level of erotic stimulation was now taken to another level, forcing Jeany's body to writhe with uncontrollable ecstasy. She at last succumbed and reached climax twice before her body couldn't take any more, as tears of release flowed from here.

Jenna at once recovered the bedding and the pillows that had been displaced during the encounter, pulling the sheets back over the naked body of her conquest. Jeany laid there in a state of enraptured release. Jenna sat there and gazed down at her quarry and felt confident that she and Jeany would now be bonded from this night on.

Though Jeany appeared to be asleep and at peace with herself, her mind was anything but. Now awoken by thoughts of Jason, her mind clicked into overdrive wondering and worrying about where he was and how he was feeling. The rude awareness that he must still be out there alone, cold and on the run, made her feel guilty. She had managed to find an inner strength from out of the ordeal and had secured a sanctuary of sorts, albeit a temporary one. Jason had neither. As both of them lay there in each other's arms, one of them was not pre-occupied with the other, but concerned about an absent partner and a lost opportunity for a better life.

ENTER INSPECTOR FANG

In the morning Jenna rose early and was busy preparing breakfast, when Jeany surfaced from the crumpled bed clothes, only to find she was all alone in the large double bed. She wasn't sure if she had been dreaming about Jason or had she really succumbed to Jenna's advances. As the realisation of what she had allowed the night before sank in, she realized the complexity of the predicament she now found herself in. A hot wave of embarrassment swept over her as she sank into the bedding. She then cleared her throat, composed herself and slipped out of bed. Without a murmur, she gathered up her clothes from the bedside chair and got dressed.

She was still somewhat embarrassed at her lack of resolve, that she had allowed herself to be groomed and predated upon by someone she had trusted. With her mind full of recriminations she ambled into the living room only to find that Jenna had prepared breakfast for her. Now wasn't the time or place to get angry at her for taking advantage of her physical and emotional state or was Jeany to blame for putting herself in that situation when she knew what type of woman Jenna was, and should have known what she wanted?

Jeany gave her a polite smile and sat down at the table, to eat breakfast. It was a simple breakfast of soy milk and warm bread, but it was the much needed sustenance her body so badly craved. As she sat there at the table she kept her thoughts to herself. Too much had happened and she needed much more time to process the events into some kind of rationale. Jenna could only guess at what was going through Jeany's mind and in order to avoid misunderstandings, she kept a cap on her curiosity and minimised her topics of conversation to the approaching winter and the Christmas sales. Jeany broke the tedious small talk first.

"Have you been able to get in touch with your contact in Beijing?" she asked, looking directly into Jenna's eyes. She smiled, relieved that she hadn't shown any revulsion about the previous night's sexual encounter.

"Yes, I emailed him earlier this morning. I told him about the rape and the local police involvement in the attack and asked him to get back to me with the name of a trusted investigator. So we'll have to wait and see. He'll reply today I'm sure. He's usually very reliable."

For Jeany, the events of the previous night would remain an issue not for discussion and for her that would be an end to it.

It was Jenna's turn to be on a late shift at the hospital and so she had time to consolidate whatever bond she could establish with Jeany by helping her quest for justice. Hers was an unrealistic goal, pursued only by the insane and the suicidal. Still Jenna believed that by standing by her in her hour of need, this would re-enforce their friendship and build mutual trust. She envisaged a relationship with Jeany and one that would last into the foreseeable future.

Although Jenna wasn't concerned about Jason, she was worried that he might reappear. There was a chance that he was out of the country, and so would never be allowed to re-enter China. Unless of course he was captured and dragged before the courts to face charges. In that case he would suffer the ultimate penalty for the murder of Bo-Cheng. Neither scenario posed a problem, which pleased and encouraged her in her quest for Jeany's heart.

At eleven in the morning, Jenna was busy doing the laundry which left Jeany alone to mull over the events of the last year. She was struggling to understand what, if anything, she had done to deserve such a cruel turn of events. Bo-Cheng had divorced her and had kept turning up to harass her. She had lost her only son in Tian-a-Men Square that June and now she had lost her lover and her only ticket to happiness. And now, to top it all, she had unwittingly been forced into the arms of a lesbian, albeit her good friend.

As she sat there wallowing in self-pity, it dawned on her that if she so wished, she could return to the language school and continue her studies, as if none of this week had ever happened. Yes, there'd be whisperings she thought, and of course Pepper may still be there. It didn't really matter that her old teacher wasn't there. Just because he was no longer on the scene, this was no reason to deny herself an education, despite the whisperings behind her back.

Though to be seen to be cohabiting with a known lesbian and so soon after Jason's disappearance was one indiscretion she could do without. At this moment she needed help and support and the kind of kinship she was unable to get from any man. With a man, she would have to consent to his wishes in order to get that support and for that, she had no appetite. For the moment she decided to bide her time, but she promised herself that the bed sharing would stop and that from now she would take the sofa and take back the control of her life.

Later that morning, Jenna received a call from a colleague at the hospital, saying that a policeman had been there making enquiries. He'd asked for Jenna's address and phone number. He'd made similar enquiries about Jin-Mei, as they'd not been able to contact her at her known home address. When Jenna told Jeany about the call, she assumed that this may be someone who had arrived in Shijiazhuang on account of Jenna's email some hours earlier. Jeany suspected that the policeman's enquiries were more likely to do with Jason, she guessed. She was sure that Mr fat man Zang Fei-Liao hadn't made a complaint because if he had, the police would have been there in force. The not knowing was in itself worrying her. After all she'd been through, what else could possibly go wrong?

Half an hour later, Jenna received yet another call, this time from an Inspector Fang saying that he would be calling round to pay her a short visit and asking if she knew the whereabouts of Jin-Mei. She confirmed that they were both at her apartment and would be there for the next hour or so. Jeany felt a sense of relief, for now she'd be able to tell her story and get the attack legally documented. Her only concern was the integrity of this policeman. Would he be like so many others and close ranks on her? Would he end up defending Bo-Cheng's actions and those of his men?

As they sat in silence, they were startled by a sharp knock on the door. Jenna answered it and came face to face with a tall, elegant gentleman in his mid-thirties. He wore a finely tailored suit and carried a briefcase, a far cry from the toady, uncouth policemen that Jeany had been used to seeing in her years as a policeman's wife.

"I'm Inspector Fang. I called earlier," he said as he reached out his hand to shake Jenna's.

"Oh please come in and take a seat," she said as she showed him the leather sofa. Inspector Fang smiled and entered the room. Without a word, he headed straight for the sofa, planting himself in a comfortable position next to Jeany, who then shuffled her rear end away in an attempt to put some space between her and the inspector, unsure of where to put herself.

"Would you like some oolong tea?" Jenna asked as she stood over the inspector and the dumbfounded Jeany.

"Yes please," he replied, he then turned and looked Jeany straight in the face.

"Ah and you must be Jin-Mei, yes?"

"Yes, but you can call me Jeany," she said.

"Jeany, I don't want to take up too much of your time, so I'll get straight to the point. I'm investigating the brutal attack on four of our officers, one of whom was the Chief of Police, a Mr Nie Bo-Cheng, your husband I believe?"

"Yes, he used to be."

"There was some discrepancy in identifying who it was who committed the attack, but we now know from the injured parties, that it was your foreign friend Jason Lamont. I believe you and he were involved in a relationship of sorts, is that true?" The tea arrived on the table immediately in front of them.

"Yes, but I haven't seen him since he set off for Beijing. I was at the hotel where I'm told the murder happened, but I didn't see anything," she said sheepishly.

"Murder? I never said there'd been a murder," said the inspector.

"But I thought."

"No Jeany — no one was hurt that badly — but bad enough to imply that he intended to do them grievous bodily harm, worthy of a lengthy prison term for sure," said the inspector looking at Jeany, with the same kind of look her father used to give her, when she had forgotten her times tables.

"That night I was driven home by one of the policemen, the same one that had raped me the day before. His name is Zang Fei-Liao. You know my husband – it was he who gave those animals the order to rape me – he's one of yours," snapped Jeany.

"You were raped? Why haven't you reported this to the police before now?" the inspector asked, with a shocked look.

"When the police do such things, where am I supposed to turn? Who can I complain to? The answer is – to no one," she said looking the inspector straight in the eyes. She pointed to Jenna.

"That's who you can trust – your friends – that's all," she remarked as she exchanged a smile with Jenna. The inspector picked up his case and extracted a small note book and cleared his throat.

"When you left the hotel, who was in the foyer?"

"There was the receptionist, he was keeping out of the way behind the bar area. Then there was Bo-Cheng and his four men – those that raped me."

"Okay and who else?"

"Oh and Pepper Lee, she was there with Bo-Cheng, arm in arm. She's Bo-Cheng's girlfriend now, so she said. I'm not jealous," said Jeany shaking her head. Inspector Fang smiled.

"What do you know about this Pepper Lee character?" The inspector scribbled in his tiny book.

"I don't know anything only that she's Taiwanese."

"Mm, Taiwanese eh!" said the inspector.

"Her name isn't in any of the injured party's reports, I wonder why?" The inspector gazed at Jeany looking for an answer, but none was forthcoming.

"You said that no one was killed, so that means Bo-Cheng is alright? He's alive? Is that what you're saying?" Jeany asked although horrified, to know that he was still out there.

"He's in hospital and will be for a while, so don't worry," said the Inspector with a warm smile. Jenna knelt down to ask him a question that had been puzzling her.

"Why did Jason say he'd killed them when he hadn't? Does that mean he's on the run believing he's a murderer, when he isn't?"

"Yes that's how it looks to us, although he is still a criminal on the run, whether he's killed someone or not," said the inspector in a stern voice.

"What would you have done if some men raped your wife? What would you do?" Jeany demanded.

"As an officer of the law, I'd have to say, that's exactly why we have the police around to protect us and administer justice," he said not looking too convinced. "I can understand Mr Lamont's motives but we can't make exceptions. Under the law we're all liable. We aren't animals and we do occasionally make allowances," explained the inspector as he rested his hand on Jeany's. She snatched her hand away as a wave of repulsion ran through her. Inspector Fang shook off the rebuff and continued. "We always take into account all the mitigating circumstances when sentencing prisoners, taking into account the level of provocation for example," he explained as he closed his notebook and raised his cup of tea.

"So Jenna, you were there then?" He asked searchingly, as he turned his attention towards Jenna, she paused for a moment.

"We were just about to pick up Jeany, when we saw her being driven away in a police car. That's when Jason jumped out of my car and ran straight into the hotel.

There was some kind of disturbance and he ran back, saying he had killed all of them. I didn't want anything to do with him or whatever had gone on. I just wanted him to leave, so I dropped him off at some bus stop on the road to Beijing."

"Can you recall which bus stop?"

"I don't remember, but he'd be long gone by now," she replied. Fang turned to Jeany.

"Where would he go?"

"I don't know, maybe the airport or over the border into Vladivostok. I really don't know. Why are you trying to catch him when rapists are getting away with whatever they like?"

"At what time did you drop him off?"

"About two o clock in the morning," replied Jenna.

"Okay that covers that, but before I leave, I need to give you these to fill in. Statement declaration forms. Please write in the time, date and place then put down what you saw and what you did. No assumptions and no opinions, okay? One set is for the hotel incident and the other is for the rape allegation. Bo-Cheng cannot be charged with rape, but inciting others to break the law is in itself a crime. I can assure you that he was in no way following normal police procedures when he ordered his men to do that," Fang said as he got to his feet.

"Here's my card. Do contact me if you hear from Jason, and of course call me when you've completed the forms. As for the rape, if it can be proved that he instigated the attack and his men are found guilty, they will be formally charged and face the full might of the law. I promise you that. They're all still in the infirmary and quite accessible, that gives us time to proceed with our enquiries. As for this Officer Zang Fei-Liao, I'll be interviewing him later today about the rape." Fang shook hands again with both of them and left.

His manner was far removed from the bully boy mentality of Bo-Cheng's circle. It made a refreshing change. By one o'clock, Jenna had gone to work, leaving Jeany alone. She was still in no state to go out and about, although she had made her mind up that when Jenna came back from work, they would both go out and try to relax over a late night meal. With that in mind she crept back into bed and stayed there, out of public scrutiny and out of harm's way.

Meanwhile, at the Shijiazhuang medical infirmary Bo-Cheng and his three comrades were recuperating in a specially assigned side ward in the head and neck department. As Bo-Cheng lay there, his neck supported by an oversized brace, his eyes were fixed on the clock, as second by second it crept towards visiting time. As the clock struck three, the noise of visitors could be heard, as they chatted and clattered down the highly polished ward. He looked up at the curtain as the tall, slim figure of Pepper Lee stepped into view, pulling it aside. She was lavishly dressed in a red patent leather mini skirt and long black socks that came just over the knee and short patent leather boots. She had over done the foundation and wore garish glossy lipstick and a low cut top designed to raise Bo-Cheng's spirits.

"Why all the fancy make up?" he snarled.

"I've a black eye and bruises on my neck. You wouldn't want me to waltz in here looking like a beaten up hooker, would you?" she retorted, as she looked down on Bo-Cheng.

"Never mind that, listen, I have two assignments for you. The first is that I need you to make it up with my ex and her lesbian friend. Say sorry or something, then you can find out where lover boy is hiding. Once you know, come and tell me – but no one else needs to know – just me, okay?" Pepper smiled.

"That shouldn't be a problem. If they know where he is, I'll be able to find out. I'm sure Jie-Na will tell me, I have a way with such women," she said with a wicked smile on her face. "What else do you need doing?" she asked, as she brushed her long silky black hair back from her face.

"Just in case that bitch takes it upon herself to press charges not that I did anything wrong, mind you, I feel she should be encouraged to keep her mouth shut. Maybe she could have an accident or maybe the boys would enjoy another session with her and give her a real going over. Maybe then she won't be so keen to mess with us," suggested Bo-Cheng. Pepper smiled and admired her long finger nails.

"I like the accident option. Rape is messy and there is always one do-gooder ready to turn informer to advance his promotional prospects, agree?"

"You're right, do it," he replied. Pepper looked down on Bo-Cheng as he lay prostrate with each limb and body part heavily bandaged.

"Leave it to me Bo-Bo. After all this has been done, when do I get the apartment you promised me?" she asked.

"When everything's cooled down and Jin-Mei is out of the way, that's when," he growled through clenched teeth.

"Right then, I have a lot to do, I need to go now," said Pepper, as she turned, and with an exaggerated swagger left the ward catching everyone's eye as she did.

Later, after lights out, whilst the patients slept, a middle-aged nurse crept into Bo-Cheng's cubicle. She leaned over him and gently kissed him. He immediately responded throwing his arms around her waist. Together they embraced. Her soft whispers were barely audible in the dead of night. Her hand caressed his upper body and then snaked under the bed sheets. Her soft lips touched his. She whispered through tears.

"I wish things could have been different Bo. You know I love you. You do know, don't you?" Bo-Cheng embraced her. She tidied his bedding and gave him a loving kiss. Then with as much stealth as she had appeared, she was gone, back behind the curtain and vanished without a sound along the deserted dimly lit ward.

Jason Goes Into Hiding

The wild chicken bus, without so much as an announcement pulled over and stopped on a dark gravely makeshift lay-by that seemed miles from anywhere. After all the passengers had disembarked into the early morning mist, Jason realised that he was now alone, a last solitary passenger at the rear of the bus. He hadn't the foggiest idea where he was or even how far it was to his eventual destination. The driver stood up and stared down the aisle at him.

"Beijing dao-le," he shouted. Jason got to his feet.

"Where are we?" he asked as he stepped down from the coach. The driver pointed down the haze covered road.

"Beijing, that way," he said, he then slammed closed the vehicle's doors and sped off into the night towards Beijing.

This left him at the side of the road with no option but to start walking. It wasn't long before the cold morning frost began to penetrate his thick leather jacket. Just a short distance along the darkened road he was relieved to see readable road signs, directing him to Beijing, written in Chinese characters and in Romanised 'pin-yin'.

It soon became obvious that the local taxi drivers knew that the illegal wild chicken buses dropped off their illicit passengers here, some distance away from the city in order not to be detected, for as he made his way along the dark desolate roadside, numerous taxis would pass him at a snail's pace offering their services much to his annoyance. He had no idea how far it was to the zoo and having many hours in hand, getting a taxi just wasn't practical. He needed to get some thinking done and clear his head, he soon realised that this was easier said than done.

As he rounded a bend, he came across a public park where an old man was practising his early morning Tai-Chi-Chuan.

"How far is it to Beijing Zoo?" he asked. The old man turned and smiled exposing his discoloured spindle like teeth and pointed down the road.

"Go north, and keep going for two kilometres, that will take you to the north west of the city," he said still smiling.

"How long will it take?"

"It's two kilometres. You decide how fast you walk," laughed the old man returning to his exercises.

Jason thought for a moment and then saw the funny side of what he had said and smiled back him. With that, he set off at a leisurely pace, preoccupied with the problems he would need to overcome. He thought long and hard about how he was going to organise his exodus from China. With the authorities looking for him, he wouldn't be able to use his passport or even his real name. He assumed that Jeany, being in custody and under extreme duress, would tell them whatever they needed to know. He wouldn't blame her for that. He had to assume that what she knew about him, they now also knew.

He had nowhere else to go and no-one else to turn to but Bunny. Douglas was back in the United Kingdom and too far removed from what was going on to help. He considered that his current situation had not as yet, become critical enough to be calling on Douglas's assistance, but he felt that such a moment was fast approaching. He looked down the road into the morning mist grim faced and tearful. He couldn't believe how suddenly his fate had turned, for here he was returning to Bunny's in less than twenty four hours after leaving her. He hadn't taken off his jacket or even his shoes since he'd last seen her. His comfortable, stable lifestyle had collapsed around him without warning.

It wasn't long before he reached the broad paved concourse outside the zoo gates. It was just twilight and far too early to be knocking on anyone's door, lest he were to alert the whole area of his presence. Wishing not to be too conspicuous, he retreated to the high brick perimeter wall of the zoo and made himself comfortable, still ruminating over what lousy cards life's fickle fate had dealt him.

He sat some distance from the road and drifted to sleep. A while later he heard the muffled noise of a patrol car cruising by. He gasped as it turned into a side street and headed in the direction of Bunny's apartment. For one terrible moment he convinced himself that they were up there looking for him. It then re-emerged a moment later, having not had enough time to have even stopped. Now was a good time to call Douglas he thought, as he searched his pockets for the mobile that Bunny had given him. He switched it on and scrolled down through the endless list of Chinese names until he got to an abbreviated 'Doughy. M'. He reckoned it would be about midnight back in London, so Douglas should be available. The phone rang a few times, and then a cheerful voice at the other end of the line responded.

"Yes Bunny. What now?"

"It's not Bunny, it's me Jason," he whispered, not wishing to be overheard speaking English in the quietness of the cold night air.

"Ah, so it is. What seems to be the problem?" Douglas asked in a patient voice.

"It's a long story, but I need to get out of China, but I can't use my passport. I need an alternative exit plan. Do you have one?" he asked, knowing that Douglas nearly always had another plan up his sleeve.

"Ask Bunny to introduce you to my old friend Wang. He'll sort you out," said Douglas calmly.

"I'll do that. Better go now."

He felt relieved that Douglas hadn't given him the third degree. If anything had happened to Bunny since he had last seen her, Douglas would have known. Her apartment must still be a safe haven, at least for the time being. Confident that she was fine he relaxed and bade his time; with his back against the zoo's cold perimeter wall he began to doze off, despite the cold November winds that curled around his squatted form. He drifted deeper and deeper into sleep.

When he opened his eyes, he was startled by the number of people milling around him. He sat bolt upright. The frontage of the zoo was teeming with visitors and street vendors, many of whom would have sauntered past him as he lay sprawled out on the freezing cold pavement. Those passing by would, no doubt, have assumed that he was just one more of those strange foreigners who had overdone their intake of alcohol. Had he not been so out of it, he would have surely drawn more attention to himself.

He scrambled to his feet, dusted himself down and rubbed his numbed legs. He made straight for the main gate, paid his entrance fee and headed straight for the comfort of the zoo's cafe. Although there was quite a large presence of police in the vicinity, the number of foreign visitors was large enough for him to mingle in and go unnoticed.

Once in the café, he ordered a coffee and retired to his favourite location near the window and the cast iron radiator. A small group of tourists came in, with loud Australian accents. They assembled themselves around a central table, from where they ordered beers and three plates of cheese and pickle sandwiches. He watched them, reassured by the presence of other westerners.

Just then, a young Chinese girl entered the cafe. She had long black silky hair that was plaited into two pigtails, which hung long and low below her exposed shoulders. Her dress was a beautiful crimson, low cut at the front and cut short at the hem and overlaid with fine embroidered chiffon. She approached the men and chatted playfully for some time with them before walking across to Jason, conspicuous as he sat there alone.

"Would you like some company?" she asked in a soft voice. He looked up into her dark eyes that could have melted a man's soul. She was barely eighteen but made up like a true catwalk professional. Her plaited hair gave her a school girl appearance. Her girlish demure and facade of innocence was probably used to seduce the latent paedophilic tendencies in her potential clients, he surmised. She leant towards him.

"Well, would you?"

"Sorry love, I don't have any money," he said, as he warmed his hands round his cup of coffee.

"I never asked you for money, did I?"

"No you didn't, but I assumed you were about to offer me a service. You'll have to forgive me if I've misread your intentions," he said.

"I was only trying to find out if you were staying in the area and needed an escort. I know a woman who can show you around and also a good time if that's what you want. Well? Are you going to let me sit down for a while and let me tell you about her? She's very beautiful," she said as she repositioned a chair and sat next to Jason, with a smile. She lowered herself down onto the chair, crossing her legs in a deliberate and provocative manner and monitored his response. She positioned herself broadside to the table, exposing the soft white flesh of her upper thigh. She saw his eyes shift in a downwards direction and smiled knowingly. He then repositioned his attention to her long, dark, almond shaped eyes.

"What's your name?" he asked, as he studied her face, her deep crimson lips both sensuous and pert. Her dress was provocative but he detected a kind of vulnerability in those deep set eyes and a look that spoke volumes. This was no hardened working girl, but a sweet young woman peddling the services of another.

"My name is Yu-Me, and you, do you have a name?" she asked still smiling.

"I'm called Jason and before you say anything else, I'm only interested in meeting one woman here in Beijing."

"You're meeting your wife?" she asked jokingly.

"No. She's called Bunny," he explained, sure that she would at least have heard about her. Yu-Mei burst into laughter.

"That's my friend, the one I was going to tell you about," she declared as she clapped her hands.

"Ah, now I can see her mark on your coat. So you've been with her then?" she asked, full of glee.

"She's a real dominatrix, did she tie you up?"

"Mind your own business. I just need to know where she is, do you know?" Yu-Me stopped smiling and got up, extracted a mobile phone from her red leather handbag and wandered a short distance away to make a call. A moment later she returned, as did her contagious smile.

"Yes she's at work today, she said she told you her schedule, she did didn't she? You know she looks after an old man, so she can't see you today," she explained in a soft consoling voice. He thought for a moment, then reached across the table and grabbed both her hands, perspiration oozed from his brow as he pleaded, a look of desperation etched across his face.

"Do you know anywhere I can stay until I'm able to see her?" he asked as he stared at her with the intensity of a man being pursued by the devil. The idea of spending one more night out in the open where he could die of exposure or worse still be identified, were not options he was willing to consider.

"You said you had no money. Even I have to pay my rent every week. Bunny helps me out and pays me for selecting suitable clients for her business. If I put you up you will need to help me pay my rent," she said as she pulled her hands free of Jason's.

"Look – I have money for rent. What I meant earlier, was that I don't have spare money to pay for companionship. That kind of money I don't have," he explained.

"How much would you accept, to put me up for a couple of nights?" he asked.

"How about a hundred ren-min-bi a night and another twenty for a cooked breakfast, agree?" She raised her eyebrows and smiled. Jason grinned and then reached over and shook her hand.

"Jason, I've spoken to Bunny, so I know you're legitimate. You need to understand that if you're staying with me, you will have to keep your hands to yourself and behave. I'm a good girl, believe it or not, and I have a nice boyfriend. Touch me and I'll call the police, do you understand?" she said in a stern voice.

"Hold on Yu-Me, no one is going to touch anyone. Did Bunny say I was like that?"

"No, but when you sleep in my room, I need to feel safe. If all you need is a place to stay and you can help me pay my rent, I'm happy with that," she said.

"How do you say it? No hanky-panky." Jason just laughed.

"You got it, no hanky-panky, I promise and I really do appreciate your help," he said as tears of gratitude welled up just below the surface. She jumped to her feet and grabbed his hand.

"Okay let's go," she said as she pulled him up onto his feet and with her arm linked in his, they headed for the main gates. The ticketing lady, who had laughed when he had left with Bunny, seemed to recognise him and gave him a friendly wave as he left with Yu-Me. He gave her a smile, although embarrassed that he must have looked like a hungry man with an inexhaustible appetite for the pleasures of the flesh.

From the large exit gates, they made their way across the paved concourse and across the road towards the apartment block where Bunny lived. She led the way into the complex, entered the tower block and then ascended the unlit stairwell, onto what looked like the very same landing as Bunny's. They made their way along and past Bunny's apartment and then stopped a few doors down where they walked straight into Yu-Me's unlocked apartment.

On entering the small room, memories of his time with Bunny came flooding back, for both rooms were very similar in size and design. The bed, the cupboard and the wardrobe were all in exactly the same position as in Bunny's room. The only extra item of furniture was a two-seater sofa pushed up against the side wall.

"That's your bed if you want it," she said as she pointed to the black leather sofa.

"Yes, that'll do fine," he said as he gave her a smile of approval. She stepped back and lowered her eyes to the ground.

"Can you pay me now, before I leave?" she asked in a quiet voice.

"Of course, I nearly forgot." She frowned.

"I shouldn't have to ask. What would people think? Here I am alone in my bedroom with a foreigner, having to ask for money. That's not very nice is it?" she said.

"Sorry Yu-Me. I never thought."

"You surprise me."

"I promise to be more tactful in future."

"Thank you, now I need to pay my rent," she said smiling. After throwing his bags onto the sofa, he reached into his leather jacket pocket and withdrew his wallet from which he extracted two red bank notes.

"Will two hundred Ren-Min-Bi be enough?" he asked as he handed her the crisp red notes. If you need a little more I can let you have it tomorrow." Yu-Me's face lit up on seeing the money, for she had defaulted on her rent recently and was facing the possibility of eviction. "There's nothing in here that a gentleman would steal, so don't worry about your belongings. They'll be safe with me," he said.

"I have to leave you now. I still owe the landlord last month's rent, but thanks to you I will almost be up to date," she said, as tears welled up in her eyes. He then glanced back into his wallet and then pulled out yet another two hundred Ren-Min-Bi.

"Here take this, it will cover my expenses for tomorrow," he said as he handed over two more crisp, clean red bank notes to her. She looked directly into his eyes.

"You have to remember what I said about me being a good girl. I am grateful for the money but all I can offer you is that sofa and breakfast, nothing more," she explained, as she tucked the notes into her small pink purse.

"I wouldn't have it any other way," he said as he slumped down onto the sofa next to his bags.

"Now I really do have to go," and with that she left him alone. The room was small and compact, and yet warm and inviting. As his body sunk into the soft leather sofa, it seemed to embrace his tired spirit and once again he succumbed to a state of slumber while still clutching his bag, as if it were a thing of endearment.

Just as he was drifting off to sleep he was shaken by a sharp knock on the door. He rubbed his eyes and then took a long hard look at his watch. It was already midday. He froze, in the hope that whoever it was that was knocking would give up and go away. Once again he heard the rapping of knuckles on the door. He sat upright and stared at the door unsure if it was locked or not. It was all too easy for him to imagine a bunch of burly grim faced policemen dashing in, intent on pinning him to the floor and then dragging him out to wherever.

The knocking ceased and silence returned to the small dwelling. He sighed. Then to his horror, a young man's face appeared at the window, with his nose and forehead pushed hard against the glass. Jason realised that the young Chinese boy peering through the window didn't seem to pose too much of a threat to him and was probably a friend of Yu-Me's. He got up and opened the door.

"There's no-one here, just me," explained Jason.

"I'm Yu-Me's boyfriend. Are you going to let me in then?" he asked, his eyes seem to stare right through Jason.

"Oh, yes of course, sorry. Yu-Me said I could stay here for a couple of days. Did she tell you about me?"

"No, but I'm not surprised; she's too kind for her own good, but if it's okay with her, who am I argue? we trust each other. We've been through a lot," he said. The young man was about eighteen years of age, clean cut and had a fresh complexion. He was tall with short cropped hair and a strangely familiar smile that Jason found endearing. He had an intelligent demeanour that was more befitting to a man ten years his senior. He went across and sat on Yu-Me's bed, kicking off his shoes as he did.

"Everyone knows me by my English name 'Peter.' I've just recently been let out of prison. Don't get me wrong I'm not a crook or an evil person. I was in the wrong place at the wrong time, if you know what I mean."

"I'm sorry to hear that," Jason replied as a twinge of guilt initiated a moment of embarrassment. He wondered what this young man would think of him if he knew what kind of crime Jason had recently perpetrated.

"I was arrested along with a large number of others while protesting in Tian-a-Men Square. We faced trial and I got six months, although I got let out a couple of weeks early for good behaviour. We're still in the democracy movement, though it's an underground movement now,"

"We know about you, we were told that you, Bunny and Douglas were going to get the tapes out," he whispered as he looked around. Jason whispered back, eager to get his own problem out into the open.

"Yes that's true but first there's something you ought to know. At the moment, I'm on the run from the police," he admitted, aware that this alone could jeopardise their hopes of getting the tapes out safely.

"What have you done that was so bad?" Peter asked with a worried look on his face.

"I killed four policemen, one of whom was the Chief of Police – some pig called Bo-Cheng," he declared, glad to be getting it off his chest. Peter was visibly taken aback by this revelation.

"Are you sure you actually killed Bo-Cheng? We haven't heard that on the grapevine and I think we would have been told if he'd been murdered," insisted Peter, with a hint of despair in his voice.

"Did you know him?" Jason asked.

"Yes I knew him, but then who didn't? There was a time when Bo-Cheng was destined for high office but he had a messy affair with someone's wife. The husband never found out, but the affair still managed to ruin his future prospects in the Politburo," explained Peter. As he talked about Bo-Cheng, there was a sense that he had some kind of sympathy with the man. The young man lay back on the bed and cupped his hands over his face, as if stifling tears. He then sat up and rubbed his eyes.

"No one can say he didn't deserve to die, but to kill him was one part brave and nine parts stupid, wasn't it?" he declared.

"I agree, but what now?"

"Tell me, how did you get involved with Bo-Cheng in the first place?" he asked curious as to why Jason had done such a foolhardy thing, and especially in a country that cared little for the human rights of prisoners.

"It all began when I met Jeany," began Jason.

"Who's Jeany?"

"Her real name was Jin-Mei and she was one of my students when I taught English in Shijiazhuang."

"What was her family name?" he asked, sitting up straight on the bed.

"Nie, her name was Nie Jin-Mei." Peter's face turned ashen. He looked down and shook his head in disbelief.

"Don't tell me she was Bo-Cheng's wife," he said amazed at Jason's talent for landing himself in the proverbial.

"She was his ex-wife. They were divorced and so she was free to see who she wanted," retorted Jason.

"Okay, go on," said Peter.

"As you know I came here to meet with Douglas and in doing so I met Bunny," explained Jason.

"Ah, Bunny, then what happened?"

"Well, we formulated this plan and I returned to Shijiazhuang, so far so good." Peter lay back down.

"Then what?" he asked with intense concentration etched across his face.

"When I arrived back in Shijiazhuang, Jeany had already been attacked by Bo-Cheng's men. Then her friend Jenna told me they were after me and that I was next. This Jenna woman then took her to a roadside hotel near Bao-Ding for her own safety. She left her there and returned to pick me up me at the Central station. When we got to the hotel she was being driven away in a patrol car. I haven't seen her since. That's when I lost it. I stormed into the foyer only to see that pig and his men enjoying a beer.

It was then I picked up a chair and went berserk. He was going for his firearm so I had to whack him. I had no choice and there's no turning the clock back, not now," he explained.

"You didn't need to charge in there like some rabid dog, did you?" Peter challenged, still struggling to understand Jason's loss of control.

"Douglas told us you were a very cool character, used to working under pressure. From what you say, you've behaved like a hot-head, and thrown away everything you had for a woman, and a woman who wasn't even yours," argued Peter.

"She's a person, and as such she doesn't belong to anyone. She's free to do what she likes," retorted Jason, exasperated.

"And you felt you were free to do what you liked, yes?"

"No, it wasn't like that."

"No? I suggest that you felt that being a foreigner, you could do what you liked and get away with it. That's the truth isn't it? Anyway, you can forget her now. No one will ever see her again, believe me. Why couldn't you have left her alone to deal with her husband?" Peter's said with his fists clenched.

"I'd do it again, I loved her," insisted Jason.

"I believe you, but what you did was paramount to suicide. For whatever reason it was a dumb move, agree?" said Peter.

"Yes I'll agree with you there," he admitted and shrugged his shoulders.

"Now we need to think about your assignment," said Peter with a business-like tone in his voice. "We need to plan your exit, and to begin with, we'll need to alter your appearance," he said. I'm not going to involve Yu-Me and Bunny anymore in this operation. As far as you are concerned you only deal with Wang and myself," he said with some authority. We both want the same thing and that is for you to leave China as soon as possible, although in your case being quick isn't our priority, your personal safety is. So it may take a bit longer than expected."

"How long will I have to wait?"

"How long is a noodle?"

"Can we make it sooner, rather than later?"

"Yes we'll try," replied Peter with a smile.

"So did you get arrested during the protest?" Jason asked.

"Yes, I was one of the lucky ones."

"Where are your family?" he asked, curious as to why he hadn't gone straight home after being released.

"I can't go back while there are brothers still incarcerated, and in any case it would be too dangerous for us to go home. We are marked people. The police and secret agents still keep an eye on us. We wouldn't want to bring turmoil and trouble back to our families," he explained.

"Can't you even tell them that you are alive and well? That wouldn't hurt would it?" Jason asked.

"It isn't that simple. They'd want to visit and spend time with us and this would expose them to possible victimisation. So for the time being, we remain dead, and when the situation changes according to each of our individual circumstances, then we will be reunited with them. But not now," explained Peter.

"What future do you have as a non-person?"

"We have a future. Next year, Yu-Me and I hope to get married. We'll tell our families then. But first we need to get you safely out of the country. Yu-Me said that she'd bring some black hair dye with her and some round clear glass spectacles to alter your appearance from how you look now. As a foreigner you're always going to attract attention. Just don't get paranoid. Government spies are not everywhere. Informers are, so watch what you say. We also need you to look older, so no shaving," he said, amused at the shocked expression on Jason's face.

"Me, with a beard? You're going to have me looking like old Douglas Murphy before too long," he jested as he scratched his salt and pepper chin, shuddering at the thought of wearing an itchy beard.

Just then the door opened and in walked Yu-Me. They embraced and then turned to Jason who still sat there contemplating the visual transformation that needed to be implemented. He felt humbled by the company he had found himself amongst. These young people were willing to risk all, even to face death to stand up for what they thought was right, albeit for their own reasons. In addition, they were going to risk all to get him out of China and in doing so, allow him to break free from the mess he had managed to get himself into.

He knew that he had put everyone at risk by his irrational and unacceptable actions. He'd been motivated by anger and had sought revenge in the heat of the moment. This wasn't the Jason of old, he used to be more calculating and divisive, not hot-tempered and brash as he had been on that regrettable night in Bao-Ding.

Yu-Me threw a box of hair dye on the bed and laughed.

"Sorry Jason, but you'll have to do it yourself," she said, laughing, as she threw her arms around Peter. Yu-Me pointed to the small hand basin and grinned.

"I'm sure you can manage to do your hair in that. If not, there's a toilet's in the back room along with a sizable bucket, that's if you haven't noticed it already," Yu-Me said with a grin. Peter had the last word.

"We have to go now, but I'll be back in a couple of hours. Then we'll introduce you to Wang. Keep your bags packed ready in case we have to leave in a hurry. And keep the curtains drawn. I'll lock you in and whatever you do, don't answer the door to anyone. You're not here," said Peter as he turned and left the room with a confused looking Yu-Me in tow.

Once the door had been locked and he had checked the curtains for exposing gaps, he threw off his leather jacket and with the hair dye in one hand, he headed for the hand basin to transform his fair but greying hair into a generic shade of black. After a great deal of painful neck bending, he managed to finish the dyeing process. He looked at himself in the small mirror that was pinned to the wall, his hair hung in ringlets, wet and bedraggled. The man staring back at him was rugged and far less sophisticated; it was as if this transformation reflected his internal deterioration, a kind of Jekyll and Hyde syndrome. Repulsed, he drew back from the image.

After a period of rest, the noise of the key turning in the lock awoke him from his siesta. As the door opened, the cold wind gushed in straight through his body, like an ice ghost escaping the daylight. Peter appeared in the doorway and behind him stood a thickset man, with the demeanour of one of those old time mafia bosses. His hair was black, greasy, brushed straight back from his strong, emotionless face and dark, deep set eyes. He was the kind of man that one would be wise not to tangle with.

"This is Mr Wang. He's the guy I told you about," said Peter as he stepped aside for Wang to shake his hand. Jason stood up and locked hands with the big man, wincing in pain as Wang's iron like grip took hold. On release, his hand not only throbbed, but it felt like each bone had been reassigned to a different position. Jason forced a smile that more resembled a grimace than a genuine smile. Peter smiled at Jason's tortured expression.

"Nice to meet you," croaked Jason, but Wang said nothing. Peter explained.

"Mr Wang has organised a place for you to stay until we can get you a safe passage out of Beijing and China. He'll visit you each day to see how you are and drop off some drink and noodles for you. We plan to hide you in the grounds of the zoo. Maybe later you can sneak onto a ship to Shang-Hai or something," explained Peter as he patted the big man on the back.

"What do I call you?" Jason asked, looking up at the big man.

"My name is Wang, call me Wang, everyone else does," he replied with just a hint of a smile. "I'm sorry, we need to go, I'll be back tomorrow at ten in the morning. We need your passport, must make some amendments. I know a man who can sort that for you, for a price," explained Wang. Peter got ready to leave.

"Don't worry about the money. We'll bill Douglas for that," said Peter, then they all left, once more locking the door behind them. Jason arranged his makeshift bedding and curled up back on the sofa.

After Wang had set off back to the zoo, Peter and Yu-Me visited Bunny. They tapped three times to be sure she wasn't busy. On this occasion she was free and invited them in. As Bunny made the tea, Yu-Me put forward her suggestion.

"Did Jason tell you about Jin-Mei getting attacked and hurt?" she asked.

"Yes, I know the whole story, I even know about that lesbian bitch who has now stepped in and is controlling things, taking advantage of Jin-Mei being weak and vulnerable. I already know everything; my informant told me the whole story. The situation isn't acceptable, what do you suggest?" Bunny asked turning to Peter.

"I can't go and help – not now – and not before the tape is out of China. Yu-Me needs to go and help," replied Peter, anxious that something needed to be done and soon.

"But isn't Jin-Mei in police custody?" Bunny asked.

"We don't know, but we need to find out," said Yu-Me, looking at Peter, who was too overwrought to say much at all.

"So we need to do something," said Bunny, then Yu-Me's face lit up, "Sha," she exclaimed.

"Yes of course, my aunt Sha. She lives opposite Jin-Mei doesn't she? She can put me up and that will give me time to find out where Jin-Mei is and get her back in her apartment and away from that Jenna." Yu-Me suggested as she gave Peter a reassuring look. Bunny set the tea down in front of everyone and smiled.

"If Jin-Mei isn't at her apartment, or if has moved out, how are you going to contact her and if she is in the local jail, who's to know?" Bunny asked. Yu-Mei seemed to have all the answers worked out.

"I can visit the hospital. It's usually crowded during the day, so no one will look twice at me as I walk round the wards," she explained.

"What if she is on night duty?" Bunny asked.

"Someone will tell me where she is and when she's on duty. If I ask around, I'll get all the information I need. If she's in trouble, the staff will tell me," replied Yu-Me.

"And what about this Jenna, won't she try to hang on to Jin-Mei somehow?" Peter said, as he rubbed his moist eyes.

"Don't worry Peter; no one is going to control her like her husband did, never again. Not if we can help it," said Bunny. Peter stood up and scratched his head.

"Jason said that he had killed Bo-Cheng, but I don't believe him," declared Peter.

"That doesn't sound true. Maybe he's mistaken," suggested Bunny.

"We haven't heard of anyone being killed in Shijiazhuang, surely we would have heard if a policeman had been murdered by a foreigner. Something doesn't add up," reasoned Peter as he slumped back down into his chair.

"That's why I have to go and find out for myself," explained Yu-Me.

"Can't we get Jason and Jin-Mei back together somewhere?" suggested Bunny.

"No way, he's trouble and the last thing Jin-Mei needs now is more trouble. No, keep them apart," snapped Peter.

"I thought you'd say that," laughed Bunny.

"Okay. I'll call my 'Aunt Sha' now and ask her if she'll be at home tomorrow," Yu-Me suggested in a determined voice. She then made a quick call on her mobile, mumbled some greetings and then asked when she'd be home.

"Well then what did she say?" Bunny asked.

"She's on nights now but she'll be home and awake after one o'clock in the afternoon. That means I can get the Wild-Chicken bus in the morning," said Yu-Me smiling. Peter gave her a big hug.

"Don't tell her I'm alive, not yet, not until that Jason has gone for good," Peter said, as he hid his face from Yu-Mei.

"Don't worry, she will be overjoyed one day, and soon," said Yu-Me as she gave him a hug.

"Then it will be my turn to have what I want," smiled Bunny.

"What do you mean?" asked Yu-Me, with a smile.

"I'm not telling, but I have plans and maybe Douglas can be very helpful." Bunny grinned.

The three settled down to sleep leaving Jason alone in Yu-Me's apartment. A storm raged throughout the night but that wasn't the reason for Jason's insomnia as the images of two spirits haunted him. As he tossed and turned, his dreams rocked back and forth between the contagious smile of Jeany and the fiery passion of Bunny. Locked between the angelic and the devilish, he desired both and yet he lay there alone and tormented.

Early in the morning, Yu-Me dressed in her smartest clothes and carrying her overnight case caught the local bus to a spot just south west of the city. There she picked up the 'Wild-Chicken' coach to Shijiazhuang. As the coach passed Bao-Ding, she kept a lookout for the hotel described in Jason's story. As the coach made one of its routine stops there, Yu-Me asked the driver to spare her three minutes to visit the ladies room. He nodded in agreement. She entered and saw the one lone bartender sat polishing glasses behind the bar.

"Bartender, is this where the policemen were murdered?" she asked.

"Yes. All dead they were," said the barman proudly. He lowered his voice to a whisper.

"Are you with the newspapers?"

"No, I'm a lawyer. Are you sure they were all dead?" she asked with a stern look on her face.

"Madam, now you mention it, no one died. I'm positive."

"Where did they take them?"

"Back to Shijiazhuang hospital I suppose. The foreigner escaped and good for him, that's what I say. I wish him luck," replied the barman, he then disappeared down into the cellar.

Yu-Me dashed back to the bus and continued her journey to Shijiazhuang with a smile on her face. 'And what of Jin-Mei, where was she? Was she in custody or at Jenna's or even back home in her apartment? Yu-Me asked herself. 'If I'm lucky I might get to see this Pepper Lee woman that Bunny told me about. Though how she ties in with everything that's going on, isn't clear,' she thought as she sat back and enjoyed the journey back to her ancestral home.

Fei-Liao's Demise

Even though Jeany was cohabiting with Jenna she hadn't got over the fear of isolation, whether in her apartment or at Jenna's. This insecurity rendered her more willing to volunteer for more than her fair share of night duties. The nightmares abated in the daylight although at night, she felt a lot safer amongst her colleagues. This night as she went about her duties, a storm raged outside. She was glad and relieved to be there amongst familiar faces and at work, where she felt safe and protected.

Jeany happened to turn and caught a glimpse of Mrs Zang heading her way along the ward. She was in no mood to argue with her and turned away in the opposite direction. Having not spoken since the day she was driven home by Fei Liao, she was ill prepared at this moment in time to start building bridges with her once best friend.

"Jin-Mei, it's me."

"Mrs Zang, how can I help you?"

"Why so formal? We've known each other years."

"Sorry Nan."

"That's better. I thought we were friends."

"I'm really busy at the moment, so how can I help you?"

"Jin-Mei, I'm sorry to have bothered you, but have you seen Jia-Na? I think she's borrowed my house keys."

"Why would she take your keys?"

"The key to the staff locker room is on that bunch. Maybe she's forgotten hers. She often borrows mine."

"Sorry but I haven't seen her tonight. Are you sure she's working?"

"Yes I saw her earlier."

"I can't help you. She could be anywhere in the hospital."

"Jin-Mei, we haven't spoken properly since that ugly incident with my husband. We should talk."

"So you know everything?"

"We still need to talk"

"How would that help?" Jeany snapped.

"If what you say is true, then he'll get what's coming to him."

"It is true."

"Then let the police deal with it."

"The police, how can I trust them? They're all the same," she snapped as she turned away from Nan, stifling her tears.

"What else can we do? What else can anyone do in this situation?" Nan said as she placed her hand on Jeany's shoulder.

"You tell me," growled Jeany.

"I don't want us to fall out, not now. We've been friends for years. Who did you turn to when your son left home and never returned? And who did you turn to when that wayward husband of yours kept leaving you? It was me and I'm still here for you, if and when you need me."

"Yes I know that," replied Jeany, turning back towards her old friend.

"Its common knowledge that my marriage is a sham, we've not been a proper couple for years," explained Nan, her eyes lowered.

"Yes I've been told that a few times."

"Mm, well yes, I'm sure you have."

"If a man wants sex outside his marriage, then he should go and find someone who's willing to accept payment to do his business with. He doesn't need to rape some helpless woman."

"But Jin-Mei, he insists that he didn't do anything."

"If being instrumental in the rape of a helpless woman isn't doing anything, then he's fooling himself. He committed a criminal act and I want to see him punished," said Jeany through gritted teeth. "If I had had a gun I would have shot him first and then shot the others, believe me," she said, trembling as she spoke.

"I'm staying with my sister at the moment. She hates him," said Nan.

"She's not alone," said Jeany her eyes narrowed as she spoke. Nan had never seen Jeany as angry as this, not in all their years of their friendship and she realised that the conversation was going nowhere. It was clear that the wounds inflicted on her friend would remain with her well into the foreseeable future.

"Jin-Mei, I really have to go now. I'm glad that we've talked. I'll call you some time. We need to get our heads together and put all this behind us. Are you okay with that?"

"Yes I promise, but give me a little more time, yes?"

"Of course, thank you and believe me when I say I couldn't feel more embarrassed and ashamed than I feel now. You're a good friend truly."

"Nan – here borrow my keys, try and get them back to me as soon as you can, I'm on my break at midnight, so I'll need them then."

"Thanks I'll do that." Nan turned and walked down the ward as Jeany stared at her sad old friend. Jeany's legs trembled as adrenaline pumped through her veins.

Anger in a vice like grip twisted her insides until she felt nauseous.

As tears welled up to the point of erupting, she made her way to the confines of the treatment room where her bottled up anger spilled out. After a few moments of release, she finally stared at her reddened face in the mirror. Her sore eyes stared back at her, void of expression and glazed.

"How could you hate your old friend so?" she asked herself. Men! That fortune teller was right, how could she have foreseen such an evil deed? But then again, did she? Maybe she was just being hateful?

As she wiped the tears from her flushed cheeks, Jenna burst into the treatment room.

"I've just been told that you and that bitch Mrs Zang have been having words. What has the bitch said to upset you?"

"She hasn't upset me."

"Oh really! Why don't I believe you?"

"No really, she was very understanding and kind."

"How could the likes of her understand someone like you, having been what you've been through?"

"Because she has had to live with that pig of a husband, that's how."

"That was her choice. You weren't given that choice. If I were her I'd be ashamed to show my face in this hospital, after what her husband did. And to work alongside someone who had been molested by her fat greasy husband is beyond belief. She should be ashamed of herself."

"She's done nothing wrong."

"Still, everyone must be talking about her. How embarrassing is that?"

"At least she had the moral courage to face me. I respect her for that."

"Jin-Mei, I'd have slapped her in the face."

"You're a doctor, so I'm sure you wouldn't have done that."

"True. But there's more than one way to slap someone in the face."

"Look I'm alright now. We both need to get back to work. It's going to be a long night shift."

"You're right. Come up and see me later when you get a break."

"Thanks Jenna, I will. Oh by the way, have you got Mrs Zang's keys?"

"No I haven't. That stupid cow leaves them everywhere. I've got my own. She ought to be more careful, blaming other people."

"Are you stopping for breakfast in the morning?" Jeany asked.

"There's a storm raging outside, I don't suppose there's any point in dashing home in that, not after a night shift anyway. So I suggest we have breakfast together?" Jenna replied with smile.

"Yes, that's an excellent idea. I'll meet you in the canteen around seven, okay?"

"Yes okay, see you later Jeany my dear," said Jenna.

She gave her a peck on the cheek and left her now feeling much better about herself. Later in the shift she had reason to go up to the second floor to the neuro-science lab to deliver some samples. She had hoped to bump into Jenna whilst there for a quick respite from her ward duties but by chance, she met the old lady fortune teller, Miss Sha her neighbour.

"Miss Sha?"

"Hello my dear, how are you now?"

"I'm much better though still as angry as ever."

"I bet you are," said the old lady with a serious expression on her face.

"Such a shocking experience takes a lot of getting over."

"You were right in your prediction."

"Yours was an easy one. Don't be offended, but women like you, divorced and hanging around with foreigners, almost always get into trouble sooner or later."

"Is that it? you sensed I would end up like I did?"

"Yes, Jin-Mei I did. Never underestimate the wisdom of age."

"I'll try not to. You could have warned me."

"Would you have listened? Jin-Mei, be honest."

"I suppose not."

"Do not worry – God has eyes. Time delivers justice as and when it deems fit to. Don't let hate destroy you like it destroyed me."

"You seem fine and well-adjusted to me." The old lady just smiled and put her hand on Jeany's shoulder.

"Embitterment and old age are troublesome bedfellows," she said, as she turned and began to go on her way.

"Oh, I nearly forgot, I need to give you these samples," Jeany said as she fumbled with the assortment of plastic bags she'd been holding.

"Thank you I'll deliver them for you. Do you finish at seven?"

"Yes."

"I can drive you home in the morning if you like? You can't walk home alone in this weather."

"Thanks but I've promised to have breakfast with Jia-Na"

"Just as long as you are sure, I'll see you around then. Don't be a stranger, yes?"

"Yes," replied Jeany, her eyes moistened and her heart touched.

Jeany returned to her ward much happier now that she had developed a better relationship with the once frosty Miss Sha, now hopefully an ally. She continued the night round, humming to herself as she did. She couldn't explain her sudden feeling of well-being but she welcomed it. Despite the storm raging outside, which had unsettled the patients, she felt that all her troubles would now dissipate. Her life's storm like that outside had to start and as such must have an ending.

That same night evil doings were afoot, not too far from the hospital grounds. A bitter wind rattled the windows of Zang Fei-Liao's house, outside the trees restless, swayed against the night tempest. Cans and bottles rolled nosily across the pavement outside. He sat and gazed at the clock, watching time slip by in the dimly lit room. At the stroke of midnight, he struggled to his feet, disrobed and slid into bed. In his recent imposed solitude, a set routine had taken over from the impulsive. Through the bedroom window, a street light struggled to be seen from behind the battered branches of a nearby tree. Despite the storm, he drifted off to sleep.

An hour later, a key slid into the front door of the little house. There was a muffled click as the lock mechanism turned. A dark figure stepped inside and then closed the door, dropping the latch on entering. The uninvited guest entered the bedroom and paused. There ahead lay the overweight, slumbering form of Zang Fei-Liao, mouth open and belly exposed to the flickering yellow street light that painted intermittent stripes across his rotund torso. Zang snorted and sniffed in his sleep unaware that someone under cover of darkness had entered his domain.

The visitor pulled up a chair and positioned it next to his bed and sat beside him. A small case was then placed on the bed's edge from which a bottle and a pipette were extracted. Some of the dark purple liquid was then drawn up into the pipette and with great care, a few drops were deposited onto his lips and tongue. He licked his lips and then swallowed. The uninvited guest glanced at their watch and sat in silence. After five minutes the visitor spoke in a soft voice.

"Fei-Liao, wake up." His eyes opened, they were red and swollen. His eyes moved but his head remained in the same position on the pillow.

"You can hear me but you can't move. Try to move if you can," said the visitor. Zang Fei-Liao's eyes narrowed as he tried to move.

"See you are helpless. Can you feel pain?" The ghost like figure like a haunting dark shadow, produced a clinical scalpel and displayed it in front of his reddened face.

"I wonder if you can feel this." The scalpel was then thrust sharply into the fat that hung around his torso and pulled, exposing the raw bloody adipose tissue that seemed to erupt from his severed skin. Zang Fei-Liao's eyes narrowed as tears ran down the side of his face.

"Ah, I see you felt that." The dark human figure gently rolled back the bedding down to his knees and then pulled his underwear in the same direction. With gloved hands, and in the same manner as one would hold a bunch of grapes, the left hand grasped that which lay between the fatty thighs tight up to the vine. And with the right hand bearing the scalpel, the dark visitor sliced, severed and separated that that was once the fruit. Blood flowed across the white bed sheets. The uninvited guest, calm and unruffled, then gathered together the implements of death, scattered an array of items of incriminating evidence around and then without a murmur exited into the cold night air. As the life of Zang Fei-Liao ebbed away he stared at the ceiling unable to move or summon help. There he lay until consciousness gave way to darkness and death.

Hurtful Disclosures

As arranged, Jenna and Jeany met in the canteen for breakfast. Most of the night staff had braved the storm that was now abating, and had gone home.

"Jin-Mei over here," Jenna shouted, as she waved to a tired looking Jeany.

"When will you ever learn to call me Jeany?" she said shaking her head.

"That was his name for you but he's gone now, hasn't he? I mean we need our old Jin-Mei back as she was," said Jenna.

"Leave it Jenna. I'm Jeany, if only to spite Bo-Cheng," she stated.

"When you came into the treatment block earlier your hair was wet. Don't tell me you ventured out into that storm, you didn't, did you?" Jeany asked laughing.

"Now you've asked I did; I had to go across to the security hut about a late night visitor and got soaked. I take it you stayed on the cosy ward and drank tea all night?"

"Maybe I did, but then my wages require me to do no more than I'm paid to do," said Jeany, as she picked up the menu.

"I'm getting my usual."

"Yes me too," said Jeany. "Oh and a cappuccino,"

"On its way," replied Jenna as she went to order, soon returning with the breakfasts. Jenna opened the conversation.

"You're so lucky to be rid of Bo-Cheng. You would never believe the things I've been told about him," said

Jenna, hardly lifting her eyes off her food. Jeany startled by the remark looked up.

"Such as?" she asked as she placed her utensils down.

"We shouldn't listen to gossip, so really I shouldn't repeat what I've heard," said Jenna knowing once out, Jeany wouldn't rest until she had heard what kind of rumours were being circulated.

"Is it about me?" she demanded.

"No, as I've said it's about Bo-Cheng."

"So tell me. Be it bad or good, what do I care?" She reached across the table and grabbed Jenna's arm. "Tell me Jenna, I want to know."

"Well if you must know, the old fox had been seeing two other women, one of them for a few years," said Jenna as she continued to eat.

"Do I know them?"

"Oh yes, of course you do. One as you now know is Pepper, that's how she knew so much about you," Jenna said.

"Yes of course I know about Pepper. She's welcome to him. So who's the other woman?" she demanded.

"I don't want to tell you, you'd be angry," she said looking her straight in the eyes.

"Tell me and then we can put the issue behind us," said Jeany, as her stomach began to churn.

"It's Nan" said Jenna.

"Zang Nan, my friend, she's been sleeping with Bo-Cheng?"

"Yes she has. She was the one whose affair ruined your husband's promotion prospects."

"But that was two years ago," exclaimed Jeany.

"They tell me she still sees him from time to time, a woman's needs and all that," said Jenna.

"Are you enjoying this? Jeany asked, almost in tears.

"You need to know the kind of friends you have," said Jenna, as she took a sip of her coffee.

"I'm beginning to find out," said Jeany, as she glared at Jenna.

"I don't suppose you know who has been admitted to Number Three orthopaedic ward? Take a guess?" Jenna asked, unable to stop herself.

"It's not Bo-Cheng is it?" asked Jeany, having not realised he was in the very same hospital as they were.

"Correct and can you guess who's on duty in Ward Four next door?"

"I have no idea," replied Jeany half knowing what was coming next.

"It's none other than your best friend, Zang Nan. She's supposedly your friend, but she's also the wife of your rapist, and your husband's lover. What nice friends you have. Your ex-husband Bo-Cheng ordered the man whose wife he had been sleeping with, to rape his own wife. How perverted is that?" Jenna said, as she leant back in her chair.

"Why are you doing this to me? Haven't I been through enough?" she asked, as tears ran down her cheeks.

"Tell me; what's worse, a cheating husband or a disloyal best friend?" Jenna asked. Jeany slammed her utensils down onto her plate.

"Husbands like to play around, but I believe a best friend shouldn't do anything to upset their friendship. So why are you sitting there raking up the dirt?" Jeany asked as she pushed her breakfast to one side.

"It's for your own good," said Jenna.

"No, it's for your good not mine. Divide and conquer. I may be stupid but I can tell when someone is

189

manipulating the situation. You're not the only person to have studied Sun-Zi," snapped Jeany.

"I'm your friend and friends don't lie to each other," explained Jenna.

"I don't need that kind of friend. Before you kept your distance, but now you're smothering me," she sobbed as she wiped her eyes with her serviette.

"That's not a nice thing to say. You have no idea what I have done for you. Everything I've done is for you."

"You want honesty, now you have it," growled Jeany.

"Don't try to be clever, it doesn't suit you," said Jenna as she stood up with her hands on her hips.

"So you think I'm stupid, do you?"

"No, just simple, life isn't as black and white as you think it is," said Jenna sitting back down.

"Listen to me. At 10 o'clock, Pepper comes to see Bo-Cheng. I'm going to tell her about Nan. What do you think she'll do when she knows Nan is still seeing him? She'll kill him," said Jenna laughing.

"Is that why we're having breakfast together, so you can hurt someone else? I know she's a bitch, but you take some beating when your venom's flowing," said Jeany.

"You flatter me. Yes I can be a bitch. I fight for what's mine and God help those who mess with me," Jenna said through gritted teeth.

"Would you kill for me?" Jeany asked.

"Oh yes, try me," said Jenna, as she stared straight into her moist eyes. Jeany had no doubt that she wasn't jesting.

"Let's go now. I'm tired," said Jeany. The strain of having to undergo such a lecture after a twelve hour shift was the last thing she needed.

"Yes, it's nearly 10 o'clock. We have to hurry," said Jenna, as she got to her feet. As they entered the foyer of the hospital on their way out, they met Pepper coming in with a huge bunch of flowers. Jeany looked at Jenna and shook her head.

"No Jenna, don't do it," she whispered. Pepper on hearing this stopped and looked at Jeany.

"Don't do what?" Pepper growled. Jeany smiled.

"Oh, nothing," she said and turned away to avoid having to explain herself.

"Hey bitch, I asked you a question, answer me." Jenna turned and smiled at Pepper.

"Do you really want to know, well do you?" asked Jenna with a smug expression on her face.

"Nothing you two can say can make any difference. Say your piece and have it done with," said Pepper as she brushed her long black hair away from her face.

"Your lover boy has been seeing another woman," said Jenna with her arms folded.

"You're a liar," retorted Pepper. Jenna smiled with confidence, knowing that deep down Pepper wasn't sure whether to believe her or not.

"Okay, so who is this woman? Look at me! Who in this grubby little town can displace me?" said Pepper, her hands on her hips.

"You're not being replaced. No. You're just being cheated on. You should know all about that sort of thing, shouldn't you? Jenna said. Jeany had wandered away in the hope that Jenna would follow, but she didn't.

"So who is she?"

"Ask Bo-Bo about Nan, the rapist's wife. You had better get your privates checked out. Who knows what kind of infection you may have picked up! Well what are you waiting for, you ask him," snarled Jenna.

"I don't believe you," shouted Pepper as she threw the flowers at her and marched into the hospital.

"Jeany, we'd better go before the firework display," said Jenna laughing.

Jeany felt sorry for Pepper, although she didn't know just how far Pepper would have gone to please Bo-Cheng. Nor did she know how far Jenna would go, to get what she wanted. Jeany just wanted to return to an ordinary life, free of complications and complex relationships.

Pepper charged onto Ward Three and threw the curtains back in a rage and stood there glaring at Bo-Cheng.

"What's got into you? Got out of the wrong side of the bed, have we?" joked Bo-Cheng as he sat up in bed.

"Tell me about Nan!" demanded Pepper.

"I don't know any one called Nan. Who's been talking?" he asked as he reached for the water vase.

"I know when you're lying. Who is she?" she demanded then dashed in and snatched the water vase from out of his hand and held it over his head.

"Don't be such a stupid bitch! Why would I want anyone else? Tell me that."

"I know her name. I'm going to do some asking around, and if you're lying to me, I'll come back and cut your slimy throat, so God help me I will!"

"She's just a friend."

"A friend you've kept secret from me?"

"I suppose so. You'd only get jealous. She's twenty years older than you and we're friends. That's all," said Bo-Cheng, as he fidgeted with the bed sheets.

"I'm going now. If I find out you lied to me, you're a dead man," she shouted so that the whole ward could hear her. She stormed out of the ward leaving the nursing staff standing speechless although relishing the spectacle of the feared police chief getting an earful from his mistress. It wasn't long before the news of the fracas in Ward Three had spread throughout the entire hospital.

Nan's Suicide

It was also common knowledge that Jeany had been raped and by whom. No one wanted Bo-Cheng and his men there in their hospital, but it was their duty to treat their wounds until they were fit enough to be discharged. The humiliation of Bo-Cheng and his men at the hands of a foreigner was a source of much amusement throughout the hospital.

Mrs Zang, having left before the incident on Ward Three, visited her home to collect items she had left behind and let herself in. The house was eerie and ominously quiet. The occasional snore or grunt she had become accustomed to on entering so late, was absent. She could hear the clock ticking on the wall, something wasn't right. As she nudged the bedroom door open, she noticed her husband laid out like a slaughtered beast. His insides had spewed out into the space between his legs. The blood had soaked into everything and dried. He was still. His eyes now glazed, fixed up at the ceiling. She noticed a few strands of black hair between his fingers and a distinct aroma of perfume. Nan felt sickened by the sight and dashed to the bathroom where she vomited. She picked up the phone and dialled the local police station where her husband had worked. Quiet and in shock she retired to the living room where she awaited the police and the coroner.

Numbed and shaken she began to cry. She had still loved him despite all his faults. Her unfaithfulness weighed heavily on her mind, although none of it really meant anything. Despite all this, she still loved him, and yet she wished she didn't. She had gone home to collect things she needed whilst staying at her sister's place. Had she not gone there, he may not have been found for days thought Nan, and who could have done such a thing? Nan knew that the police would leave no stone unturned in their efforts to find the killer of one of their own. It would only be a matter of time before the killer was brought to justice, thought Nan. As she sat there in silence she reminisced, her mind drifting back to better days.

It was just over three years ago, when Fei-Liao had gone under cover in Tian-Jin on the east coast. Bo-Cheng had sought her advice as he was having problems with Jin-Mei who was demanding the kind of affection Bo-Cheng was incapable of. She had wanted flowers, presents and flattery, all of which was lost on Bo-Cheng. Nan was a true romantic and would have risen high in social circles had it not been for her loyalty to her husband, a man chosen by her father as a sound investment. Nan had begun by showing Bo-Cheng some dance moves and how to flirt and surprise a woman. It was this kind of intimacy that had turned the hard man into an affectionate devotee. A few days passed and each began to yearn for the company of the other. Time after time, when he could assign Fei-Liao to an operation away from Shijiazhuang, they would meet up at a nearby hotel.

Jeany never knew about her husband's obsession with this older woman, whose skills in seduction had turned the tables on her. There was no way Nan could have owned up to Jin-Mei, her best friend, and to turn her back on Fei-Liao now, a shadow of his former self, that would have been heart-breaking. An affair was acceptable, but as time went on, for her the love grew stronger, as unrequited love does.

Now in her moment of anguish, what was left? Where could she turn, she asked herself? Time had roughened her smooth skin and cracked her dry lips. Gravity had all but sent her skin, once tight now sagging. There was nothing else desirable to offer only memories of illicit love unvoiced and selfishly cherished.

As the forensic men worked in the bedroom around the body of Fei-Liao, he lay there still visible through the plastic sheeting. Tears ran down her dry and chapped cheeks. The room was dirty. She had never noticed just how unkempt the place was. She had neglected her duty as a wife in more ways than one. She had let herself down.

"Oh mom – I want my mother! What shall I do? I need you! Where are you now when I need you? Why are you never there? Why did you go away and leave me?" Nan cried. There was no reply from the dark corners of the dimly lit room as she wept, no one was there, just the shadow of a lone sad woman lamenting her past misdeeds and life, and wishing the end of it.

As the muffled sound of the forensic men continued like white ghosts behind a translucent cloud, Nan rummaged around in her bag. There were the sedatives which were given to her by one of the policewomen as well as numerous other tablets. In the living room drawer she found some sleeping pills and an assortment of painkillers that had accumulated over the months, such were the perks of being a nurse. She took all she could swallow and washed them down with Fei-Liao's whisky. He won't need it, not now. She sat there and looked up at the clock ticking loudly counting the minutes of her remaining life. Zang Nan drifted off to sleep, her tears now dry white lines on her pallid skin. In the dimly lit room, the life of Zang Nan ebbed away.

The forensic men now finished for the day were ready to wheel out the body of Fei-Liao and convey him to the mortuary. On seeing Mrs Zang asleep, they slipped out of the front door careful not to disturb her unaware that she was now beyond being troubled by anyone.

Two hours passed and Nan's sister arrived only to find her older sister alone in the dark and not breathing. Saliva had dried as it had run from her mouth during her last breaths. Her sister rang the police who wasted no time in returning. Nan was then taken to the mortuary and laid next to her husband. There would be no enquiry regarding her death. No one had ever questioned her loyalty, nor would they ever.

Yu-Me Visits Miss Sha

When Yu-Me's taxi arrived at Jeany's apartment complex, she noticed two police cars outside the main entrance. She sat back and sighed. 'What now?" she thought. As she climbed the concrete stairs, she could hear muffled male voices from above. On the top floor she noticed her Aunt Sha and two police officers stood outside her apartment. She dashed up the last couple of steps to greet her aunt. Miss Sha spun round in amazement.

"Yu-Me, how have you been? I haven't seen you since you left for Beijing back in May."

"Never mind me, are you getting yourself arrested?" she joked.

"They're looking for Jin-Mei."

"Sorry to interrupt your home coming, I'm Inspector Fang and this is my colleague Inspector Lu. We need to know the whereabouts of Nie Jin-Mei or the foreign teacher Jason Lamont. Have you seen either?" the Inspector asked.

"I've just arrived from Beijing and haven't seen anyone for over six months. I really can't help you, sorry," she said as she placed her bags on the floor.

"Inspector, I've told you all I can. Jin-Mei has been staying with her friend Jie-Na. She's a doctor at our hospital. Have you tried asking around there?" Sha asked.

"Not yet, but we will. You said you saw nothing. Is that right?" Fang asked.

"I saw the state she was in after they had left. So I made sure I saw them all and I can recognise them," she replied.

"Thank you. I may have to visit you again, and we need you to write a statement. Is that alright?" the inspector asked.

"No problem, officer. If that's all, can we leave it for now?" she begged, keen to get in and spend some time with her niece.

"Yes of course. Please let me know if you see either of them. Here's my card," said Inspector Fang. They then left and descended the dimly lit stairs mumbling to each other.

"Yu-Me, come on in and tell me about Beijing," she said as she helped her in with her bags.

"So where is she?" Yu-Me asked.

"Like I told the police, she's with Jenna. She's helped her a lot but I can't see Jin-Mei staying with her for long."

"And why not?" Yu-Me enquired.

"Jenna has a preference for women, if you know what I mean."

"They were both on duty last night, so I expect they'll be at Jenna's fancy apartment trying to sleep," Sha said and then she chuckled to herself.

"What's so funny?"

"That woman is like a typhoon.

"Which woman?"

"Jin-Mei of course, everywhere she goes, there's trouble, it seems to follow her. That Jenna woman, now she's trouble waiting to happen. If ever there was a person to be avoided she'd be it," laughed Sha as she shook her head.

"Did Pang-Xi ever come back?" Yu-Me asked, knowing full well that he hadn't.

"No my dear, he never did. I think he was one of those who perished in the June 4th incident," she said as she looked away, visibly touched by the issue.

"How did Jin-Mei deal with the loss?"

"She managed. Misery seems to have followed her most of her life. But you and Pang-Xi were the best of friends when you were at school. Are you telling me you don't know how he died?" Sha asked, as she placed her hand on Yu-Me's.

"I think he may still be alive but I can't say either way. No one knows," said Yu-Me as she stood up.

"What are we going to do about Jin-Mei? Sha asked.

"We'll visit the hospital tonight, to see if we can catch her at work. That's if she hasn't been arrested by then," Yu-Me said with a laugh.

"Let's sort your bed out first and then we can sit and chat," suggested Sha.

Inspector Fang and Lu went through the hospital gate and stopped at the gatehouse. The gatekeeper leant out of his window and greeted them.

"We're looking for a Doctor Jia-Na and a nurse called Nie Jin-Mei. Have you seen them?"

"They left together at about 10 o'clock this morning. Did they upset someone?" The gatekeeper asked and then gave out a hearty laugh.

"What's so funny?" Fang asked.

"Some crazy woman marched in here this morning with a bunch of flowers and started ranting and raving at both of them. She ended up binning the flowers. It made my day. It really did," laughed the gatekeeper.

"Do you know the woman's name?" Fang asked.

200

"Aye, we all know that one. She's the Chief of Police's foreign mistress and a sharp tongued bitch at that," said the gatekeeper with a grin. She's called Pepper Lee."

"10 o'clock this morning, you say?"

"Yes, right on the stroke of ten every morning like clockwork. You need to go into the foyer and ask at reception if you want to know any more," said the gatekeeper, suddenly aware that he had probably already said far too much.

The two detectives drove in and parked their car. During their visit they passed through Ward Three and paid their respects to Bo-Cheng. When asked about Pepper, he was less than helpful.

"Who told you about her?" Bo-Cheng growled.

"We believe she will be able to assist us in our enquiries," Lu replied.

"That bitch is only good for one thing, and it isn't being helpful. Whoever killed Fei-Liao needed a reason. She and Fei-Liao got on well together. They were part of my team, so you had better look elsewhere," he suggested.

"That foreigner did it. What better motive than revenge? I take it you are looking for him?" he said glaring up at them.

"Yes, of course."

"You'd better find him or I reckon he's got some crazy plan to come here and get me. After all, aren't I supposed to be the villain here?"

"Your ex-wife seems to think so," said Lu, cocking his head as he spoke.

"And so does her lover boy. So you two had better get moving and clap that long nose in irons or do I have to get out of here and do it myself?" Bo-Cheng snapped.

"So this Miss Pepper Lee, can she be eliminated from our enquiries?" Fang asked.

"Yes. Now leave me alone and get me some protection. Who knows who's going to be next," he said as he turned away and curled up in his hospital bed with his back to them.

After making a few more enquiries, the two inspectors left with Jenna's address and a list of staff that were on duty on the night in question and duly inscribed in their notebooks.

"This Pepper Lee sounds like she's got a bit of a short fuse. From what I've heard, she gave poor old Bo-Cheng an earful when she arrived. She turned up just after 10 o'clock. Make a note Lu. It may be unimportant, but then again it's a clue of sorts," said Fang as they drove towards Jenna's residence.

After showing their identity badges to the security guards at the barrier, they were allowed entry into Jenna's apartment complex. They rang her bell and spoke into the intercom.

"Miss Jie-Na?" Fang asked and for a moment there was no answer, then a voice replied.

"Hello, are you the gentlemen who just signed in?" Jenna asked.

"Yes we are."

"Please come in. I'm on the second floor. You can take the elevator."

When they reached Jenna's landing, she was already standing outside her door to greet them.

"Inspector, please come in. How can I help you?" she asked with a smile.

"We really wanted a word with Mrs Nie Jin-Mei, is she here? Fang asked.

"Yes she is. Please come in and sit down. She's in the bedroom. Jin-Mei," she shouted, as Jeany strolled in, still in her dressing gown.

"Is it about the rape?" Jeany asked.

"We are looking into your allegation as part of our enquiries," replied Fang.

"Jeany, I believe you were working last night, is that so?" asked Fang.

"Yes, but what has that to do with the rape?" she asked, as she stared at the men. Her brow furrowed and her lips tensed.

"It does have some bearing on the rape. Please bear with me, and then I'll explain. Last night Mr Zang Fei-Liao was murdered and I believe he was one of the culprits named in your rape allegation."

"He was there and it's not an allegation. He was involved in the rape," insisted Jeany.

"Well now he's dead. We need to eliminate you from our enquiries. You're the main suspect. At the time of the murder, you said you were at work. Can you corroborate that?" Jenna stood up.

"Yes, she can. We were both at work on the same night shift."

"Jeany, did you at any time leave the hospital?" Inspector Lu asked.

"No; there was a storm all night," explained Jeany.

"Who else was on the ward with you?" Lu asked.

"No-one, but I saw many nurses throughout the night, who can verify that I was there."

"So you could have crept out easily and at any time, yes?" Lu asked.

"Yes, I could have, but I didn't," insisted Jeany.

"Didn't you? Lu challenged, as he stared at Jeany, eyebrows raised.

"And killed someone? I couldn't kill anyone. If I had wanted to kill him, I had a chance when he drove me home. Bo-Cheng allowed me to carry a knife for protection but I never used it. I could have got away with killing him then but I didn't."

"But you wanted him dead, didn't you?" growled Inspector Lu.

"No, I wanted him in a court of law," snapped Jeany.

"Well, there's little chance of doing that now," said Lu.

"Jie-Na, where were you last night?" Fang asked.

"The paediatric ward with the children. Except for an hour, that's when I had my break."

"And what time was that?" Lu asked.

"At midnight."

"I see," said Lu, as he gave Fang a meaningful look.

"No, you don't see. We medical practitioners spend our breaks together," said Jenna.

"Would you like more tea Inspectors?"

"Why thank you. You're very kind," replied Fang.

"How was he murdered?" Jeany asked.

"I was wondering how long it would take for someone to ask that," said Lu as he turned to Jenna.

"Don't look at me. I don't care how the fat pig died. I'm only glad he's dead," Jenna said, as she brewed the tea.

"Did you kill him?" Jenna smiled at Lu.

"No, I didn't."

"Jeany, I have to ask you. Did you kill him?"

"No, inspector I didn't." Inspector Lu turned to Jenna and smiled.

"You both have sound and verifiable alibis. So what about this Jason Lamont? I bet he would have loved to kill the fat pig, to use your euphemism, yes?"

"Yes, I'm sure he would. You'll have to ask him yourselves," said Jenna, confident that he was well out of the area by now.

"Yes we will, I'm sure the assault on Bo-Cheng and the murder of one of his men is sure to be connected. We have a lot of questions for that man, and rest assured, he will not be leaving China in a hurry."

"I know him, he wouldn't kill anyone," insisted Jeany, as she shielded her face from view.

"Jeany, we're not animals. If he's done this, we have the law and he'll have every chance to have someone in his corner to help," said Fang in a soft voice. Lu interrupted.

"Jeany if you know where he is, you must tell us." Lu frowned at her.

"I don't know; I don't know. I'm telling you the truth," she insisted, now in tears. For a moment the police sat and drank their tea, allowing Jeany some time to compose herself.

"Jenna, what do you know of this Pepper Lee woman?" Fang asked.

"That bitch is Bo-Cheng's whore," sneered Jenna. "You should know more about her than we do. She's the Police Chief's illegal immigrant belly warmer. In any other country, she'd be sent back to where she came from. But not here."

"You don't like her very much, do you?" Fang asked.

"No, I don't like her."

"Yesterday, you, Jeany and Pepper had words I believe?" Fang asked.

"Oh, you're good. How did you find out about that?" Jenna asked, smiling.

"Well, are you going to tell me what happened?"

"Yes. I just happened to tell her that Mrs. Zang and her lover boy Bo-Cheng had been playing around with each other behind her back," said Jenna with a satisfied look.

"Why did you tell her? What business was it of yours?" Lu asked.

"I just thought she ought to know," replied Jenna.

"And maybe Fei-Liao's death may have had something to do with what you said," suggested Fang.

"Oh no, could Pepper have killed Fei-Liao?" Jeany blurted out as if shocked by, what was to her, a distinct possibility.

"We don't know yet, but we'll know a lot more when the forensic boys have finished with the crime scene," said Fang.

"Where is Nan Zang now?" Jeany asked. Both inspectors looked at each other and shrugged their shoulders.

"We cordoned off the bedroom and left her in the front room. Her sister said she would pick her up after she finished work. So she should be okay. The forensic people are there," said Lu. He got to his feet and together they left, leaving more questions than answers in their wake.

Jeany began to worry about her old friend Nan, was she traumatized or withdrawn? Did she discover his body? The police hadn't actually said how he'd died. Was it sordid or a simple death? She had to know.

"Jenna we have to go now and find out how Nan is," demanded Jeany.

"Don't get involved. For all you know you may get charged for murder. Stay away, I would." Jeany grabbed her coat and brushed her hair, as she stared at her tired face in the mirror.

"I'll be back as soon as I can," she said, determination etched on her tired face.

"Okay, if you really have to go I'll drive you, but I'm staying in the car," insisted Jenna. With that, they headed towards the hospital. The Zang family home was but a five minute walk from the gate house.

"We'll park at the hospital and you can walk to their house. The police may have cordoned off the area. So it's best to approach the house on foot," suggested Jenna as she began to get ready to go out.

As agreed they arrived at the hospital and walked to the house. The police vehicles were there as well as Nan's sister's car. Jenna stayed away, while Jeany approached the house on foot.

"Jeany, they're not here," said Nan's sister as she wiped her eyes.

"Where's Nan? We heard about the murder," said Jeany.

"She's dead."

"But we heard it was Fei-Liao that was murdered?" Jeany asked, her hands hiding her face.

"Fei-Liao is dead but so is Nan." Nan's sister broke down in tears. Jeany embraced her and held her close.

"She killed herself," she whispered. "How could she still have loved him after all he'd done, and to you, her best friend? How could she do this to us?" she cried. The police and the coroner have taken them to be with each other in the mortuary. I'll have to go there and go through the identification procedure."

"I'll go with you. She was my best friend after all, wasn't she?"

"Yes she was. Thank you Jin-Mei." Jeany ambled back to the car to explain why she was going to the mortuary.

"What about me?" Jenna asked.

"You go on back home. I'll make my way back after I've finished at the hospital," said Jeany, her arm still linked with Nan's sister. Jenna turned her face away and started up the car and without looking back, headed off towards her home. Jeany went with Nan's sister and they identified the two bodies.

"Now that's done I need to go home and break the news to the family, before they hear it from other sources," Nan's sister explained.

"Would you like a lift anywhere?"

"I don't want to take you out of your way but I'd like to check my apartment. Just to be sure no one has broken in. What with some murderer on the loose. Can you take me there?"

"I'll drop you off there. Do you need me to wait for you?"

"No I'll get a taxi home or even call Jenna. A lift there would be very helpful," she said as she gave her a hug.

Less than fifteen minutes later, Nan's sister dropped Jeany off outside her apartment complex. She looked up at her window; the curtains remained closed and inhospitable, dark and dismal. As she trudged up the concrete stair towards her apartment, she heard the chattering of female voices descending the stairwell. Jeany stopped by one of the few stair wall lights and waited for the strangers to appear. As they became visible, Jeany recognised Miss Sha. She was chatting as she came down the dim stairwell. At first Jeany didn't recognize the young lady beside her.

"Jin-Mei is that you?" the young girl asked. "It's me Yu-Me. I'm back from Beijing."

"My God, do you have any news about Pang-Xi?" Jeany asked.

"I can't say. He could be anywhere, I just don't know." Yu-Me replied. Sha placed her hand on Jeany's shoulder.

"Let's talk in the car. I can drive you back. Are you still at Jenna's place?" Sha asked.

"Yes, for now."

"Your apartment's fine. There's no need to check it out. Had a bad day, have we?" Sha asked.

"Yes, a terrible day. I'll tell you all about it in the car," said Jeany, happy to have someone to share her misery with.

Yu-Me sat in the rear seat with Jeany, while Sha navigated the dark, twisty road ahead. As they drove, Jeany mentioned the murder. Sha seemed unsurprised and dismissive. It was when Jeany described how Nan Zang had committed suicide that both Sha and Yu-Me seemed moved and upset.

"She used to be your best friend, didn't she?" Sha asked.

"Yes she did. Fei-Liao spoilt all that. I can't say I'm sorry he's dead," said Jeany.

"I'll second that" said Sha. Men like that are no better than animals."

"I'll miss Nan though," said Jeany, her eyes moist and conscious of the well of tears bubbling up just below the surface.

"I'll miss her too," said Sha.

"Jeany, you almost forgot what I looked like, didn't you?" Yu-Me asked with a smile.

"How could I forget you? Yes you've changed but then it's only been six months since you left. I must admit you've altered your appearance so much that I truly never recognised you," said Jeany, as she looked across at Yu-Me's young and vibrant face.

"I'm so sad; I only wish that Pang-Xi could see you now. He always liked you." Jeany began to weep.

"Don't cry, Jeany. Be strong for Pang-Xi. I'm sure he's with you in spirit." Yu-Me turned to Jeany and held her hand.

"If you like, you can call me your daughter." suggested Yu-Me.

"What about your real mother?" Jeany asked.

"She's gone away, that was years ago," said Sha.

Jeany smiled at Yu-Me and gave her a big hug. Sha looked over her shoulder.

"If you're serious Yu-Me, we can draw up the marriage proposal and papers sometime, okay?"

"Yes let's do it," said Yu-Me as her enthusiasm bubbled over into laughter as she gripped Jeany's hand.

"Remember, if he were ever to turn up alive, you'd still be his wife," warned Sha.

"Here's hoping he does," said Yu-Me with a laugh.

"We're there now," said Sha, as they pulled up outside Jenna's complex.

Jeany embraced Yu-Me for it was as if, she had somehow retrieved a small part of her son back. She was the next best thing, a daughter-in-law. There was an old law dating back to ancient China that permitted a girl to marry the dead son of a woman and so become the woman's daughter in law, which in turn afforded her the obligation to care for the woman and in so doing gave her inheritance rights. Jeany turned to Yu-Me as she clasped her hand.

"How long are you staying in Shijiazhuang?"

"I hope to return one day and in the not too distant future. My dear mother, I will return as soon as I can," said Yu-Me as she threw her arms around Jeany. They kissed and then Jeany stepped out of the car. Yu-Me smiled at her and handed her a name card with her mobile number on it.

"Wo-de Po-po," she said, which meant 'My mother-in-law. Jeany laughed and then closed the car door. She felt like she was floating on air. 'What a day,' she thought.

It was then she decided she would return to her own apartment but when? and how would she break the news to Jenna?

Pepper meets Jenna

Jenna yelped, jumped out of bed and began dashing around the room picking up clothes.

"I'm late. Jeany, you have the day to yourself. What are you going to do?" she asked, as she pulled on her last boot.

"I'm meeting Yu-Me at Century Park and then we are going for something to eat," she said, stretching her arms high above her head as she gave out a monstrous yawn.

"I shan't bother cooking for you then," said Jenna with a hint of disapproval in her voice.

"I suppose not. Have a nice day" croaked Jeany.

"Thanks a lot. How would you like to spend the day with twenty-six sickly children? A nice day! Highly unlikely!" groaned Jenna, as she left.

Jeany slithered back beneath the bed clothes and smiled. Yu-Me was such a pretty young woman, Pang-Xi would have been so pleased to know she had agreed to become his mother's daughter-in-law, she thought. She reached for the name card Yu-Me had given her and dialled her number. A cheerful voice answered.

"Jeany, is that you?"

"Yu-Me – how would you like to spend some time in Century Park and then go for a meal?"

"Okay, I'll see you there in an hour," said Yu-Me, her voice full of excitement. Jeany laughed at Yu-Me's exuberance and energy. She thought back to the last time someone had evoked such mirthful spirit in her. It was then that memories of Jason flooded back. Where was he and what was he doing? He had to be in hiding somewhere, where no one can find him,' thought Jeany.

Her suspicious nature was never far below the surface and at this moment, the whole sordid affair suddenly seemed to make sense.

"Jason's the murderer," she thought as a hot flush ran down her whole body. "Now it all makes sense, it's my Jason who is the killer; he's meted out justice on my behalf. He didn't run away at all, he is still here in the area somewhere. I'm sure he's taken on the job of being my avenging angel and punishing the wicked," she whispered to herself. On realising what he was doing for her, she was overjoyed. Then it sank in that two people had died and one was her old friend, who had been so full of remorse that she had taken her own life. Her eyes opened wide and her jaw dropped.

"My God, Bo-Cheng is next," she cried out aloud, she then hesitated.

"Why should I save his skin?" she asked herself.

"Didn't he say 'he didn't care what those pigs did to me'? Well now it's my turn to turn away and let someone else administer God's judgement," she mumbled.

She knew that Bo-Cheng would be safe during daylight hours. This gave her plenty of time to decide what the best course of action was, if any. Right now, Yu-Me would be on her way to Century Park and she would have to hurry to get there on time.

Jeany jumped out of the taxi just outside the huge iron park gates and hurried across the forecourt towards the water feature and Century Tower. Though the park concourse was crowded, she felt that someone was shadowing her. She glanced over her shoulder and caught a glimpse of Pepper a few paces behind. She turned and hurried in through the park gates, daring not to look back. Maybe Pepper hadn't seen her she thought as she entered the park. Just as she passed the water feature with its knee high perimeter wall, someone pushed her in the back from behind, knocking her off balance, over the retaining wall and headlong into the icy cold water. Her shin bones were now grazed, bleeding and her elbows bruised by the impact against the pond wall.

She looked up at the crowds looking down at her but Pepper was nowhere to be seen. Bystanders stood by and stared at her. Two young teenagers stepped into the pool and helped her out of the water. She looked up at the sea of faces around her and noticed Yu-Me with her arms outstretched.

"Yu-Me, thank God I've found you," she gasped.

"Was that Pepper?" Yu-Me asked.

"I think so. Bo-Cheng and her make a nice couple, don't they?"

"I wouldn't call them nice. Evil more like," said Yu-Me with a smile.

"Let's get away from the water and dry off," Jeany suggested as she shivered in the cold air. Yu-Me took her large army style coat off and wrapped it around her. They made their way to one of the many park benches to recover. A tall man then approached them. Jeany looked up at him and recognised Inspector Lu.

"Jeany, I saw that. I've been following you and from what I've just seen, I believe someone is out to harm you. I don't know what could have motivated her to do that. She tried to hurt you, but why?" Lu asked.

"I don't know. She and Bo-Cheng hate me. Maybe they're jealous?"

"No, I don't think so," replied Lu shaking his head but failed to explain why he thought so. Jeany sat with Yu-Mei and massaged her sore arms and legs while Lu sat beside them.

"All I know is, that this Pepper woman, and maybe even Bo-Cheng were in some way involved in the murder. I intend to find out why and how," explained Lu, resolve written across his sullen face.

"Why were you following me?" Jeany asked, as she looked up at the Inspector.

"It's just a precaution, in case Jason accosted you or worse," he explained.

"Jason wouldn't hurt me, why should he?"

"I don't know. You tell me?" He said as he shrugged his shoulders.

"There's a coffee shop near the back gate of the park. I suggest you go there to dry off. If you don't mind, I'll stay around and keep an eye on you. The attack on your person has been duly noted and will be recorded as an assault. We'd like a chat with this Pepper woman about other matters and this gives us a legitimate reason to pull her in," he explained.

"The police don't need a reason to pull people in, not in my experience," said Jeany.

"I'm sorry you think like that," said Lu.

"Nothing changes," groaned Jeany.

"I think things are changing, especially in the Police."

"And so they should," snapped Jeany.

"Jeany, you can't say that to a policeman. You'll get arrested," laughed Yu-Me.

"That's alright, let her speak, but in future keep your opinions to yourself, it's safer that way," he replied with the hint of a smile.

Yu-Me and Jeany headed for the coffee shop and Lu followed behind at a distance. As they sat and talked, Jeany explained why she believed that Jason had committed the murder in retaliation for what Fei-Liao had done to her.

"It was because I was raped by Fei-Liao that Jason killed him," she said convinced that she was right. Yu-Me didn't remember the word 'rape' ever being used in her conversations with Jason, although at this moment in time, she was not in a position to contradict her version of what had transpired. Yu-Me sat and thought long and hard.

"If it wasn't Jason, then who was it?" she asked.

"I don't know and to be honest, I'm past caring. I'm only worried that he has got himself into all this trouble on my account."

"The police think its Jason. That policeman isn't following us for fun. They want to get to him," Yu-Me said, as she stared into her coffee. Her brow furrowed.

"So do you think he did it?" Jeany asked.

"How would I know? I've never met him and how would I know if he was the sort of man to do such a thing? I wouldn't, would I?"

"It's obvious he did it. Isn't it?" she asked again.

"It's far too obvious, and what if he didn't? Who did?" Yu-Me asked as she leaned back in her chair. Jeany furrowed her brow.

"It must have been Pepper."

"Why Pepper? Why would she do that to one of Bo-Cheng's gang, a gang she also belonged to?" Yu-Me challenged.

"Shall we just forget it and try to live a normal life, like any other mother and daughter," Jeany suggested.

"That sounds great, more coffee?" Yu-Me asked with a broad smile on her face.

The hospital wasn't far from Century Park and during her lunch break, Jenna decided to walk there. She often went out midway through her shift to get some air. On her way to the park, she would pass by the local street market, where she decided to buy some provisions to take home after work. As she made her way through the market, she felt an arm slide around her waist. Jenna spun round and came face to face with Pepper, their faces almost touching as their eyes met. She gave Jenna a warm flirtatious smile. Jenna was taken off guard and shocked by her audacious manner. She was so startled that she was rendered unable to respond appropriately, all she could do was to smile back at her.

"I'm sorry I lost my cool the other morning. Someone needed to tell me and you were right, he had been cheating on me," confessed Pepper, her arm tightened around Jenna's waist.

"Our bumping into each other today isn't a coincidence is it?" Jenna asked, as she looked Pepper straight in the eyes.

"No, I've been feeling guilty about my anger the other morning and think we've started off on the wrong foot, so to speak," explained Pepper.

"I've just half an hour break, so you'll need to get straight to the point, if you have one," replied Jenna, turning so that they were face to face. Pepper's hands remained on Jenna's waist as they spoke.

"I was hoping to seduce you, but I guess I chose the wrong place and the wrong time," said Pepper looking down at her frontage. Jenna looked up at Pepper and cocked her head.

"You seduce me? What made you think I'd fall for that one? You're with that slob Bo-Cheng aren't you?"

"I was, but not now," said Pepper, as her fingers caressed Jenna's lower waist.

"And you expect to bounce off that slob onto me? You're hetero aren't you?"

"I'm both ways. Sleeping with people you don't like is an acquired taste. You get used to it and it pays the bills," explained Pepper.

"What kind of woman do you take me for?"

"You've got the brains and a nice lifestyle. All I need is to be valued and needed. I'm begging you to take me on. Just give me a chance to please you, that's all I'm asking," she pleaded with her eyes moist and her body trembling. Jenna could see she was desperate, lowering herself to plead with someone she had previously stood up to.

"If I were to take you on, who'd be paying the bills then?" Jenna asked with a business-like look on her face.

"I'd make it worth your while and I'm a lot younger and prettier than that ugly old bird Jeany," she said, as she pulled her head back, allowing Jenna to see what she was getting at close quarters.

"You're not going to ingratiate yourself with me by stabbing my friend in the back. Jeany is a special friend. Do you hear me?"

"Yes I do, but Jeany isn't gay, she never will be. As for being seductive, well? Jenna, stop and look at me. Don't pass me up for a wet fish like Jeany."

"I don't know. I hardly know you. What if Bo-Cheng comes back and I get what Jeany got?" Jenna said as she put her hand on her shoulder. Pepper smiled, aware that Jenna was being swayed by her obvious charm.

218

"We're finished, trust me. He belongs to the past," she said as she looked Jenna in the eyes, luring her closer, daring an illicit kiss.

"Are you really willing to move in with me?" Jenna asked, as her pulse raced at the prospect of someone who had offered themselves openly.

"You've reduced me to begging. Do I have crawl on my hands and knees for you to accept me?" Pepper asked, rubbing Jenna's outer thigh as she did.

"Nothing is more alluring than an offer of availability. If I accept your offer, where does that leave Jeany?"

"I just saw her with a pretty young woman back there in the park. They were holding hands. She's already moved on, if not now then soon," said Pepper as she held Jenna's hand.

"She's a cousin's niece visiting from Beijing," Jenna explained. Pepper groped in her bag for her name card.

"Here, please call anytime when you are free. Will you?" Pepper begged.

"Yes, I will but only when Jeany decides to leave and of her own free will. No monkey business from you, do you hear me?" she said, pointing her finger at Pepper, who then gave her a warm smile of approval. Jenna turned and made her way back towards the hospital, all the time aware that Pepper's eyes were focussed on her, watching her every move.

Jeany left Yu-Me at Sha's apartment and returned to Jenna's to get some sleep in preparation for yet another night shift. At 7 o'clock in the evening, Jeany bumped into Jenna in the hospital foyer as she ended her twelve hour shift.

"I bought some things for us to eat tonight, I forgot you were on night duty, never mind it will keep until tomorrow," said Jenna, as she looked in her carrier bag and sighed.

"Never mind we'll talk tomorrow. Yu-Me is going back to Beijing soon. After Christmas she wants to come and live with me," said Jeany, looking down at her feet.

"With us?" Jenna snapped.

"No, at my place."

"And what about me, are you leaving me?"

"She would have been my son's wife. I can't turn her away. Can I?"

"But you can turn me away," growled Jenna.

"Don't be like that. I do care about you, I really do," said Jeany, her knees shaking in the cold evening air.

"I'm going now. I'll see you in the morning, we'll talk then," said Jenna as she turned and marched away towards her car. Jeany felt a little better now she had told her about her plan to move out.

Jenna went back to an empty apartment. She opened a bottle of burgundy and sat there, her mind ruminating over the conversation she'd had with Pepper. She put the opened bottle onto the highly polished table and reached for the phone. The person at the other end of the line answered in a whisper.

"Hello, who's calling?" The voice said.

"It's me Jenna."

"Are you alone?" Pepper asked.

"Yes, quite alone."

"Is Jeany there?"

"Like I said, I'm alone."

"How long are you going to be alone?"

"All night until daybreak."

"Would you like me to come over for a few hours to cheer you up?" Pepper asked in a soft voice.

"Yes and why not? We could start getting to know each other," said Jenna, butterflies fluttering inside her as if she were a blushing teenager once again.

"Pick me up outside the market where we met today, give me half an hour. I'll be waiting for you near the bus stop. Okay?"

"I'll be there," replied Jenna.

A Bad Day for Bo-Cheng

Jeany smiled as she made her way to her ward on the second floor. She felt empowered, having plucked up the courage to tell Jenna about her change of heart and that she now wished to return to her old apartment. On her arrival on the ward, one of the other nurses approached and whispered in her ear.

"Jin-Mei, your husband's still on Ward Three. Why don't you go down there when you have time and rattle his cage? They sent him a bodyguard today and would you believe it, it's one of his own men. They must be worried that your foreigner friend will turn up out of the blue and slit his throat."

"It never occurred to me that I could visit him down there. I suppose now he's all wired up, he won't be able to get violent."

"If he gets too angry we'll have to sedate him, won't we?" the nurse said with a smile.

"I think I will. I'll go see him later and give him a piece of my mind," she said.

"That's what we've all been waiting for, good for you Jin-Mei."

"Jason isn't a killer. So I really don't know who's doing this, I really don't," she explained, only half believing what she had said herself.

"Ah but Bo-Cheng doesn't know that does he? Jason's probably back in England now, so there's no harm in saying he's still out there, gunning for him, now is there?" the nurse suggested, excitement written all over her face.

"Do you think he is scared?" Jeany asked.

"I would be in his place, whether he's out there or not, it doesn't matter," said the nurse as she placed her hand on Jeany's shoulder.

"You're right. Maybe it's time for him to learn something about fear and what it's like to lie awake afraid to close your eyes. It's only what he deserves," said Jeany, her pulse now racing. They both laughed and then went about their duties.

At midnight, her relief turned up so that she could take her break. She left the ward, via the elevator and went down to the ground floor to Ward Three. She made her way to Bo-Cheng's cubicle, where she saw him laying there, his guard beside him. She recognised the fat grotesque looking guard as one of those that had raped her. They were enjoying a game of cards on the bed. The sight of this disgusting man enjoying his time with Bo-Cheng made her feel nauseous. She turned and dashed away secreting herself in the treatment room, where she vomited.

She rummaged in the drawer her hands shaking uncontrollably. With her blood all fired up, she took out a scalpel. The powerful urges she had experienced when she'd been in the back of the patrol car with Fei-Liao came flooding back to her. Gripping the surgical instrument as tightly as she could, she returned to the cubicle. The two men laughed at her having seen her dash off distressed into the treatment room. Having now composed herself, she stood at the foot of the bed and raised her hand bearing the scalpel. She stared at the blade; in her mind's eye she could see herself butchering these good for nothing human beings.

"Hey, put that knife down you crazy bitch," shouted Bo-Cheng, keen to alert the whole ward that he was being threatened. The fat guard stood up and glared at her.

"I hope you weren't relying on that fat pig to stop me cutting you up. Did you hear that fatso?" she challenged as the guard sank back into the seated position.

"You don't scare me bitch," said the guard, gripping the chair arms as he spoke. She gritted her teeth and glared at them.

"So I don't scare you? You're able to rape a helpless woman that's being held down. I have a knife now, come and get me. Come on, why don't you come and rape me now? Ah!! Maybe because now I'm able to defend myself, am I right?"

Behind her, a gathering of nurses had assembled eager to hear what these men had to say for themselves. Once again the guard got to his feet and growled at her.

"You're just an old frustrated whore, that's all you are, bitch," said the guard as he spat at her.

"Pang, watch your lip. No one asked for your opinion," snapped Bo-Cheng as he pulled the guard back into his chair.

"Jin-Mei, leave now before you get into even more trouble," said Bo-Cheng.

"It's Jeany, if you don't mind, and don't try to charm me, you ran out of that years ago."

"What do you want?" he asked in a weary voice.

"I'm here to warn you. Jason is coming to get both of you, you'll see," she stated, waving the scalpel in the fat guard's direction.

"If Jason's coming to get us, why are you waving that knife at us?" the guard said, pointing towards the blade aimed in his direction. Bo-Cheng laughed.

"Don't worry; she hasn't the nerve to use it. She had the chance to skewer poor old Fei-Liao but she didn't, isn't that so?"

"He's dead now, isn't he?" she said as she glared at the guard. Bo-Cheng laid back and smiled.

"Don't worry Pang. She had to wait for lover boy to do it for her. He wouldn't dare show his face in here. That would be suicide," he boasted.

"If I were you, I wouldn't sleep tonight. They tell me Jason's back in town and he's very angry," she said still clutching the blade.

"He doesn't know of my involvement in the so called rape. Not unless you told him," said the fat guard. Whispers of astonishment came from behind Jeany.

"I appreciate your confession but it's probably too late now to save you," she jeered. A nurse from behind Jeany spoke out.

"Now we all know you're nothing but a couple of filthy rapists! Pigs," she shouted, as if in a court of law. Jeany pointed to Pang the fat guard and Bo-Cheng.

"These are dead men – no pity shown, no pity given," she declared, as both men, open-mouthed remained silent, stunned by Jeany's audacious behaviour.

"Pity! Who do think you are talking to?" Bo-Cheng grunted.

"You have confessed in front of these witnesses. The rape has been reported to Inspectors Fang and Lu and the law requires you to write a statement to support your confession," she said with determination etched across her face.

"Go to hell! You must think we're stupid," he said, he then threw the deck of playing cards at the onlookers now standing around his bed.

"Poor Fei-Liao, they tell me he had his guts cut open. What an end! And Bo-Cheng that's how you're going to end up, maybe tonight," taunted Jeany.

"Leave us alone! Get out!" screamed Bo-Cheng, his face red and bloated. She stood as near as she dared with the scalpel at the ready, brimming with confidence.

"I'll see you regret the day you sent Pepper Lee after me. She's a clumsy assassin. When she's arrested, and she will be, she'll tell them everything."

"Just let it rest will you? I can't turn the clock back. You can tell lover boy to vanish and that will put an end to it. You're now free to do what you want, I won't interfere anymore, I promise. The murder can stay unsolved, who cares?"

"I do and it's too late to apologise, not now."

"Me apologise? Go to hell. I was offering you a way out, bitch!"

"I'm not the one going to Hell," she proclaimed.

"Just leave me alone," growled Bo-Cheng, as he turned his back on the assembled audience. She turned and smiled to her colleagues.

"See the big man now, on his death bed," she pronounced with a triumphant tone to her voice. There was muffled laughter and murmuring as the hospital staff drifted away. She then returned to her ward on the second floor with a contented smile on her face. She had won a battle, although she knew the war was far from over.

At about 3 o'clock in the morning, the dimly lit ward was quiet except for the occasional snore or grunt emanating from the occupied beds. Beside the slumbering Bo-Cheng the fat guard slept, slumped back in his chair with his mouth gaped open. His arms hung limply down each side of his chair and with his legs fully outstretched, he posed no threat to the unseen figure approaching from out of the dark. The hunched figure strolled without a sound past the nurse's station and the napping night nurse, with her eyes shut and both arms folded.

The soft white shoes came to a halt outside Bo-Cheng's cubicle then they stepped inside. After entering, the visitor pulled up a chair and sat next to him and with great care, placed a small case on the edge of his bed. A small vacuole of neuro-toxin was produced and a pipette. Three drops of the toxin were then dripped into his mouth and outer gums. As if time were of no consequence, the agent of death sat back and waited.

After five minutes, Bo-Cheng was prodded with a sharp implement. His eyes, red and blood-shot opened. His swollen eyeballs rotated towards the face looking down at him. His eyes widened as fear seized him, although this was the only bodily movement he was capable of. The uninvited guest stood up and walked around the bed towards the fat guard, who remained oblivious as to what was now imminent. His swollen eyes followed in horror as the would-be assailant deposited a few drops of the toxin into the fat guard's gaping mouth. Bo-Cheng's eyes bulged as he strained to scream but his screams echoed only inside his cranium. Beads of sweat oozed from his pallid skin, as he recognised his would-be assassin.

A few minutes later, the noise of chair legs being pushed back sounded, as the ward nurse got up and began walking in their direction. The night witch like a shadow in the night, slid behind the curtain that formed the cubicle. The drapes were pulled back and the night nurse looked in at Bo-Cheng, whose eyes wide open stared at the nurse, as if beckoning her to come in and save him.

"Not sleeping. Ah well must be your conscience. I'll call by later with a sedative, try to sleep now," said the nurse after which she headed for the elevator.

Once the elevator showed that it had stopped on the third floor, the night caller spoke.

"Bo-Cheng, I hope you are watching, because you are next," whispered the figure, moving round the bed towards Pang, then with the sharp end of the scalpel the dark figure prodded the fat guard. His blood shot eyes sprung open, but he too was unable to respond to the fear that now seized him. Pang began to sweat, perspiration running freely down his fleshy cheeks. A face etched with evil intent glared at Bo-Cheng and then produced a surgeon's scalpel and waved it across the fat guard's face.

"Bo-Cheng, are you watching?" the avenger asked in a whisper as the fat guards trousers were undone and pulled down over his knees and then his underwear pulled down in a similar fashion. With his shirt pulled aside, the fat guard lay there helpless, yet fully aware of what was going on and what this night witch's evil intentions were. Bo-Cheng watched in horror as the fat guard's genitals were pulled as if they were weeds being tugged from the dry earth. With a steady hand the scalpel sliced at the base allowing that which was being pulled to separate from the body. The fat guard's eyes swollen and red rolled upwards as the pain churned inside him. Blood gushed down onto the floor and down his exposed legs.

The visitor turned to Bo-Cheng who was now in a state of shock. With saliva dribbling from his gaping mouth, he stared blankly at the assassin. His bed sheets were rolled back and his nightwear pulled down to just above the knee. With great care his genitals were cut away. Each time he passed out, the surgeon would stop. When he recovered, the surgery would continue dissecting and dismembering the component parts of his groin. When the deed was done the uninvited guest rolled the bed sheets back over him so that nothing looked unusual. Pang was covered with a blanket, as if someone had taken pity on him being cold and had draped it over him. The assassin then gathered together the implements of death and disappeared into the stairwell.

At 6 o'clock in the morning, the night nurse raised the alarm on seeing a lake of blood covering the floor beneath and around the guard's chair. The duty doctor was called and Pang was pronounced dead. Bo-Cheng's vital signs were checked and although there was just a glimmer, there were still signs of life. He was rushed to the intensive care unit and placed on a life support machine. Despite his ordeal, he was still alive, although his body remained in a state of neuro-paralysis and shock.

The local police were called in and the ward was cordoned off for forensic work to begin. The names of all staff on duty that night were taken and the night nurse when she had recovered from the shock was well and truly interrogated to the point of tears. All the staff that had been on duty that night were kept back for further questioning. Photos were taken of the crime scene and of the body positions.

The floor was vacuumed and the materials at the scene including the curtains and bedding were taken away in sealed bags to the forensic laboratory for detailed analysis. Each member of staff on duty that night was asked to write a statement before they were allowed to go home. Many mentioned Jin-Mei's bold threats to Bo-Cheng, and how she predicted his death so publically. Jeany was held back and detained for further questioning. Fang spoke to the forensic team away from the hospital staff.

"For the time being let no-one know that Bo-Cheng is still alive. Only a select few know that he is still alive. At all costs, don't let Jin-Mei or the ward staff know this," ordered Fang.

It was made out that Bo-Cheng had also died to avoid the assassin returning to finish the job. The murders of Fei-Liao, Pang and the mutilation of Bo-Cheng had shaken the local police force into action. They had lost three of their men in less than a week. With few leads to go on, they concentrated their energies on Jeany and Jenna whose homes were targeted as soon as the murders had come to light. They already knew that Jeany was at work but then she had the opportunity and a good motive. She had also threatened Bo-Cheng on the very night that he was the subject of a murder attempt, and this made her a prime suspect in the gruesome mutilation murders.

Enter the Police

On hearing of the murders, Inspector Lu, as instructed, made his way to Jenna's out of town apartment. It was seven o'clock in the morning and Jenna was alone, Pepper having left in the early hours.

"Come in Inspector, what brings you here at such an unearthly hour?" she asked as she closed the door behind him.

"Are you telling me you don't know?"

"Don't know what?" she replied, as she brushed her hair, tugging at its knotted ends.

"You'd better sit down," said Lu in a calm voice.

"What are you going to tell me that is so important, that you have to deprive a lady of her beauty sleep?" she asked.

"Bo-Cheng is dead and so is Officer Pang. They were murdered last night," said Lu. Jenna burst into laughter and gave Lu a broad smile.

"That wasn't the reaction I'd expected," said Lu looking disgusted.

"Sorry Inspector. So Jason got his man in the end," she said with a smile.

"Where were you last night?"

"I was at home all night," she replied.

"Alone?"

"Yes of course."

"Really?"

"Yes."

"Did Miss Pepper Lee visit you at 8.30pm last night, or have the gate staff been telling me lies?" Lu asked with a crooked brow. She had a look on her face that needed no interpretation. Lu could see that she was not being altogether truthful, but concluded that a woman with her profile was unlikely to be the perpetrator of this horrific crime. She looked up at Lu and put her hands together as if she was about to pray.

"If I tell you, will you promise not to tell Jeany?" she begged. Lu shook his head.

"I can't make such promises. What I can assure you is that should anyone find out, it will not have come from me," replied Lu, smiling as he did.

"I was with Pepper, but she left early in the morning."

"How early is early?"

"I can't recall the exact time," replied Jenna.

"Make a guess," said Lu.

"I can't; maybe 3 o'clock?"

"Let me refresh your memory. The gateman said she left at midnight. That means she would have had plenty of time to get to the hospital and kill Bo-Cheng, agree?"

"She has no car and she may have had to walk back," she suggested.

"Wrong again. The gateman said she stopped a taxi just past midnight."

"I wasn't to know how she got home," argued Jenna.

"Yes, that's if she went home of course."

"I don't know where she went after she left me," insisted Jenna.

"Did you stay here after she'd gone?"

"Why don't you ask the gatekeeper?" she snapped.

"We did, but we need to hear you start telling us the truth, and not just when you feel it's convenient."

"I stayed in my bed," she said.

"Forgive me if I'm wrong, but did you spend most of your time with Pepper together in bed?" Lu asked with his eyebrows raised.

"That's none of your business," she hissed.

"Jenna, I'll tell you when something isn't my business. In the meantime, just answer the questions, did you hear me?" Lu growled, determined to maintain his authority.

"Yes, I'm sorry."

"How often does she come here?"

"Oh, this was the first time."

"Oh, really?"

"That's the truth. She asked to come over," she replied. Lu looked puzzled.

"Are you telling me that she came here tonight for the first time, and last night of all nights, her lover was murdered?"

"I couldn't say. What are you trying to say?" Jenna asked.

"Maybe she was looking for an alibi and hadn't known the gateman would be clocking her time in and out. That's what I think," said Lu with a smug smile on his face. She fell silent and slumped back into her large leather sofa.

"The bitch and I thought she was attracted to me," she said with an annoyed look on her face.

"You were taken in by her. Don't feel bad about it. Such women spend their lives pretending to be something they're not," said Lu, now sure he had a vital lead. I need to go now. We'll expect you to report to the central police station at five this evening for further questions. And if you see that Pepper woman, get in touch with us immediately."

"I will, you can be sure of that," said Jenna through clenched teeth. Inspector Lu left, sure that this Pepper woman was either in league with the killer or knew who the killer was.

Both Jenna and Jeany arrived at the central police station in downtown Shijiazhuang. Jeany had been given a thorough interrogation the morning before and was dreading a re-run of the same thing over and over again. On their arrival they were both ushered into the same interview room and left alone. Fearing that they were being taped or recorded neither spoke, they just sat there and waited. Inspector Fang then entered the room followed by his associate Inspector Lu.

"Sorry to keep you waiting ladies," said Fang, smiling as he sat down opposite the women. Lu sat at the end of the table and produced a recorder. Fang smiled at Jeany and leant back in his chair.

"We need to tape this interview to be sure we miss nothing out. I need to tell you that the questions will only cover recent events and not the rape allegation."

"Aren't you going to investigate the rape?" Jeany asked looking directly at Fang.

"Yes we will, but at the moment, we're more concerned as to who is killing your suspects. We have no case if they're all dead," said Fang with a faint smile. Lu switched on the recorder.

"Jenna, did you kill Fei-Liao, Officer Pang or Bo-Cheng?"

"No I didn't," she replied.

"Jeany, what ward were you on, on the night when Pang and Bo-Cheng died?" Fang asked, aware that either of them might have discovered that Bo-Cheng wasn't in the morgue.

"I was on Ward Five all night."

"And did you at any time venture down to Ward Three?" Fang asked.

"Well yes, I had words with Bo-Cheng at about midnight," she explained.

"And did you threaten to kill him?"

"No, I just said that Jason was out to get him. I was angry," she explained.

"So do you think Jason Lamont killed Bo-Cheng and the guard?"

"I suppose so," she replied in a soft apologetic voice.

"So we're wasting our time talking to you ladies, if the perpetrator is still out there on the loose, yes?" Fang asked.

"I think so," Jenna continued. "You need to be out there catching that killer. We can't help you at all."

"Let's turn to you Jenna, where were you last night?" Fang asked.

"I was at home," she replied, as she folded her arms.

"Were you alone?" he asked, as he looked down at his notes.

"Yes I was," she insisted.

"We commandeered the security log book of your housing complex and it shows you had a guest. Are you still telling us you were alone?"

"I had a friend visit but they left at about midnight," she said, anxious for the questions to end there.

"Who was the visitor?" Fang asked with a smile.

"You know, so why ask me?" she snapped. Jeany looked on as Jenna became more and more agitated.

"For the tape, we need you to give us a name," he insisted.

"She was a friend," replied Jenna.

"A name please?"

"Pepper, Pepper Lee," she whispered with her eyes lowered. Jeany stood up and looked down at her.

"A friend, and since when did you and that bitch become friends? You two-faced bitch! I trusted you," growled Jeany, her voice almost breaking.

"She just wanted to talk, I couldn't say no, could I?" Jenna explained. Jeany glared at her.

"Inspector Fang, how long was she at Jenna's apartment?" Jeany asked, her eyes switching between Jenna and Inspector Fang.

"Jenna, answer the lady. How long was she there in your apartment?"

"You have the log book," Jenna argued.

"I'm asking you."

"About four hours, maybe less," she said shrugging her shoulders. Jeany sat down and covered her face.

"That was a long conversation. What did you talk about?" Fang asked.

"Use your imagination why don't you," Jenna said through pursed lips. Jeany stared at her, her mouth open.

"How could you jump into bed with that painted witch?" she sobbed as she shifted her chair away from Jenna's.

"So that's why she attacked you in the park. She was jealous," said Lu.

"Yes I'm sure. But what has this to do with the murders?" Jeany asked looking across at Fang.

"Jeany I'm not sure, we've found some puzzling forensic evidence that we're at a loss to explain. We have examined Bo-Cheng's apartment and found traces of Miss Pepper Lee there and some paperwork including Bo-Cheng's diary," said Fang.

"So where is Pepper now? I thought she shared his apartment," Jeany asked.

"She's moved out. I don't suppose Jenna can enlighten us as to where she is?" Lu asked, with a wry smile on his face.

"I don't know. Like I said, she's only been to my place once and we made no plans to see each other again," explained Jenna.

"The murders were meticulously carried out and with a fair amount of medical knowledge. Someone like Miss Pepper could not have perpetrated these crimes on her own. Someone with medical expertise must have helped her. And if it was the foreigner Lamont he would also have needed the same kind of help," said Fang turning to Jenna.

"Don't look at me. There's a hospital full of people who had the skills. Why point the finger at me?"

"Because you and Jeany were very close weren't you?" Fang said leaning back in his chair. Jeany sat up straight.

"She didn't think that much of me when she was seducing that Taiwanese bitch. Such a fickle person wouldn't dream of murdering someone for anyone but herself," said Jeany. Fang looked down at his notes and then turned to Jeany.

"Can you tell me who Jason went to see in Beijing?"

"I remember it was to meet an old friend, I think he called him Douglas," she said.

"Why did he attack Bo-Cheng in the first instance?"

"The rape, why else?" replied Jeany.

"Ah! Yes, the rape."

"How did Jason find out about the rape?"

"I told him. He needed to know," replied Jenna. Fang cocked an eye brow and gave Jenna a puzzled look.

"Yes he did, but then didn't you drive him to the hotel in Bao-Ding, where you knew he would come face to face with Bo-Cheng? You set him up, didn't you?"

"I didn't know they were there," insisted Jenna. Fang smiled at Jenna.

"A coincidence was it, yes?"

"Yes it was."

"Was Jason getting in your way? What I mean is, had he had become a stumbling block between you and Jeany. That's true, isn't it?" Jenna looked down and shook her head.

"That's not true."

"So you were happy with Jason being with Jeany, leaving you on the side-lines, eh?" Fang asked.

"Well, not really."

"I see, so having Jason flee to Beijing or wherever was rather convenient, wasn't it?" he suggested.

"I suppose so, but I didn't plan it like that, truly I didn't," she replied looking across towards Jeany.

"And was Pepper there at the hotel?"

"Jason said that she was there, but I didn't see her."

"And yet another coincidence," Fang said smiling.

"I suppose so," said Jenna.

"What kind of scheme are you and Pepper cooking up behind our backs?" Fang asked, as he stood up, allowing Inspector Lu to continue the questioning.

"Do you know where Pepper is now?" Lu asked as he twizzled his pen over his fingers.

"No, I don't know. If she isn't at Bo-Cheng's place, I don't know where else she might be," said Jenna.

"Jeany, do you know where she is?"

"I don't know or care where she is," she replied as she glared at Jenna.

"Jenna, did you stage that argument with Pepper outside the hospital?" Lu asked.

"No, I've never spoken to her before that day."

"So why go out of your way to upset her?"

"I confronted her because I hated Bo-Cheng."

"Did you hate him enough to kill him?" He suggested leaning towards Jenna.

"Yes. But I didn't. That pleasure fell to Jason Lamont," said Jenna through pursed lips.

"Jeany, we have questioned both staff and patients and they are all able to corroborate your alibi. For the time being we have no more questions for you. I don't need to remind you that if you do see Pepper or Jason, you are duty bound to inform us immediately," said Lu.

"Jeany. Where will you be staying tonight?" Fang asked. She looked at Jenna with a tearful expression on her face.

"I want to go home. I want to go back to my apartment, sorry Jenna. I was planning to leave anyway. I don't hate you, you are what you are, clever and predatory just like a man, and I don't need that," she said as she stood up. Fang turned to Jenna still sitting at the interview table.

"Will you help her to move her things?" he asked. Jenna forced a smile and nodded. Fang lead Jeany out of the interview room and flagged a taxi for her.

"Do you have your keys?"

"Yes Inspector, and thanks for everything," she said on the verge of breaking down as she shuffled into the rear seat of the taxi. Inspector Fang watched as the taxi sped off with Jeany. Jenna was in no mood to talk as she climbed into her car; now alone she headed home to her apartment now full of bittersweet memories.

Jeany's Visitors

On her arrival, Jeany felt relieved to be back home and beholden to no one but herself. After a brief rest, she picked herself up and began tidying the living room. She found a bowl and filled it with hot soapy water and began to clean the windows and the window sills that had managed to accumulate a thick layer of dust in her absence. She stripped the bed linen and bundled each sheet and blanket into a black bin bag to dispose of later in the day, intent on buying a new set, clean and unviolated.

She was then startled by a sharp knock at the door. She waited with bated breath in the hope that whoever it was would get tired of knocking and leave. The rapping of knuckles on the door continued which began to annoy her. She threw the damp rag she was holding into the bowl of water and grabbed a kitchen knife from its hiding place. Then with great care, she opened the door.

In the hallway were two men in police uniforms, one was short and the other much taller. Repulsed she at once recognised them. She felt somewhat reassured when she noticed the stocky frame of Miss Sha standing directly behind them having been disturbed by their persistent knocking; she had come out to protest. She glared at the back of their heads with distain etched all over her lined face.

"What do you two want?" Jeany asked, the knife trembling in her hand.

"We need to talk to you," said the tall man.

"Well, I don't want to talk to you," she said as she began to close the door on them. Miss Sha picked up a brush that had been conveniently placed by the door and beat the shorter man over the head from behind.

"Bloody rapists, leave her alone you freaks," she croaked. She then retreated into her doorway out of harm's way hissing at the two unwelcome visitors as she did.

"Don't worry Sha, I have a knife and I'll use it," said Jeany, as she tried to shut the door. The shorter of the two men put his foot between the door and the door jamb preventing her from closing it. Now furious, she pulled open the door and lashed out at the men with the kitchen knife, just missing the tall man's face.

"I'm sorry," cried the short man, as he leapt backwards, almost falling into Miss Sha's open doorway. The tall man raised his hands up, in a gesture of peace and spoke in a mild mannered voice.

"Jeany, forgive us," he said.

"You called me Jeany. Why are you here?" she asked, as she hung onto the door and the knife out at arms' reach.

"We have come to beg your forgiveness and apologise for our misdeeds," the tall man pleaded.

"Don't trust them Jeany. Those hyenas will just laugh at you behind your back if you forgive them. They're mocking you," she shouted as she waved her broom handle at the couple.

"Why now?" Jeany asked.

"We're the only two left out of five, your foreign friend has mutilated three of us. We know we did wrong and we're here to make it up to you," said the tall man.

"Then why haven't you turned yourselves in and confessed if you feel so bad about what you've done?"

241

The short man produced some paperwork and offered it to her.

"We have written statements admitting what we did. Take a look, here." She glanced down but was unwilling to let either the door or the knife out of her grip.

"Let the lady behind you read them and then I suggest you take them to Inspector Fang before sunset if you know what's good for you," suggested Jeany. Sha snatched the documents and nodded to Jeany to say that they were what the men said they were. Sha threw the papers down at their feet for them to pick up.

"Is that all?" Jeany asked, as she glared at the men whose drawn faces expressed fear for their own hides but to Jeany, they showed little or no remorse for their past misdeeds.

"We're going now and we'll hand ourselves in today. We only ask that you tell your foreign friend that we've admitted our part in the crime and that no good can come of cutting us up like the others. Please tell him we're sorry," begged the short man, as he fell to his knees in front of her.

"Ah, so you're scared are you? You're afraid that Jason is going to come and get you in the night. You are, aren't you? You're not sorry at all, you're afraid," said Jeany as she looked into their eyes oozing with fear. Sha couldn't resist compounding their fear as she chanted behind them.

"It's no use. He's coming to get you for what you did to his woman. You're as good as dead," she chanted.

"Will you be quiet, woman?" the tall man said. Sha gripped her broom tightly and puckered her lips.

"I'm going nowhere. I'm not leaving you rapists alone with her," Sha said. The tall man joined the shorter one on his knees.

"Jeany, I don't want to end up like Bo-Cheng. I have two daughters and a wife at home. Can't you find it in your heart to have pity on me, Jeany please?"

"Would you forgive anyone who had raped your daughter?" The tall man just lowered his head.

"I didn't think so, and did you spare me when you had a chance?"

"I did as I was told," retorted the short man.

"No moral courage. You're cowards both of you."

The tall man reached into his jacket and produced two red envelopes.

"We've collected all our savings and converted them into American dollars to offer Jason as payment for sparing our lives. There's enough to keep him in clover for years," said the tall man as he offered up the envelopes.

"I don't want your money. You invaded my body and now you're offering me money. You must really think I'm a whore. Well I'm not. I didn't sell it; you stole it and stole my life along with it. Get out, I despise you both," she growled now in tears.

"They'll pay when Jason catches up with them," snarled Sha seething at their shameless audacity.

"We're not offering the money to you. We wouldn't insult you so. We're offering this to the foreign assassin in exchange for our lives. We have the written statements and the money to buy off the foreigner. Please accept it and at least give it to him and beg his understanding."

"I'll not touch the money; you keep it for your burial costs." The tall man's hand reached in under Jeany's arm and tossed the envelopes through the door and onto the carpet.

"Just deliver the envelopes. We can see that he gets out of China safely. We have our ways to help, if he needs it."

"Leave me alone!"

"We're going," said the taller man, as they both got to their feet. The two men turned and began to make their way down the concrete stair. Jeany threw open her door and shouted down at them.

"Don't you ever come here again, or as God is my judge I'll cut you up myself," she shouted. Sha stood next to her at the top of the stairs and joined in with her deep voice echoing down past the two men to the basement.

"I hope he gets you and cuts you into little pieces you filthy rapists," shouted Sha trembling with rage.

"Sha don't be angry. They're cowards, afraid of dying."

"And so they should be. Those animals that raped Nan-Jing got away and escaped justice, but these two will have nowhere to run," said Miss Sha as she embraced Jeany.

Jenna Meets Pepper on the Run

As Jenna drove home, she constantly reprimanded herself for her poor judgment and naivety. Jeany was a gentle and loving individual; although lacking in passion and genuine sexual attraction, she was comfortable to be with, and adequate. Pepper on the other hand was exciting and ready for anything that Jenna would throw at her, although lacking in sincerity, she was the real thing. She yearned for a partnership like Pepper, morally illicit and yet highly desirable. As she waited at the traffic lights just a short distance from her compound, she saw Pepper stood by the wayside as if she had known Jenna would pass that way. She turned the corner, pulled over and then switched off her engine. As she looked in the rear view mirror she could see Pepper approaching. She wore a black leather coat and a red top and jeans. She was slim and leggy and moved well. She looked beautiful with her long black hair blowing wildly in the cold wintry wind.

Pepper ran up to the car, opened the passenger door and slid in. She took one look at Jenna and then threw her arms around her. She looked into Jenna's weary eyes and kissed her. Her deep red lips, soft and tender throbbed with sincerity, which startled Jenna.

"You're not playing with me, are you?" Jenna asked, as she looked into Pepper's deep dark eyes.

"I was before, but then I was desperate to find somewhere to live and I was willing to make a deal with what I could offer. Now that I've found you, I want to hang onto you, and for keeps," she said.

"You are impossible, you know?"

"Jenna, what am I going to do?"

"You know the police are after you, don't you? They think you're a murderer."

"Yes, but they were my gang. Bo-Bo let me order them about and made them do things for me. Why would I want to murder them?"

"You can't stay at my place, but the security guards list everyone who comes and goes."

"They don't search your car, do they?"

"No, but then again, if you hid in my car, they'd be sure to spot you as you climbed out and they'd be sure to notice you entering the building," explained Jenna.

"I know, I'll wear a disguise and you can give them a false name," suggested Pepper. Jenna smiled and nodded.

"Okay, you go to the supermarket and buy some flour to grey up your hair and I'll go back to my apartment and bring you some of my old winter clothes. You'll need to lose that lip gloss and the make-up though. I'll see you back here in half an hour."

"Good idea. I'll see you later, I won't be long," she said and with that she slid out of the car and headed back down the street. Jenna was in two minds not to return, but the idea of having Pepper to herself was far too compelling an opportunity to pass over.

As promised, Jenna was back at the same parking spot her mind preoccupied with whatever future delights were to come when Pepper knocked on the window. She was at once taken aback by the plain looking woman outside, with no make-up she was barely recognisable as she slid into the car.

"Here put these on, and before you do, you have to rub plenty of flour into your hair. It'll make you look much older." Pepper did as instructed and then dressed accordingly.

"Right – just say nothing, let me do the talking," instructed Jenna. Pepper nodded and they set off for Jenna's apartment complex. As they drove in, the gatekeeper approached the car. Jenna lowered her window.

"Jie-Na and my cousin Xun, she will be staying a few weeks," said Jenna smiling. The guard nodded and wrote their names down in their log book. On driving through she whispered to Pepper.

"Remember not to sway your hips too much; you don't want to attract their attention, do you?" With this advice in mind, Pepper tottered into the apartment block with her back arched and knees bent, stifling her amusement. Once inside, they both burst into laughter.

"That was so much fun," said Pepper. Jenna hadn't laughed so much in years. To Jenna, this wild woman was like a breath of fresh air, exciting and dangerous with it.

"Are you hungry?" she asked.

"I'm starving. I haven't eaten anything for a couple of days," said Pepper grinning. They drifted into the kitchen and side by side began to prepare what was to be their first meal together. Both women knew that there would be no freedom of movement for Pepper, not at least until the crimes committed against Bo-Cheng and his team were solved. Jenna began to pack away Jeany's things that were still littering the living area and the bedroom. She took them and loaded them into the back of her car with the intention of delivering them the following day. For Jenna this marked the end of one episode in her life and the beginning of another.

With no blood relatives left, Bo-Cheng had no one to pay for his intensive care and hospitalisation. The police department were willing to pay for someone to care for him but just for a limited period of time. With his prognosis being so poor, he was not expected to live out the next six months. He was unable to speak, he couldn't urinate without a catheter and his paralysis extended from his neck downwards. Though Miss Sha had no sympathy for her old neighbour, she offered the police force her services, at a reasonable cost. For a price she would take him into her apartment and care for him until his eventual death. At Sha's he would be close to his ex-wife, not that she would be visiting him. He would also have the best medical help anyone could wish for. Miss Sha drew up the papers and agreed on a weekly sum paid into her bank account. Bo-Cheng was then duly dispatched to Miss Sha's apartment just across the corridor from his old home.

Although he was unable to speak, his eyes looked on as he was lifted up the concrete stairs and then wheeled into Sha's apartment. He had never liked Sha, and on seeing who had volunteered to look after him, his moist reddened eyes stared into oblivion. Locked in an eternal hell, his internal screams began, as he lay there expressionless and silent.

YU-ME TELLS JASON

As soon as Yu-Me arrived back in Beijing, she contacted Wang to find out where Jason was. He told her that he was comfortable, having been given a place to hide out deep in the bowels of the zoo grounds. It was a vacant room usually reserved for visiting officials. He had been told to keep his door locked and not to switch on the lights, and had been given instructions on what to do if he needed to hide for any reason. This was in the cellar situated in a far corner of the room via a small hatch sunk into the floor and covered with carpet. The cellar was rarely used and was thick with dust. Cobwebs hung in festoons across the wooden beams. The darker reaches of the cellar were occupied by an assortment of rodents that came and went as they pleased.

It was early in the morning and he was startled by a knock on the door.

"It's me, Yu-Me," she whispered. He turned the key.

"I thought you guys had forgotten me."

"No, we've been busy. Yesterday on my way back from Shijiazhuang, I met an Australian couple on the train. They said their mobile battery had died, so I gave them the battery out of mine. In return they gave me their spare phone also flat. It's a cheap one but it works in China. Here – you have it – it's charged up, you can call Jeany." He stood there, overwhelmed by the thought of hearing her voice again.

"So she's alright then, can I actually call her?"

"Yes. If she's at work you'll get a messaging response, I can't remember if she's on nights or on days, sorry."

"You're an angel, Yu-Me. How can I thank you?" he said clutching the phone.

"I can't remember her number," mumbled Jason. Yu-Me laughed.

"It's on the phone. Just scroll down. I put it there last night."

"What plans do you have to get me out of China?" he asked as he sat down on the bed. Yu-Me sat beside him and put her hand on his shoulder.

"Jeany can't go with you."

"Why not, can't Douglas fix it for her?"

"No he can't. There's a murder enquiry going on, and Jeany is one of the suspects. So at the moment she can't go anywhere, with or without you."

"So who's been murdered?" he asked, puzzled as to why anyone would suspect Jeany of a violent crime.

"Bo-Cheng has been murdered."

"But I killed Bo-Cheng at the hotel. The barman saw the whole thing."

"You put him in hospital, but you didn't actually kill anyone."

"So I'm in the clear then?" The colour rushed back into his cheeks.

"No Jason, the police are looking for you. Someone is killing the men that raped Jeany."

"Raped? No one said that she'd been raped! Why didn't anyone tell me?" He stood up and kicked the sofa. "Why didn't Jenna tell me, why?" He clenched his fists and sat back down, covering his face.

"I think she wanted Jeany to herself."

"And did she manage to do that?" he asked looking up, his eyes glazed.

"No she didn't, she's back home and on her own again."

"I ought to go back. If I'm not guilty of anything why can't I?"

"I didn't think you'd want to go back, what with her being raped and all that."

"How can you say that?"

"Jason, men are strange creatures. They love to sleep around with women, whose job it is to have intercourse with many men, but if their wives or girlfriends are raped, they don't want them anymore."

"I'm not like that."

"No?"

"No." He then paused.

"You surprise me,"

"So who did kill Bo-Cheng?" he asked, as he rubbed his moist eyes.

"No one knows. But according to the police you did, and maybe with Jeany's help."

"How did he die?"

"Bo-Cheng, his guard Pang and his driver Zang Fei-Liao were all cut up. Then Nan, Fei-Liao's wife killed herself, so they are all dead. The police are expecting you to return and kill the last remaining rapists. So innocent or not, you're still a fugitive."

"Why were so many murdered?"

"Jeany was raped by the four policemen. Two are now dead, along with Bo-Cheng."

"And they think I did it?" Jason retorted.

"I would be proud to have done it, if she was my kin, and I would."

"I don't want to distance myself from what's happened, but that's gruesome. I couldn't do that, no matter what they'd done," declared Jason.

"I thought you were made of tougher stuff than that. I should turn you in and let you grovel to the police, protesting your innocence."

"Don't be like that."

"You'll still end up with a bullet in the back of your head, innocent or not."

"I really do need to leave China, don't I?"

"Yes, you do. I'm going now. Remember, they can trace your call after three minutes, so call just once. Okay?" Yu-Me said as she slid out of the door.

Jason sat there and considered Yu-Me's words of wisdom. He had to admit that he had willingly taken to the seductive Bunny and had no feelings of distaste at her comings and goings with whomever. Yet here he was, contemplating leaving China and turning his back on his beloved Jeany. Was he punishing her for being a victim? Was Yu-Me right? Should he have stayed and sought revenge on those who had perpetrated the rape? Should he or could he have protected her? He sat there with his head in his hands and tormented himself with these imponderable questions to the point of distraction.

An hour passed and having struggled with his inner self, he decided to call her and tell her that he still loved her. As the phone rang, his stomach began to churn. It was as if he had never spoken to her before. A quiet timid voice answered the phone.

"Hello."

"Jeany. It's me, Jason."

"Jason? Is that really you? Where are you?"

"I can't say and I don't have long, I just needed to tell you that I still love you."

"You don't know what has gone on here."

"I don't care, what's done is done, the past is like water passing under the bridge, it's gone. Just remember that I'll always love you."

"And I you Jason, but you can't come back. They're after you."

"Do you think I'm a murderer?"

"Jason, just don't kill any more; it's finished. We're all tired of death. Please stop what you're doing," she begged.

"Jeany, I won't kill anyone, that's a promise."

"When can we see each other again?"

"I don't know. I'll call you again but later. Maybe we can meet up here in Beijing, but not now. I'll call you again when I can arrange a safe place for us to be alone together."

"Take care of yourself Jason, and no more revenge."

"No revenge, I promise. Jeany, we'll meet up soon. I love you." and with that he cut the conversation short.

Yu-Me returned to her apartment block and called in on Bunny, who was in a cheerful mood packing her suitcase. Yu-Me looked puzzled.

"Bunny, where are you going?"

"Nowhere, Just sit down I have a plan. Listen carefully. Tomorrow we are taking Jason out of the zoo. Tell him to arrange a meeting with Jeany in Starbucks, the one in Xi-Dan. Make it ten thirty. We'll drive him there," said Bunny with a smile.

"What about the police?" Yu-Me asked.

"There's a parade tomorrow. The whole force will be out on the streets, along with a hundred or so foreign faces, more than you can count," laughed Bunny.

"So after we've moved him, then what?"

"There's more I need to tell you, but for now get back to Jason and get him to make that call."

"Yu-Me preferring not to use her phone, dashed back to the zoo hideout to deliver Bunny's instructions. Once again he called Jeany. Her tired voice answered the phone.

"Hello, who's that?" she answered, not expecting it to be Jason again.

"Can you meet me tomorrow morning in Xi-Dan?"

"Yes, of course I can, where?"

"I'll be in Starbucks at ten thirty."

"I'll be there. I can't wait to see you again. Will it be safe?" she asked.

"I'm told it'll be fine. See you tomorrow. Jeany, I love you."

"I love you too, just be careful."

"I will, bye."

He put the phone down and smiled at Yu-Me.

"After our meeting, what do we do then?"

"You don't need to know, Jason. Wang will drive you somewhere very safe and then out of China. Are you okay with that?" she asked.

"Yes – what choice do I have?"

"None Jason, none at all."

"Have you prepared my documents?"

"It's all been done. You'll see Bunny tomorrow."

"I'll miss Bunny, she's unique."

"Yes she is and so is Jeany," said Yu-Me, as she gave him a playful scowl.

"I didn't mean anything by it," he said, his face reddening. Yu-Me just laughed.

"I'm going now, I'll see you early in the morning. I'll bring you some clean clothes and some socks that don't smell as bad as those," she said as she slipped out of the door and vanished into the zoo grounds.

As the morning sun flooded through the shutters, there was a knocking at the door which startled Jason into consciousness. He threw the bed clothes back and dashed to the door pinning his ear against the wooden slats.

"It's me, Yu-Me," she whispered. Jason dragged on his jeans and pulled open the door. Yu-Me slithered in sideways.

"Is there a problem?"

"No Jason, but I do need you to do me a favour."

"Yes, anything," he replied as he watched her pull out a writing pad from her leather bag.

"You can use the table over there."

"What do you want me to write?"

"Both you and Jeany are the prime suspects as far as these murders are concerned. You can run but Jeany will be left alone and at the mercy of the police. We can't let that happen can we?" she said.

"I agree, so what do you want me to write?"

"Whatever you write will not be shown to anyone until you are back in the UK. You trust us, don't you?"

"Yes, now tell me what you want me to say."

"Say that because your friend Jeany was raped, you were angry and that you and you alone killed Fei-Liao, Officer Pang and Bo-Cheng. Tell them you cut their balls off."

"I did what?"

"Yes you did."

"Tell them that Jeany wasn't involved and that by the time they get this letter, you'll be in Marseilles in the south of France."

"I wish," he said with a smile as he made notes.

"You need to sign it," said Yu-Me.

"Do you need me to finish it now?"

"Yes, Wang has your new passport. It has the same photo of course but you are now Douglas Murphy. He came by a while ago and left his passport. We just switched the photos."

"When do I fly?"

"Wang will pick you up. Just be patient. You're meeting Jeany at ten thirty, aren't you?"

"Yes, we're meeting at our favourite coffee bar in Xi-Dan," he said. Yu-Me just smiled. He then finished writing the letter and signed it 'Jason Lamont'. She picked up the letter, folded and sealed it.

"Jeany has you to thank for saving her life – that's how important this letter is to her. Oh, can you address it 'care of Inspector Fang'?" He did as she asked and wiped the perspiration from his brow.

"Wang will pick you up when he's ready. It's still far too early," she said as she stood up and turned to leave.

"When are you coming back?" he asked as he stood up. She turned around and gave him an apologetic look.

"I'm not coming back. I have places I need to be. Wang will pick you up at about 9 o'clock, just relax." She forced a smile and then slipped out of the door for the last time.

He slumped down onto the bed and fell sideways into a foetal position and tried to sleep. He remembered that first day when he had seen the lone woman standing there in the foyer of his school and how she evoked that mirth in him. He recalled that smile and those eyes, enticing, dark and deep. Tears rolled down his cheeks, as he contemplated flying out of China, leaving behind in his wake a trail of misery and regret. As he lay there, he felt empty and haunted by the faces of those he was about to leave behind.

Jenna and Pepper at Breakfast

Pepper opened her eyes and threw her arms around Jenna.

"Wake up Jenna, I'm hungry." Pepper gave her a gentle kiss on the lips to which Jenna rolled onto her side and embraced her. With the red curtains fully drawn the room was awash with a seductive crimson hue.

"Pepper, so you want me to cook you breakfast, do you?"

"I didn't mean that. Are you sorry you took me in?" she asked as she stroked Jenna's long black hair, pushing it back from her face.

"No, but we need to work out who is doing what. I assume it isn't you who's murdering those attackers."

"We both know its Jason. But how can we prove it?" said Pepper.

"It's not our job to prove anything. That's why we have the police," replied Jenna. Pepper rolled onto her back.

"Forget them, forget them all, come hold me," she said, as she pulled Jenna towards her. Pepper kneaded Jenna's fleshy back, sending tingling ripples up and down her exposed body. She responded by grabbing Pepper's wrists, pulling them away from her back and pinning them down against the soft mattress. With Jenna looking down at Pepper, she lowered herself gently on top. As both naked bodies touched, they kissed. Their unleashed passion swiped the bedside light off the table.

The huge smothering duvet was kicked aside. The nuisance pillows were discarded onto the floor, as both lovers wrestled as one. At that sweet moment, nothing really mattered. They were oblivious to the outside world.

A short time later when the heat of the moment had passed, there was a knock at the door. Jenna pulled on her clothes and ran a brush through her hair. It must be a neighbour, she thought, as the gatehouse hadn't rung to say she had visitors. Jenna looked through the spy hole. Her head shot backwards.

"It's that Inspector Fang," she whispered. Pepper threw her clothes on and crawled under the bed. Jenna then opened the door. In front of her stood Fang, he put his right foot in between Jenna's feet and with both hands pushed her in the chest, sending her flying backwards onto the floor.

"What did you do that for?" she protested. Fang looked down at her.

"Murder is a serious business and to kill a policeman is seriously foolhardy. To murder three is tantamount to suicide," said Fang as three police officers ran in past Fang to search the place.

"So where is your cousin Xun, out shopping is she?" Jenna remained silent.

"Inspector, there's a body under the bed," said one of Fang's men.

"Oh really, is it a dead one?"

"Shall I kick it and see?"

"Use your own judgment, but get it out from under there. No doubt this is your cousin Xun. Shy is she?" The officer pulled at Pepper's leg, causing her to squeal as the underside of the bed caught her clothes pulling them adrift.

"Ah, Pepper. How nice to meet you at last," said Fang with a smile. Pepper picked up the bedside lamp and hurled it at the Inspector. The young officer who had discovered her, tried to restrain her, but got more than he'd bargained for, as she punched him squarely on the nose. Fang escorted a calm Jenna to a waiting patrol car while the three other officers struggled with Pepper. After a great deal of effort, Pepper was bundled into another patrol car. The two women were then taken to police headquarters and formally charged with the murders of Fei-Liao, Officer Pang and the attempted murder of Bo-Cheng.

"Bo-Cheng is alive?" Pepper screamed, still boiling over with anger.

"Why don't you ask him who tried to kill him? He'll tell you it wasn't us," snapped Jenna. Fang shook his head.

"He'll never talk again. He's in a vegetative state and unlikely to recover."

"It wasn't us," claimed Pepper, her fists clenched and shaking. Fang sat down and folded his arms.

"I suggest that you both sit down and gather your thoughts." The two women looked at each other and then pulled their chairs next to each other.

"How very touching," said Inspector Lu. "You weren't so affectionate when you were pushing Jeany into that water feature were you?" Pepper lowered her eyes and said nothing.

"Pepper, can you explain why strands of your hair were found in Fei-Liao's bedroom and by Bo-Cheng's bed? Fang asked, looking straight into her eyes. Pepper looked up and stared straight back at him.

"Anyone can plant evidence. That doesn't prove that I was there."

"I think it does," replied Fang, as he leant towards her.

"Why would I kill old Fei-Liao? He idolised me."

"That perfume you're wearing, I detected that fragrance at both murder scenes, is that planted too?" Jenna looked at Pepper with a worried look on her face.

"Jenna, I didn't do anything to anybody, and they know it."

"We have to work on the evidence, not on how we feel. We are legally obliged to detain you and hold you in custody until a trial date can be set. Murder is a capital crime. If neither of you own up, both will be executed." Pepper held onto Jenna's hand.

"Can we stay together?" Pepper asked as she squeezed Jenna's hand. Fang thought for a moment and nodded.

"If it helps to extract the truth from you, I don't mind," said Fang.

"Where will you take us?" Jenna asked.

"There's a remand centre near Beijing. You'll be sent there and I'll tell the governor to put you together," promised Fang. Pepper looked at Fang.

"We're innocent," she said. Fang nodded and sighed.

"It really doesn't matter what I think but if it makes you feel better, I believe you. Only God knows how you are ever going to prove it," replied Fang as he turned away with his head bowed.

Jason's Surprise

There was a gentle knock at the door but Jason just sat there contemplating his rendezvous with Jeany, then it dawned on him that maybe it was time to go. He opened the door and came face to face with Wang as he towered over Jason. Wang stared at his watch.

"It's time to go."

"Sorry Wang, I was just doing some thinking."

"Are you ready?"

"Yes." Jason scrambled to his feet.

"Let's go, we need to hurry."

"Are we late?" Jason asked, staring at his watch.

"No, we just need to be on time." He scratched his head in puzzlement.

"I'm sure Jeany wouldn't mind if we were a few minutes late. She's not the most punctual of women herself," he mumbled but his humour fell on deaf ears. Wang remained straight-faced, turned and left the tiny compound. Clasping his bag he followed Wang through the zoo's grounds and out of the main gates. The lady gatekeeper recognised him and gave him a wave, as they passed out of the zoo and onto the concourse beyond which a parked car awaited them.

Without a word being said, Wang jumped into the driver's seat. No sooner had Jason occupied the passenger seat than Wang sped off, leaving the main road and entering the narrow streets of old Beijing, in a convoluted route that led them out of the city and onto a country road. Jason stared out of the window, as they drove past ploughed fields and haystacks.

"Where are we going?" he asked as he gazed out over a bleak countryside with dark overcast skies. Wang turned to him and for a rare moment he smiled. His eyes then returned to the road ahead. At some distance along the road, Wang made a left turn and headed towards some large, featureless buildings that were reminiscent of the hangers he remembered from his air force days.

"Is this is an airport?" he asked, his voice one octave higher than usual.

"Yes Jason, that's exactly what it is," replied Wang.

"What are we doing here?" Wang just smiled, as he drove into a parking bay and switched off the engine.

"We need to get going," said Wang.

"And go where?"

"Your plane departs in half an hour; you need to check in now."

"What about our rendezvous with Jeany?"

"What about it? You need to leave China and don't forget your name is Douglas Murphy," said Wang as he handed over Jason's documents and his hand luggage. The couple then dashed into the departure lounge and up to the check-in desk. The air stewardess smiled at Jason. "Mr Murphy you are just in time."

Once on the plane, Jason squeezed between a large overweight businessman intent on reading his broadsheet newspaper and a young woman dressed in red lace curled up asleep. He reflected on the occurrences over the last few weeks and how he had been so fortunate to have had a well-paid job and a good woman, along with the perks of having been a popular figure. He found it incredible that it had all evaporated in front of his eyes. He had done nothing wrong, bar a fracas with Bo-Cheng. Now here he was, on a plane to wherever.

The voice over the public address system apologised for the delay and announced that the flight to Geneva would take off in just a few moments. He leant back and sighed, 'That's Douglas Murphy's haunt' he thought as he placed his passport and documents into his bag. 'The old fox,' he thought to himself, as he closed his eyes and smiled with contentment, for soon he would be back amongst kindred spirits. A message came over the tannoy instructing the passengers to fasten their seatbelts. Two slim oriental stewardesses made their way down each side of the plane ensuring that everyone had complied. When they came to Jason's row, she touched the young woman's arm to wake her up. As he had his seat belt fastened he was more interested in reading the fat man's newspaper than the lady in red next to him. The headlines read, 'Jason Lamont still at large, killer of four government workers'. He shrank into his seat.

As the plane began to taxi towards the end of the runway he turned and looked to his left in order to look out of the window and he noticed the young woman now sitting upright with her surgical mask fitted across her face. It was the type of mask generally used to prevent airborne infections spreading. He continued to peer out of the oval shaped window, his attention fixed on his last view of China. As he looked out he suddenly felt the young woman's hand slide across his upper leg where it gripped the fleshy part of his inner thigh making Jason wince with pain.

Startled he looked her in the face, and although he couldn't see her entire face, he felt that he recognised those eyes as they narrowed into a smile.

"Do I know you?" he asked, his face inches from hers.

"No. Would you like to?"

"What am I supposed to say?"

"You're not shy are you?" she said as she smiled from behind her mask.

"Why are you wearing that mask?"

"I have a cold," she said as her sharp nails dug into his now sore thigh.

"Will you stop that and take the mask off, you can't be so ugly as to not want anyone to see your face," he said, now amused by the situation. He raised his hand towards her face and hooked his finger behind the mask. Two bright eyes stared at him daring him to pull it from her face.

"Well do I pull the mask off or will you do it?" he asked as he stared into her narrowed eyes.

"I'll do it," she said, as she pulled his hand away with her left hand and removed the mask with her right hand. It was Bunny.

"I guessed it was you by the way your nails bit into my leg," he declared, rubbing his sore leg vigorously.

"I take it you are going to Geneva?" he asked.

"I am."

"I assume you're meeting Douglas there, are you?"

"No. Douglas has mislaid his passport in China somewhere."

"So why are you going to Geneva?"

"Where you go, from now on I go," said Bunny.

"So you want to stay with me?"

"Yes Jason, just you and me. Good eh?"

"But you're not a one man woman. Be honest, you're not, are you?"

"I'm a Chinese woman. I can be whatever kind of woman you want me to be."

"So you want us to be a couple?"

"Yes. Jason – do you still think I'm beautiful?"

"Yes I do. You're a real stunner," he said as he glanced down at her skirt, barely halfway to her knees.

"Well then, that's all that matters, isn't it?" she said, as she rested her head on his shoulder.

"No more selling your body, okay?"

"I've never sold it. I took what I wanted and got paid for it. I was always the one in charge and never lost control. But I'm too old for that now."

"Bunny, you'll never be too old to pull."

"Not now Jason, I have you. Kiss me?" Bunny said, as she pulled him towards her.

"Okay, Bunny you've got me. Now tell me what's been going on with these murders."

"Okay Jason, from what Yu-Me has told me, Jeany will be alright. She's been given cash which will buy Peter and Yu-Me somewhere to live, and she still has your pension coming in." Jason nearly choked.

"Ah, my pension, I forgot to cancel it," croaked Jason.

"Don't worry we can both live on mine."

"You have a pension?"

"I was an operative and a good one, but not now."

"And what about those murders, tell me, who did them?" Jason insisted.

"You killed them all."

"No, I didn't," he insisted, adjusting his sitting position, as he sprang to his own defence.

"I know that, but the police believe you did and didn't you write a confession?"

"Yes, but that was to clear Jeany of any involvement."

"It was good of you to do that."

"I assume you know, so tell me who did kill them?" he asked in a whisper.

"Many years ago, Bo-Cheng tried to rape Aunt Sha. She never told anyone and certainly not Jeany who was Bo-Cheng's wife at the time and was sure to have defended him. When Bo-Cheng's men attacked Jeany, Aunt Sha realised that Bo-Cheng had to be stopped, along with any man who would dare to do such a vile thing to a lone woman.

"I never met this Sha woman."

"No Jason, she wouldn't have liked you. She's not like me, not at all."

"Why kill them?"

"She'd suffered under the Japanese as a comfort woman and later under the Guo-Ming-Dang troops of Jiang-Kai-shek, and later the Red Guards. She tells fortunes and hears the stories of women like Jeany and if she chooses to help them, I wish her luck," explained Bunny, as she fisted the air.

"Does Jeany know?"

"No she doesn't,"

"So is Jeany free now?"

"Oh yes, quite free, and from what I hear Jenna and Pepper have been arrested for the murders."

"Pepper and Jenna, were they in league with each other, really?"

"And a nice couple they are, believe it or not."

"So they're in prison instead of Jeany then?"

"Yes, but your letter should exonerate them soon enough. But if it doesn't work, Aunt Sha will have to sacrifice two more filthy rapists to prove their innocence and secure their release," explained Bunny through pursed lips. Jason laughed.

"Fancy Jenna and Pepper together – what a combination," he said with a broad smile. She slipped her arm into Jason's.

"Yes I know," said Bunny with a smile. He looked at her and smiled back.

"Yes and now it's just you and me."

"Yes Jason, till death do us part."

JEANY ENTERS THE COFFEE SHOP

The wild wind howled behind Jeany as she entered the coffee shop. For a moment she stood there and glanced around but she didn't see anyone she recognised. Left with no other option, she made her way to the counter where she ordered a cappuccino. She then ambled across to a vacant table next to the main entrance and beside the window. Many people entered the shop with their faces covered under hoods or behind scarves.

As she stared out of the window, she thought she recognised Yu-Me approaching with someone beside her. The person beside her had their head covered beneath a fur trimmed hooded garment so that their face wasn't visible. She sat upright and brushed the hair back from her face. As the couple drew nearer her heart sank on realising that the person next to Yu-Mei was far too short to have been Jason. She shook her head in despair. Jeany stood up as they entered, Yu-Me's companion still concealing their identity below their hood.

"Mom, are you alright?"

"Where's Jason?" she asked.

"He's on his way back to Europe. He couldn't make it. He's very sorry," whispered Yu-Me as they embraced. Jeany lowered her eyes, as tears streamed down her cheeks. The young man stood back, still unrecognisable as he distanced himself from the shielded conversation. Yu-Me whispered into Jeany's ear.

"I have no doubt that the call Jason made to you was listened in on and that the authorities should now believe that he will be here soon. So I've brought this young man in his place," explained Yu-Me.

"You're so clever Yu-Me, so who is he?" she asked. Yu-Me smiled at Jeany.

"He's my husband," she replied. Jeany's mouth dropped open.

"But I thought you and Pang-Xi were…" The young man turned and looked directly at Jeany and smiled.

"Mom, don't you recognise me?" he said, as he spread out his arms to embrace her. Jeany cried out aloud. Everyone in the coffee shop turned to see what was happening. Pang-Xi stepped up to his mother and held her close, as tears of joy dampened their cheeks. Her hand touched the back of her son's neck and sensed the warmth she had never dared dream of again. Yu-Me stood aside and clapped with sheer delight. The occupants of the coffee shop on seeing such a reunion clapped along with her.

From out of this sea of happiness there were some that were not so caught up by the occasion. The police, who had been sitting around the coffee shop in plain clothes ready to pounce on an unsuspecting Jason, stood up and surrounded the small gathering. Inspector Fang dashed across from where he had secreted himself and pulled Pang-Xi's hood back. He looked surprised to see a Chinese face.

"Where is he?" Fang asked his face red with embarrassment.

"He hasn't turned up yet. You're welcome to wait. He said he should be here at about 10.30," said Yu-Me, as she sat down, followed by the others.

"We'll wait. No one move until I say so. Do you understand?" Fang said through clenched teeth, his face screwed up like a spoilt child's. He then turned to his men, as they stood around, afraid to say anything to annoy their inspector further.

"What are you lot looking at? get back to your seats and act normally. Can you manage that?" growled Fang.

"We were about to ask him to turn himself in. We would have handed him over to you, but maybe you've frightened him off," she said looking up at Fang.

"There are two women back in Shijiazhuang who have been charged with these murders. We've enough evidence to convict them, but deep down I believe your Jason friend is behind these murders. What kind of man escapes and lets two women go to prison for a crime he committed?" Fang asked as he turned and made his way back to his remote seat.

Jeany reached across the table and held Pang-Xi's hands.

"I thought you were dead. In my mind, I've buried you a hundred times. How could you let me believe such a terrible thing?" she asked, still tearful.

"Sorry Mom. I was only released from prison a few weeks ago and didn't want the authorities to harass you because of my actions," he explained, his eyes now red and moist.

"I'm sorry to have to tell you this, but your father's dead," said Jeany, looking directly in to her son's eyes.

"I know," said Pang-Xi, as he turned to Yu-Me and smiled. Yu-Me placed her hand on Jeany's.

"Actually he's not quite dead. Miss Sha has offered to look after him until he passes on. He hasn't long to live and the police have offered to pay her a decent amount to care for him in her apartment," she said.

"That's very kind of her to offer to help," said Jeany, with a slight look of puzzlement on her face.

"She's all heart," said Yu-Me smiling as she gripped Jeany's hand.

"What do we do after they realise that Jason isn't going to turn up?" Jeany asked.

"Can we all go back home to Shijiazhuang? Can we Mom?" Yu-Me asked, as she gave Pang-Xi a hug.

"Yes of course we can. What a silly question. We're a family once again and I have a new daughter in Yu-Me," said Jeany as she leaned across the table and threw her arms around the young couple. They sat and chatted as the plain clothed police like pillars of salt, stared into their lukewarm drinks. After an hour, it became obvious that they were going to be disappointed. Fang stood up and ordered his men to return to their vehicles and then made his way across to Jeany's table.

"I assume that you're all going back to Shijiazhuang. We have space to take you all back if you like," said Fang looking directly at Jeany.

"Yes that would be very kind of you. We're sorry he didn't turn up. If it's any consolation, we're sure he killed those people and that Jenna and Pepper are innocent," said Jeany.

"I lost my father. He wasn't a good man, but we would never dream of being involved in his murder or protecting his killer," said Pang-Xi, as he shook Fang's hand.

"I believe you. I really hope we can get these women cleared somehow," said Fang, as he led the way out of the coffee shop, followed by Jeany, Yu-Me and Pang-Xi. As they walked towards the police car, Fang slid his hand behind Jeany's arm.

"I have a great deal of sympathy for you, since the investigation began."

"Why is that?" Jeany asked, giving Fang one of her sweetest smiles.

"I've read Bo-Cheng's diary, along with Fei-Liao's and Nan's. I can't tell you what they wrote, but I'm sure your life was made a living hell by those you should have been able to trust," he said.

"You're very kind. Now I have my son back and a new daughter-in-law, what else could any mother wish for?" Fang pulled a tissue out of his pocket and dabbed his eyes.

"My wife died some years ago. I still miss her."

"Is there no one else in your life?" Jeany asked as she placed her hand on Fang's arm.

"There's someone I like, but maybe I'm too old to start thinking about such things."

"Never say that. Tell her and let her decide," said Jeany, as she looked into his moist eyes.

"Do I know her?"

"Yes, you do."

"Is it me?" Jeany asked, smiling at Fang.

"Is that a surprise?"

"Yes, but a nice one."

"Well then, what about a meal out some time?" he asked.

"I'd love to." Jeany stopped and gave him a long hard look. He wasn't bad looking and Jason wouldn't be coming back. Bo-Cheng was no longer able to pose a threat and Pang-Xi seemed to get on well with him. She linked her arm through Fang's and gave him a smile.

"What do I call you?"

"Just call me Fang," he said, his eyes flitting between her seductive eyes and her adorable smile.

As they drove along the road back to Shijiazhuang, they passed Bao-Ding and the hotel from where Jason had fled. Pang-Xi and Yu-Mei were sitting in the rear of the police vehicle arm in arm. Jeany sat in the front next to Fang, who from time to time would turn and smile at her. For once in her life, she felt that she had landed on her feet and although the opportunity that had presented itself was sure to have its trials and tribulations, she was old enough and now wise enough to ride out the storms, come what may. To Jeany, Bao-Ding and all the memories that were associated with it, were now well and truly behind them as the patrol car sped past towards Shijiazhuang and a brighter future for all.

'NIGHT WITCH'

This is a murder mystery novel set 1989 in Shijiazhuang, north China, the year of the June 4th incident in Tian-a-Men Square and it centres on the miserable life of *Jin-Mei*, the divorced wife of the local Police Chief *Bo-Cheng*. Her life changes when she meets *Jason Lamont* a Head Teacher from her local language school with who she envisages a better life.

Her life is turned upside down when she is raped by four of her ex-husbands' police department colleagues on *Bo-Cheng's* orders. The consequences of the rape are far reaching as *Jason* goes on the run for assaulting *Bo-Cheng*. *Jin-Mei* is then taken in by a *Dr Jenna* a lesbian colleague at the hospital where both she and *Jin-Mei* work.

One of the rapists, *Fei-Liao* is brutally murdered and a suicide ensues. *Bo-Cheng* is then mutilated in his hospital bed and his guard *Pang* is murdered as he slept. The police search for *Jason* who evades capture with help from *Douglas* an old colleague and so the finger of suspicion then moves to others in the complex puzzle. *Jason* is then torn between the love he has for *Jin-Mei* and his fascination for *Douglas's* operative, a playgirl named '*Bunny*'.